FAULT LINES

WINNER OF THE PRIX FEMINA

Fault Lines
Nancy Huston

McArthur & Company
Toronto

English edition first published in Canada in 2007 by
McArthur & Company
322 King St. West, Suite 402
Toronto, ON
M5V 1J2
www.mcarthur-co.com

This paperback edition published in 2008.

Library and Archives Canada Cataloguing in Publication

Huston, Nancy, 1953- [Lignes de faille. English]   Fault lines / Nancy Huston.

Translation of: Lignes de faille. ?ISBN 978-1-55278-664-2 (bound).
--ISBN 978-1-55278-730-4 (pbk.)

I. Title. II. Title: Lignes de faille. English.
PS8565.U8255L5313 2007   C843'.54   C2007-903976-6

Printed in Canada by Friesens

The publisher would like to acknowledge the financial support of the Government of
Canada through the Book Publishing Industry Development Program (BPIDP) and the
Canada Council for our publishing activities. The publisher further wishes to acknowledge
the financial support of the Ontario Arts Council for our publishing program.

10 9 8 7 6 5 4 3 2 1

For Tamia
and her song

'What was it – that burning, that amazement, that endless insufficiency, that sweet, that deep, that radiant feeling of tears welling up? What was it?'

R. M. RILKE

FAULT LINES

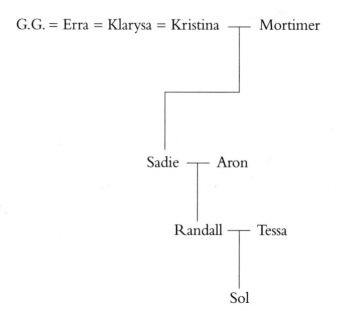

G.G. = Erra = Klarysa = Kristina ——— Mortimer

Sadie ——— Aron

Randall ——— Tessa

Sol

I

Sol, 2004

I'm awake.

Like flicking on a switch and flooding a room with light.

Snapping out of sleep, clicking into wakefulness, a perfectly functioning mind and body, six years old and a genius, first thought every morning when I wake up.

My brain floods into the world, the world floods into my brain,

I control and own every part of it.

Palm Sunday   early   G.G. here visiting   Mom & Dad still asleep

A   sunny   Sunday   sun   sun   sun   sun king   Sol   Solly   Solomon

I'm like sunlight, all-powerful, instantaneous and invisible, flowing effortlessly into the darkest corners of the universe

capable at six of seeing   illuminating   understanding everything

In a flash I'm washed and dressed, my hair is combed and my bed is made. Yesterday's socks and underwear are in the dirty laundry basket, later in the week they'll be washed, dried, ironed and folded by my mother, then returned to my top drawer ready to be used again. This is called a cycle. All cycles have to be controlled and supervised, such as the food cycle. Food circulates through your body and turns you into who you are, so you have to be careful about what you let in and what you keep out. I'm exceptional. I can't allow just anything into my body: my poop has to come out the right colour and consistency, this is part of the circulation.

I'm actually never hungry and Mom is very understanding about this, she only gives me foods I like because they circulate with ease, yoghurt and cheese and pasta, peanut butter and bread and cereal, she doesn't insist on the whole vegetable-meat-fish-eggs aspect of eating, saying I'll get around to that when I'm good and ready for it. She makes me mayonnaise sandwiches and cut the crusts off for me, but even then I eat only half or a quarter of the sandwich and it's enough, I nibble at the bread and wet the small pieces with the saliva in my mouth and swish them up between my lips and gums to let them gradually dissolve because I don't want to actually swallow them. *The point is to keep my mind sharp.*

Dad wishes I'd eat like a normal growing American boy. He worries about how I'll manage at the cafeteria when I start school next fall but Mom says she'll pick me up and bring me home for lunch, that's what stay-at-home moms are for!

God gave me this body and mind and I have to take the best possible care of them so I can put them to the best possible use. I know He's got high intentions for me, otherwise I wouldn't have been born in the wealthiest state of the wealthiest country in the world, with the most powerful weapons system capable of blasting the whole human species to kingdom come. Fortunately God and President Bush are buddies. I think of heaven as one big Texas in the sky, with God rambling around in a cowboy hat and boots and checking to make sure everything's in order on his ranch. Taking an occasional pot shot at a planet for the fun of it.

When they dragged Saddam Hussein out of his rat hole the other day his hair was all matted and dirty, his eyes bleary and bloodshot, his beard unkempt and his cheeks gaunt. Dad sat there in front of the TV set and cheered. 'Boy, that's what I call *defeat*,' he said. 'I hope all those Muslim terrorists know what's in store for them.' 'Randall,' said Mom, who was just then setting down a tray in front of him with an icy glass of beer and a bowl of peanuts, 'we should be careful about what we say. You wouldn't want to give Solly the impression that all Muslims are terrorists, would you? I'm sure there are Muslims living right here in California who are very nice people, I just don't know them personally.' She said this in a joking tone of voice but I know she was also telling the truth. Dad took a long swig of beer and said 'Yeah, you're right, Tessie, I'm sorry,' and burped quite loudly which Mom decided to take as a joke so she laughed.

I've got wonderful parents who love each other which isn't the case of most kids in my kindergarten. You can tell they love each other because their framed wedding photos are still standing on the buffet along with all the congratulations cards even though they got married seven years ago! Mom is actually two years older than Dad, I hate to admit it and she certainly doesn't look it but she's *thirty years old,* some of the kids in kindergarten have moms in their forties and my friend Brian's mom is *fifty* which is older than my Grandma Sadie. That means she had him when she was forty-four years old which is disgusting, I can't believe people go on screwing in old age. Yes I know how babies are made, I know everything.

It's actually Grandma Sadie who chose my name for me. She always regretted not giving Dad a Jewish name, so when the next generation came along she didn't want to miss her chance a second time and Mom said it was okay with her. Mom's an easygoing person, she basically wants for everybody to be as happy as possible, and I guess Sol can be a Christian name too.

That's about the extent of my grandmother's influence in my life because luckily she lives far away in Israel and I almost never see her except in the photos she sends us which are always close-ups so you can't see she's sitting in a wheelchair. I say luckily because if she lived any closer she'd try to interfere with us and boss us around like Dad says she always does. Even though he's her own son he dislikes her, but at the same time he's scared of her and doesn't dare to stand up to her so whenever she comes here for a visit there's quite a lot of tension in the air which upsets my mother. As soon as Grandma Sadie's back is turned, Dad gets courageous and attacks her, once he said she was to blame for the death of his beloved father Aron who was a failed playwright at the age of forty-nine, and Mom said that as far as she knew Dad's father was killed by smoking cigarettes rather than by his wife, but Dad said there was a well-known connection between cancer and repressed anger which I'm not sure what that means, repressed.

My father once lived in Israel himself when he was my age and he loved the city of Haifa so much that of all the places to live in the United States of America that's why he chose California, because the eucalyptus and palm trees and orange groves and flowering bushes reminded him of those good old days. Israel is also where he started not liking Arabs because of some Arab girl he fell into and out of love with there, which I don't know anything about because whenever he talks about it he gets all tense and clams up and even to Mom it's a mystery what happened with this childhood sweetheart of his.

Grandma Sadie is a cripple and an orthodox Jew unlike anyone else in the family. She wears a wig because when you're an orthodox Jewish female you're not supposed to show your hair to anyone except your husband in case they covet you and want to screw you out of wedlock. Given that she's widowed and confined to a wheelchair, I'd be surprised if anyone would like to covet and screw her but she still refuses to take off the wig. Recently this rabbi in Florida ordered Jewish women to stop wearing wigs made out of Indian women's hair because in India they bow down to gods with six arms or elephant heads or whatever and their hair gets all sullied by praying to these gods so Jewish women will also get sullied by wearing wigs made out of it so they have to buy new synthetic wigs *at once*, the rabbi said, but Grandma said that was going too far.

The wheelchair is because of a car accident she was in many years ago but it certainly doesn't keep her from getting around, she's been to more countries than everyone in our family put together. She's a famous lecturer and her own mother Erra (namely my great-grandmother who I call G.G.) is a famous singer and when Daddy gets around to enlisting for Iraq he'll be a famous war hero and it's up to me to decide what I want to be famous about but that'll be no problem at all, fame runs in the family.

Unlike my father, whose mom was away hectoring in universities all the time when he was little, I have an excellent mom who

7

decided to be stay-at-home out of her own free will and not because it was women's destiny like in the olden days. Her name is Tess but I call her Mom. All children call their mothers Mom of course, and sometimes in the park another kid yells '*Mom!*' and my mother spins around, thinking it's me. I can't *believe* she could confuse me with anyone else. 'It's like when someone else's cell phone has the same ring as yours,' she says. 'You sort of snap to attention and then realise—oh, nope, it's not me they want.'

It's *not* like a cell phone. I'm unique. My voice is MY VOICE.

At kindergarten and elsewhere, I amaze everybody with my reading skills because Mom taught me to read when I was just a little baby. I've heard her tell the story a thousand times, how I'd be lying there in my crib and she'd flash these cards at me with words printed on them and pronounce the words, which she did for twenty-minute periods three times a day practically from the day I was born so I pretty much learned to talk and read at the same time and I can't even *remember* when I didn't know how to read. Mom says my vocabulary is awesome.

Dad's away from dawn to dusk every weekday because he commutes more than two hours each way to work in Santa Clara at a job of programming computers in a very demanding capacity. He earns an excellent salary so we're a two-car family—'We've got more cars than kids!' they sometimes say laughingly because Mom comes from a family where they had six kids and only one car. Her family was Catholic which meant my grandma wasn't allowed to do family planning so she just kept on having babies until they got into deep financial waters and then she stopped. My father had a Jewish upbringing, so when he and Mom fell in love they decided to find a church halfway between Catholic and Jewish, and what they finally decided on was Protestant so they're allowed to do family planning, basically what that means is the wife takes a pill and her husband can screw her as much as he likes without putting babies in her stomach, which is why I'm an only child. Mom wants to have another baby some day and Dad says they should be able to afford it a year or two down the line, but no matter how many kids they have I'm not worried about sibling rivalry, Jesus had a whole slew of brothers, too, and you never hear about what *they* did with their lives, there's just no comparison.

Once a month my Dad goes to a men's group where they talk about what it's like to be a man nowadays since women started working. I'm not sure why he needs this group given the fact that my mother doesn't work but anyhow they all take turns sitting in the hot seat and telling the truth about their problems and then they're supposed to follow the group's advice and if they disobey they're punished with lots of push-ups and sometimes the whole group goes out and does manly things together like hiking and swearing and sleeping out in the wild and enduring mosquito bites because men have more stamina than women.

I'm sure glad I was born a boy because it's far more unusual for boys to be raped than girls, except if they're Catholic which we're not. On the sobbingweb which I stumbled on one day when I asked Google for images of the war in Iraq you can see hundreds of girls and women being brutally raped for free and it says they were really and truly harmed in front of the cameras. They sure don't look as if they're enjoying themselves especially when they're gagged and tied up. Sometimes the men are not only screwing them in their mouth or their vagina or their anus but also making as if to cut their nipples off with craft knives, although you don't see the nipples actually getting cut off so it might just be make-believe. Mohamed Atta and the other 9/11 terrorists also used craft knives when they flew the planes into the Twin Towers when I was three years old, I can still remember Dad calling me in to watch the towers falling down over and over again and saying 'fucking Arabs' and drinking beer.

I've got my own little computer on my desk in my room, surrounded by all my stuffed toys and picture books, my drawings from kindergarten neatly taped to the walls with Magic ©Scotch tape that won't tear the wallpaper when you take it off, and also my name in wooden letters on wheels—S—O—L—which my mom painstakingly covered with gold leaf so it would shine and shine. My computer allows me to play games all by myself because I don't have any brothers and sisters which is the main reason my parents bought it for me, so I wouldn't feel lonely. I can play Scrabble and checkers, snakes-and-ladders, and a bunch of idiotic little computer games for kids, where you get to shoot people who are climbing up the walls of buildings and watch them tumble to the ground and then you get a point, or whatever. But given that my room is right next to my parents' room, and given that I've got perfect control of my body and can walk on tiptoe without making a sound, it's a cinch for me to slip into Mom's computer while she's doing the housework downstairs and get on Google and learn about what's happening in the real world.

My mind is huge. As long as I keep my body clean and the food circulating correctly, I can process any amount of information, I can be President Bush and God combined, guzzling google. Dad told me the word *googol* used to mean the biggest number you could imagine—one followed by a hundred zeros—but now it's pretty much the same thing as infinity. You just have to download and you can get the girls being raped or screwed in the anus by horses or dogs or whatever else you want, click click click, with animal cum dripping out of their mouths which are half-smiling. Mom almost never uses her computer and also she sings as she does the vacuuming so how could she possibly hear me clicking with my right hand on the mouse as I put my left hand on my crotch and start to rub. My mind is racing my stomach is almost empty I'm an exciting machine. I'm not allowed to but it's easy to be two people a thousand people plus all the animals, everything will be fine as long as it's carefully controlled and timed and structured.

did Dad…?

good thing I'm a boy

The corpses of Iraqi soldiers lying in the sand is one of my favourite things to click on. It's a whole slide show. Sometimes you can't even tell what body parts you're looking at. Torsos maybe? Or legs? They're sort of wrapped in rips and strips of clothing and they're lying in the sand, partially covered by the sand which has absorbed their blood, it's all very dry. You can see American soldiers standing around them, looking down at them and thinking *There but for the grace of God…was this a human being?*

When I was really little and my dad worked right nearby in Lodi, at a job that didn't have as good a salary but didn't take as long to commute to, he used to sing to me at bedtime, giving me a paddle-whacking like his father used to give to him. Now I'm usually asleep by the time he gets home so he doesn't sing to me anymore but I know he still loves me as much as before and he's just working so hard to keep us up with a good standard of living and be able to meet the mortgage payments for a two-garage house in one of the cushiest real estates in the country. Mom says this is something to be proud of, even if I miss those bedtimes with my dad.

Anyway one of my favourite songs he used to sing was called 'Dry Bones':

> *E-ze-kiel cried, 'Dem dry bones'!*
> *E-ze-kiel cried, 'Dem dry bones'!*
> *E-ze-kiel cried, 'Dem dry bones'!*
> *Oh hear the word of the Lord*
> *The foot bone connected to the—leg bone,*
> *The leg bone connected to the—knee bone,*
> *The knee bone connected to the—thigh bone*

He'd go paddle-whacking all the way up my body in semi-tones, then all the way down again. I used to love it, and I always think about that song when I see the dead Iraqi soldiers or the photographs of people sliced in two by a car accident, like wow, this is *not reparable,* not even by God when they get to heaven, you know what I mean? This torso is—all alone. This leg bone is connected to—nothing at all. It's pretty scary because when you're little and you watch old-fashioned cartoons on TV, you see characters like Tom and Jerry or Bugs Bunny or the Roadrunner getting crushed by heavy stones, whammed and blammed by cement mixers, sliced and diced by electric fans, or plummeting down cliffsides and splatting flat as pancakes on the highway, and then a couple of seconds later they're all in one piece again and ready to go on to their next adventure. But with those Iraqi soldiers you can really tell there are no more adventures in store.

Mom is very much against violence, she gets emotional about it which is only natural because women are always more emotional than men. She's just an extremely positive person and I don't see any point in sullying her illusions. She supervises everything I watch on TV which means yes for 'Pokemon' and no for 'Inuyasha', yes for 'Gummi Bears' and no for 'The Simpsons'. As far as movies go she says I'm still a bit too young for *Harry Potter* and *The Lord of the Rings*, which is unbelievable. I remember she didn't even want me to see *Bambi* when my friend Diane from kindergarten gave me the DVD for my fifth birthday, even if it's just an old cartoon she was afraid I'd be upset about the scene where Bambi's mother gets killed. She thinks I'm too young to know about death so I do my best to protect her. Last week we saw a dead sparrow at the edge of the road and she started stroking my hair and saying 'It's all right, darling, he's in heaven with God now' and I clung to her leg and sobbed to make her feel better.

To her, Arnold Schwarzenegger is nothing but the governor of California. She's never seen any of his films but I have thanks to my friend Brian or rather his parents. They've got lots of old videos in their rec room down in the basement, all three *Terminators* plus *Eraser* plus *Collateral Damage*, to say nothing of the complete collection of *Star Wars* and also *Godzilla* which is like a remake or rather a pre-make of 9/11 with the Manhattan skyscrapers tumbling down and New Yorkers screaming in panic and running around in all directions. We watch them to our heart's content because Brian's mom isn't stay-at-home and his babysitter doesn't mind as long as she can paint her toenails and talk to her boyfriend on her cell phone. Schwarzenegger as a robot is totally awesome, he's unbeatable and indestructible, if his human skin surface gets damaged he's got no qualms about cutting open his own arm or cutting out his own eyes with a scalpel, so I'm definitely not going to be jittery about my mole operation next July.

Dad is not an athlete or a sportsman by any stretch of the imagination but in the summertime he plays softball with guys his age in the neighbourhood. He takes it quite seriously because it was one of the things he used to share with *his* dad when they lived in New York City. He bought me a game called Base, which means there's a T-ball stand you set the plastic ball on and you practise hitting it with a plastic bat, someone runs to pick up the ball for you and then you start all over again. During Dad's softball games, Mom and I play *Base* together. Some of Mom's friends are surprised to see her running to pick up the ball about a hundred and seventy-five times in a row, clapping and cheering for me and saying 'Hooray, Sol! Good for you!' every single time. They think it must be boring for her but I know it's not; it goes along with her love for me. Instead of boasting to them about my great destiny, she just shrugs and tells them it burns off calories.

I'll be starting real school in the fall and I intend to listen to everything, record everything and get sterling grades while still keeping a low profile; for the time being I don't want anyone else to know that I'm the Sun King, Only Sun and Only Son, Son of Google, Son of God, Eternal Omnipotent Son of the World Wide Web. WWW turned upside down is MMM: apart from My Miraculous Mother to whom I've allowed brief glimpses, no one has the vaguest notion of the brilliance, the radiance, the fabulous radioactivity in my brain that will one day transform and heal the universe.

I've only got one defect which is this mole on my left temple.

It's the size of a quarter, round and raised, brown and fuzzy. A tiny defect—but on the temple of Solomon, even tiny defects have to be eliminated. Mom's making arrangements for it to be surgically removed in July. Dad's a bit against it, but he'll probably be in Iraq by then.

The war in Iraq has been over for almost a year now but lots of American soldiers are still getting killed over there and when Dad gets upset about this Mom tries to gently change the subject and get him thinking about something pleasant instead. 'There's no point in getting all het up about things you can't change, Randall,' she says. 'All we can do is try to keep this world as safe a place as possible, each at our own level. President Bush is doing his job, you're doing yours and I'm doing mine.'

Mom's job is to keep *me* safe and I think we've probably got the safest house on the planet. It's *childproofed*, which is a word Mom explained to me a couple of weeks ago. (She always insists on explaining things to me as fully, honestly and clearly as possible, and the minute she tells me something I know it forever as if I'd invented it myself.)

'Our house is childproofed,' she said, 'which means we've done everything in our power to make it safe for children.'

'And our fence is burglarproof,' said Dad, 'which means we've done everything in our power to make it safe for burglars.'

'No, no,' said Mom. 'There's a difference between *proof* and *proofed*. An umbrella is rain*proof*, which means that rain can't get through it.'

'And my whisky is 70-*proof*,' said Dad, 'which means it's forbidden to people over 70.'

Mom laughed because Dad kept on trying to make jokes, but

the way she laughed made it clear that he should stop interrupting; then she went on telling me about how they childproofed the house. For instance, all the electrical outlets are covered over in case I try to stick my fingers into them and get electrocuted with my hair all sticking out in all directions and my eyes popping out of their sockets like a cat in a cartoon or like one of the guys that gets sent to the chair by President Bush for being on Death Row. There are soft plastic rounded corners added to every right-angle table and counter in the house so I won't bang into them and get a deep gash in my head with lots of blood spurting out of it, then have to be rushed to the hospital and get stitches as my parents stand next to my bed, tearing their hair out with anguish and guilt. Also the burners to the stove have a special blocking mechanism so I can't turn them on by accident and burn myself by sticking my hand into the flame or setting fire to the curtains, which would set fire to the whole house and leave me nothing but a little pile of charred flesh like an Iraqi soldier amidst the smoking ruins of our house, whereas Dad just took out a second mortgage on it. Even the toilet is childproofed so the lid won't fall on my penis while I'm peeing, which I guess would really hurt. When I want to poop I have to call Mom to come and unhook a hook and let the lid down very carefully.

Mom knows about all this stuff thanks to a course she took on parent-child relationships. It wasn't only about child-proofing, it was about all the other aspects, like how you should respect your children and listen to them and not treat them as if they were stupid idiots the way parents used to treat their children in the olden days. I must admit that Mom has never made me feel like an idiot. It's like with Mary and Jesus. Mary would never go against any of Jesus's wishes because she knew he had a special destiny cut out for him, so she just kept all these things in her heart and pondered them. The main difference is, I don't plan to end up nailed to any old Cross.

Mom always comes to say prayers with me at bedtime. We invent a different prayer every night, we can ask God to help us bring peace to Iraq and make all the Iraqis believe in Jesus, or we can have a special thought for the health and happiness of our family members, or we can thank God for giving us such a nice neighbourhood to live in. Praying's like a private conversation between you and God except you can't really hear the answers, you've just got to trust in them.

'You're the most precious thing in the world to me,' Mom said once as she was kissing me goodnight after prayertime.

'More precious than Dad?' I asked her.

'Oh, there's no comparison,' she said, laughing, and I'm not sure what her laughter meant but I got the feeling it meant *Yes*. I think she basically sees Dad as the breadwinner in the family and a helper around the house, and they talk over important things together like whether they'll be able to afford a new kitchen next year, but she's also acutely aware of his defects. For instance, Dad's the sort of person who sometimes loses his temper in an unpredictable way. Once the three of us went up to Sequoia National Park, it was a nice October day, we were all in a good mood and sort of ambling down the road hand in hand. The nature was so beautiful that it made Dad nostalgic for when he used to live out East, so he started trying to tell me about one time when he and his father drove up to Vermont together and slept out in a field, but because Mom loves us so much she's always watching to make sure we don't get run over by cars or trucks so the minute she hears one coming even half a mile away she tells us to be sure to stay on the edge of the road and this kept on interrupting Dad's train of thought until finally he broke off and muttered, 'Ah, forget it.' 'Oh, darling, I'm so sorry,' said Mom, 'please go on with your story. We just need to make sure Solly knows how important it is to keep off the road when he hears a car coming, that's all.' But Dad refused to tell us about what happened that day in Vermont.

Or another time we were at home, they'd already had supper and I didn't feel like having any so I didn't join them at the table, and then we went upstairs to watch a non-violent family viewing film on TV together and in the middle of the film I started feeling a bit hungry so I asked Mom to bring me something to eat. She went down and got me a tray ready with milk and cookies, which I really appreciated because meanwhile she was actually missing the best part of the film, I said thank you but suddenly out of the blue Dad said in a loud voice: 'Tess, it's time you stopped waiting on this child hand and foot. You're his *mother,* not his slave! Being his mother means that *you're* in power, *you've* got the authority, not *him*, for Christ's sake!' And Mom was so taken aback by his use of language especially the word Christ in vain that her hands were trembling when she set the tray down in front of me.

'Let's talk about it later, Randall,' she said. In the parent-child relationship course they probably said it wasn't a good idea for kids to sit in on their parents' marital quarrels. Mom has taken all sorts of classes in meditation and positive thinking and relaxation and self-esteem, and she's gotten really good at it so later on in bed I heard them talking things over and trying to pinpoint exactly when the tension started rising in the course of the evening.

'Maybe it reminded you of a scene from your own childhood?' Mom suggested very gently. Dad grunted. 'Or maybe, in a way, you're jealous because your own mom never took care of you the way I take care of Solly?' A few more grunts and reluctant murmurs and sighs from Dad. I guess they managed to iron things out and repair their marital relationship though I must say I've never heard them screwing despite the fact that my room is right next to theirs with just a plywood door in between. Maybe married people screw in silence unlike what you see on the Brutal XXX sites where they pant and roar.

One thing my parents agree on completely is that I should never be slapped, spanked, or given any form of corporal punishment whatsoever. This is because they've read lots of books where it shows that battered children turn into battering parents, molested children into paedophiles and raped children into pimps and prostitutes. So the important thing is you should always talk, talk, talk, ask the child why it misbehaved and give it the chance to explain itself before pointing out, as gently as possible, how it might be able to behave better the next time around. You should never hit it.

This seems to me an excellent principle, and the thing about Jesus I disagree with most is the idea of turning the other cheek and letting other people hurt you. If I was Jesus, when the Roman soldiers came to arrest me I'd never have let them tie my hands behind my back without putting up a fight, to say nothing of crowning me with thorns or spitting in my face or flagellating me. That's where Jesus made his big mistake in my opinion and it led him straight to the Cross.

Mom has made this very clear to me: '*No one* has the right to raise so much as a finger against you, Solly,' she tells me, looking deep into my eyes. 'No one in the world. Do you hear me?' And I nod solemnly and think Boy, good thing we're Protestant because

Protestant ministers (like Jewish rabbis) are allowed to get married and screw their wives so they don't molest and rape little boys the way Catholic priests do, according to what we've been hearing about in the news these days.

Anyway. So far only one person in the world has dared to transgress this rule about corporal punishment, namely my mom's own father Grandpa Williams, and I doubt if he'll make another attempt in the near future. Last summer we were on vacation at their place up in Seattle, which (visiting other people's places) is already a problem because of mealtimes; no one makes the food I like and Grandma Williams refuses to change her way of cooking so Mom has to do a special daily shopping just for me.

One afternoon Mom and Dad went out to the movies and Grandpa took me with him to the neighbourhood park. He doesn't have a Base game like we do, and when Mom described it to him he said, 'Oh, come off it, it's time this young rascal got a taste of the real thing!' So what he brought along was a real bat and softball and glove, and even though at five I was already very strong and well coordinated for my age, that bat weighed a *ton* compared to the plastic one. I was at the plate, Grandpa was on the pitcher's mound, he kept throwing me these incredibly fast and nasty curve balls and I kept missing them one after the other. 'Strike one, strike two, strike three, you're out!' he said, which made me furious so I threw the bat in his direction. It missed him by a mile but still, his eyes popped out of his head when he saw that and he yelled at me. 'What the hell do you think you're doing?' he said, which I found deeply offensive with the word *hell* in it which you're not supposed to use in front of children. He went and picked up the bat and brought it back to me and said with a serious look on his face, 'Listen, Sol. I know you're used to plastic bats, but wooden ones can be *extremely dangerous*. So don't you *ever* do that again, do you hear me? Okay? Shall we continue?'

Okay, I said, but I was upset by the way the afternoon was going with my own grandfather humiliating me, apparently not realising I was Number One and that he was supposed to say 'Hooray, Sol! Good for you!' the way Mom does, instead of talking to me in that condescending way. We started over again but Grandpa just went on throwing me those mean curve balls and because of feeling so upset I swung the bat even more wildly than before. 'Strike one, strike two, strike three, you're out!' he said, and this time when he pronounced the words *you're out* I saw red and threw the bat again as hard as I could, not caring where it went, and it landed on his foot. It can't have hurt that much, but it sure made him fly off the handle. He strode over to me and grabbed me by the wrist and lifted me up until I was practically dangling in the air and then— *whack, whack, whack*—hit me on the bum three times with the flat of his hand.

I was shocked beyond belief. The smarting pain on my rear end flowed straight into my bloodstream which was like a lighted match meeting gasoline. It caught fire and I erupted like a volcano, overflowing with scream after burning scream of rage and indignation because *no one* has the right to raise a finger against Solomon. I could tell that Grandpa was aghast to see what a problem he'd made for himself with his *whack whack whack* and I wasn't about to stop because I wanted to teach him a lesson once and for all. I screamed all the way home in the car, and when he parked the car in the driveway and led me back into the house I screamed so loud the neighbours must have wondered who was being murdered.

Grandma's anxious questions, soothing words and comforting gestures couldn't silence me and I was still screaming when Mom and Dad came home from the movies an hour later.

Mom rushed over to me in a panic and took me in her arms and I fell silent at once. 'Solly, Solly! What happened?'

When I told her that her father had spanked me, I could feel her whole body harden underneath me and I knew for sure that Grandpa would regret what he'd done.

'Did you turn the other cheek?' asked Dad.

'Randall,' Mom said sharply. 'That's *not* funny.'

We packed our things and left their place without even staying for supper. As Dad drove us back to California, Mom tried to explain a bit so I wouldn't hate her father for the rest of my life. 'He's got old-fashioned ideas about education,' she said. 'That's the way he was brought up and that's the way he brought up his own kids, so you have to forgive him. Plus, don't forget there were six of us! If he hadn't been careful about discipline, that household would have turned into pandemonium.'

Still, I'm pretty sure Mom didn't speak to her father again until he sent her a written apology, along with the solemn promise never to hit me again.

I AM POWERFUL.

All that happened last summer, when I was five and a half. That was Mom's side of the family. Now I've turned six and it's Palm Sunday (which is when Jesus returned to Jerusalem on donkey-back—definitely not a good move on his part) and we're dealing with Dad's side of the family. G.G. flew in yesterday from New York City. My father gets along much better with G.G. than he does with Grandma Sadie who is his own mother, in fact he almost worships G.G. but Mom has strong reservations about her—for one thing because she smokes and for another because she doesn't go to church.

When I go out onto the verandah she's there already, sitting in the white wicker rocking chair with a book in one hand and a little cigar in the other, her white hair standing up in little wisps and catching the sunlight.

I don't like it that she's up.

I want always to be the first one up, the one who greets and creates the day.

'Good morning, sweet Sol,' she says, glancing at her watch and slipping a bookmark into her book. 'Goodness, it's barely seven—what an earlybird you are! I've got an excuse, I'm jet-lagged.'

I don't deign to answer. She's in my way, clogging up my thought processes; I wish I could grab a remote control and zap her.

'Speaking of earlybirds,' she continues, beckoning to me—'come over here!'

I cross the verandah sluggishly, dragging my feet so she won't think I'm interested in whatever it is she wants to show me.

'Look!' she whispers, gathering me onto her lap and pointing towards a hibiscus bush in the garden just below. 'Look! Isn't it *exquisite?*'

I look, and see a hummingbird hovering among the bright scarlet blooms. But as a general rule I don't like it when people point stuff out to me—I would have noticed that hummingbird all by myself if G.G. hadn't been here.

'And look, darling!' she says again, pointing. 'Over there—the diadem!'

Against my will I look, squinting into the jagged blaze of the rising sun, and see a spiderweb spun between two bars of the garden fence, its every line glittering with diamond dewdrops. I would have seen that, too, if only she'd given me the time, if only she hadn't gotten out here before I did, if only she hadn't made a point of noticing everything first just so she could beat me to it. She rocks a little bit in the chair with me, singing 'Itsy-bitsy Spider' to me as if I were two years old or something. Sure, her voice is amazing no matter what she sings but I feel uncomfortable being on her lap because she seems unclean to me. Her body gives off pungent odours of sweat, cigar smoke and oldness. Didn't she even take a shower when she got in last night? To fulfil God's purpose I have to stay clean—that much I know. So I scramble off her lap and down the steps, as if I had some important business to take care of in my sandbox under the verandah.

What with G.G. visiting and there still being a couple of hours before church, Mom whips up a fabulous breakfast of pancakes and sausages and scrambled eggs and maple syrup, fruit salad and coffee and orange juice. We all join hands around the table, bow our heads and Mom says grace, 'For these and all thy blessings, Lord, we are truly grateful.' Dad and I chime in to say 'Amen' with her and G.G. says nothing. Then Mom and Dad both kiss me and clap for me which is a family tradition they started when I said 'Amen' for the first time when I was a little baby and then they got into the habit of doing it at every gracetime so now it's become part and parcel of the ceremony, which means that God and Sol are being celebrated together.

G.G. is surprised to see that I help myself to only one pancake, cut up by Mom into tiny pieces which I absorb one at a time, rolling them slowly between my lips and gums instead of chewing them, often going up to my bedroom between bites.

'Won't you stay at the table with us, Sol?' she asks, as I head for the staircase.

'Oh, no,' Mom answers for me at once. 'Sol has always been a bit particular about food. Don't pay any attention to his wanderings—he's fine. We see to it that he gets a balanced diet.'

'I wasn't worried about that,' says G.G. 'I just thought it would be nice to have him around as company.'

'He's a fussy eater,' says Dad. 'And since Tess gives in to all his caprices, he's not about to change.'

'Randall,' says Mom. 'Do you think that's a pleasant way of putting it—in public?'

At this point I close my bedroom door and by the time I get back they've changed the subject; now they're discussing my mole. Mom must have told G.G. about our plans to have it removed this coming summer, and G.G. is thunderstruck.

'Surgically removed?' she says, putting down her fork. 'At age six? Whatever for?'

'My dear Erra,' says Mom with a look of patience and sweetness on her face. 'Randall has visited pretty much every website there is on the subject of congenital pigmented nævuses, and believe me, there are a *number* of good reasons for having it removed at this time.'

'But Randall,' says G.G., turning to my dad. 'You can't...you won't let her do that, will you? What about...your little bat? Would you have wanted Sadie to have *it* removed?'

This goes back to some game they had when my dad was a kid, in which *his* mole, which is located on his left shoulder, was a fuzzy little bat that used to talk to him and whisper advice into his ear. G.G.'s got a mole, too—in the crook of her left arm—that's what congenital means, it's been handed down in the family for generations although it keeps turning up on different parts of the body and it skipped a generation; Grandma Sadie doesn't have one.

'Erra,' says Mom. 'Forgive me, but we need to get out of the metaphorical world here. I know you and Randall have always had special feelings about your moles, they've been like a secret connection between you, but Solly's is a whole 'nother ball game. So let me tell you, realistically. Reason no. 1: the mole being extremely visible, virtually on his face, he could be teased about it at school; even if this is *not* the case, it's liable to make him self-conscious and give him an inferiority complex. Reason no. 2: unlike the two of you, Sol has what is known as a *nuisance mole*. Being right at the junction between his temple and his cheek, when he starts shaving ten years or so down the line, daily contact with the razor is bound to irritate it. Reason no. 3, by far the most important one, is of course the risk of developing melanoma. I hate to point this out, but Randall's father having died of cancer, there's a family history that makes Solly all the more vulnerable to this possibility. As I said, Erra, we've read up on the subject. We've also consulted a number of specialists, and reached the decision that *we prefer not to take that risk.*'

'Oh,' says G.G.

'There are two options open to us,' says Dad. 'A shave biopsy or an excision biopsy. The excision cuts deeper but virtually eliminates the possibility of his developing cancer later on. I think we're going to go for it.'

'Oh,' says G.G.

'That won't change anything about *our* moles,' Dad goes on reassuringly. 'Solly has never felt one way or the other about his—have you, Solly?'

'Yes I have,' I say.

'Oh?' says Dad, a bit startled. 'How's that?'

'Negative. I feel negative about it.'

'You see?' says Mom triumphantly. 'Reason no. 4! So we've scheduled the operation for early July. That way he'll have the whole summer ahead of him for his skin to heal, and be able to start school in September without a care in the world.'

G.G. looks down, strokes the mole in the crook of her left arm, and says something that sounds like *lute*.

'I beg your pardon?' says Mom.

'I liked mine so much I gave it a name—it's called Lute,' murmurs G.G. with a smile, and I see Mom glancing briefly but pointedly at Dad as if to say You see what I mean? She's losing it…and Dad looking fiercely at Mom as if to say Shut up. This is something I do *not* want to witness, so I scuttle back to my room.

When I return to the kitchen the atmosphere has changed again because it's time to start getting ready for church and Mom has asked Dad to help her clear away the breakfast things and Dad is doing so without a word.

At ten-thirty we get into Dad's car and he backs smoothly out of the driveway and we head for church. I'm in the back seat with my safety belt attached and as we drive slowly down the beautiful calm tree-lined streets of our neighbourhood Dad starts telling us a story. 'I remember once when I was your age, Solly, and spending some weeks alone with my dad—my mother, as usual, was off on some trip or other—Erra and a friend of hers suggested we all get together on Sunday for a picnic in Central Park.'

'Excuse me, Randall,' says Mom, 'but I have to point out that you're not really stopping at the stop signs. You're just slowing down.'

'Boy, I was so excited! I couldn't wait for it to be Sunday. But just when we had the picnic basket all packed and were about to leave the house, it started raining cats and dogs.'

'I mean, *stop* means *stop*, darling—right?' murmurs Mom, gently stroking Dad's hand on the steering wheel. 'You wouldn't want Sol to think that driving rules are optional, would you?'

Dad sighs and obeys—only now he purposely brakes hard when we come to the stop sign at the end of every block, as if to under-line the fact that he's obeying.

'So you had to cancel?' I ask, to bring him back to his story.

'No, no...We went down to their place on the Bowery and had our picnic—on the floor!'

'On the *floor?*' says Mom with a grimace. 'Given Erra's reputa-tion as a housekeeper, that must have been a rather...er...dusty meal!'

'It was a terrific meal,' says Dad, braking violently and accelerating just as violently. 'As a matter of fact it was one of the most wonderful meals I ever ate.'

'Be that as it may,' says Mom after a few moments, 'I wonder if you could ask G.G. to refrain from smoking in our household.'

'She doesn't!' says Dad. 'She goes outside to smoke.'

'Well as far as I know, the verandah is part of our household,' says Mom. 'Not only that, but she smokes around Sol. He can inhale the smoke, it can damage his lungs.'

'Tess,' says Dad, pulling onto a bigger road with thank heavens no more stop signs on it, because I was starting to feel woozy from getting jerked back and forth, 'Erra happens to be one of my favourite people in the world and I *truly* wish you'd try to make her feel at home on the rare occasions when she comes to pay us a visit, which is about once every three *years.*'

'Oh,' says Mom, on the verge of tears. 'Because that enormous breakfast I just made you guys, which took me an hour to cook and cost me a considerable amount of time and money to shop for yesterday—that didn't live up to your standards of hospitality?'

'Of course it did, darling. Of course it did. I'm sorry.'

'No matter what I do, I can't seem to be able to please you where Erra is concerned. She's this—goddess or something...'

'I said I was sorry. I apologise. What do you want me to do, stop the car and get down on my knees?'

Just then we arrive at the church and Dad parks the car.

'Frankly, Randall, I would say it's not me you should be getting down on your knees to, it's God. I would say you should do some serious praying to try and find out why it is that the arrival of your grandmother makes you so incredibly hostile towards your wife.'

'Why doesn't G.G. go to church?' I ask, as the three of us join the throngs of worshippers now converging towards the church doors at a pace which is neither fast nor slow. There are clumps of purple and white pansies on either side of the sidewalk, and a manicured lawn holding them in. This is structure; this I like.

'Because she doesn't believe in God,' says Dad matter-of-factly, as if he were saying she prefers Pepsi to Coke. The idea of not believing in God seems to me preposterous, but from the expression on Mom's face I can tell she won't be eager for this conversation to be continued on our way home.

God is everywhere, everywhere, how can you not *believe* in Him?
    He is the Power and the Glory
        the Prime Mover   the Maker   the absolute source

the secret of everything that swells and bursts
from the tiniest dandelion in the lawn
to the frenzied horse's cock spurting cum all over a woman's
    face
from the boiling bubbling heart of a volcano on the verge of
    eruption
to the mushroom cloud of a nuclear bomb
all of this is God   God   God
this energy, this opening and throbbing
this *movement of matter*

That's what I think about during the church service as we march in procession up to the altar carrying palm branches and singing *Hosanna! Hosanna in the highest!*—God is the Power and the Glory and all of us are sinners because Eve ate from the tree of knowledge and nowadays the tree of knowledge is the Internet with its billions of branches extending in all directions, we keep on eating its fruit and sinning more and more with carnal knowledge so we'll always need purifiers and if I want to be a purifier like Christ or Bush or Schwarzenegger, I have to know everything there is to know about evil.

> *From Olivet they followed,*
> *mid an exultant crowd*
> *the victor palm branch waving*
> *And chanting clear and loud!*

The minister launches into a sermon about the situation in Iraq, which reminds me of the stumps and lumps of dead Iraqi soldiers in the sand which reminds me of the women being raped and this hardens my penis so I use the hymn book to hide what I'm doing, rubbing myself gently all the way through the sermon until I almost faint with the images. At night sometimes in my bedroom—*All glory, laud and honour*—imagining I'm the foaming horse or the shooting machine gun or the exploding bomb—*To thee, Redeemer, King*—I rub myself raw with the sense of power rising in my entrails and after the service my parents wend their way through the milling crowd outside on the sidewalk, shaking hands with people and saying 'How are you?' 'Good to see you again' 'See you on Easter Sunday, then' and 'Isn't it just a *beautiful* day?'

In the afternoon it gets really hot out so I go down to my favourite place to play which is in the sandbox under the verandah, I take some Legos down with me just to prove to Mom that I'm not addicted to my computer games which she sometimes worries about for my mental health. A while later Dad and G.G. come out and sit on the verandah under the parasol and I can listen in on their conversation which is something I like to do because I learn stuff while nobody's watching and later I can amaze everybody with my knowledge.

'Tell me about your new job, Ran,' says G.G.

'Oh...' says Dad, and it's clear that for some reason the question makes him squirm. 'There's not much to tell. Computer programming...'

'Any interest in it?'

'Yeah, well, the seven percent interest on my long-term savings plan.'

'Ah, I see...What about your co-workers?'

'Bunch of nerds.'

'Oh, that's too bad...'

'Well…not everyone can be an artist, hey?'

'No, that's true.'

'But I mean the salary's good, my chances for promotion are very good, and I do derive a certain amount of satisfaction from knowing I'll be able to send Solly to an excellent college on the East coast without having to ask for help from anybody.'

'*Anybody* being…your mother, I suppose.'

'Naturally.'

'How *is* Sadie?'

'The same…only more so.'

'God help us.'

'You said it. How long since *you* last saw her?'

'Tell you the truth, Randall, I don't know. Must be nearly fifteen years now…Ever since she published that dreadful book—what year was that?'

'1990. *Rockabye Nazi Baby*…I remember because it came out just a few months before Dad died.'

'Almost killed me, too.'

For some reason this makes them laugh; they must be drinking martinis or gin tonics or something.

'So she's still at it?' says G.G. after a pause.

'She's still at it.'

'Jesus.'

'What about yourself, Erra?' says Dad. 'How's life been treating you?'

'I'm fine, darling,' says G.G. 'I can't complain. All in all I've had a marvellous life.'

'Don't say all in all, as if it were over…You're only—what?—sixty-five now?'

'Yup. And a half.'

'Hell, you've got *decades* ahead of you! And I swear you don't look a day over…ah…*forty-seven* and a half.'

'Thanks, dear. But I must admit I'm beginning to feel my age. Not only did I have a fairly genuine heart attack a couple of months ago, I don't have a tooth left in my head!'

The two of them laugh at the same time.

'Is that why you stopped singing?' asks Dad. 'You were afraid your dentures might fall out during a performance?'

More laughter.

'Oh, no!' says G.G. 'I simply realised that my voice wasn't up to scratch anymore…But it's not a painful thing. I sat down and took my hand and said to myself: Listen, kid, you've recorded countless hours of music and given concerts all over the world, you've made a mint, and an impact, and from now on you should undertake to seriously enjoy life and nothing else. Read the books you want to read, see the people you love, take Mercedes with you to all those wonderful countries you saw too briefly…'

'I'm sorry about Mercedes, by the way,' says Dad.

'Careful, Ran.'

'What?'

'Careful about this *I'm sorry* thing. You must've said *I'm sorry* a dozen times since I got in last night. It's a dangerous habit—not good for you. Not good for your soul.'

'I mean, Tess is an open-minded person in so many ways, but for some reason when it comes to homosexuality…'

'She was afraid it would traumatise Solly to see two old ladies holding hands?'

'I'm sorry, Erra.'

'See what I mean? Stop it!'

They laugh. I can smell the smell of G.G. lighting up a cigar.

33

'Speaking of Solly,' she says after a while, 'I wanted to buy him a present before I left New York. I had a rather hilarious experience wandering up and down the aisles of *Toys 'R' Us* on Forty-Fourth Street…I kept thinking of Tess's obsession with safety, so I'd go: Well, let's see, now, this is a beautiful crane but Sol might swallow the hook and it would get caught in his intestines and cause internal hæmorrhage…Ah, here's a great chemistry set but it's full of things that scare and flare and could be poisonous if swallowed…Um, well, this looks like a great electric train but he might accidentally electrocute himself…Hm…One by one, every toy in the store turned into a deadly weapon intent upon attacking and destroying my great-grandson. So I gave up, and arrived empty-handed.'

Now they're both laughing uproariously.

I feel miffed. I wish she'd bought me one of those presents.

I go past them into the house, where Mom is getting an appetiser dish ready with carrot sticks, celery sticks with cheddar cheese, radishes, cherry tomatoes, sliced mushrooms, crackers and dip. I nibble at a piece of cheese and help myself to some Wonder Bread in the fridge. She knows I won't be joining them for supper.

'Did you know G.G. has false teeth?' I ask her.

'Sure I do, sweet. She needs a glass on her bedside table to put them in every night before she goes to sleep.'

'Oh, yuk…How come she lost all her teeth?'

'I think it's because she was malnourished as a child.'

'You mean her parents didn't give her enough to eat?'

'Oh…it's a long story…I think she was in a refugee camp or something…She doesn't much like to talk about it.'

I think to myself: so you can have false teeth like G.G., or false hair like Grandma Sadie, you can have false eyelashes, false breasts…'What about a false heart?' I say out loud.

'What do you mean? A heart transplant? When they put somebody else's heart in your chest? Yes, that's possible.'

'And false feet?'

'I guess pretty much everything can be replaced nowadays.'

'And a false brain?'

'Hm, I'm not sure. I don't think so.'

'A false soul?'

'Nope,' says Mom, smiling now as she arranges the raw vegetables on an oval plate in a striking multicoloured sun pattern. 'That much I *do* know, Solly. Your soul belongs only to you and God. Forever.'

I can feel it   Sol's soul   feel it is eternal and immortal   one
in a billion trillion googol   one that will change the world

Holy Week draws to an end, G.G. flies back to New York City and our daily routine starts up again. One day I come home from Brian's house and find Mom very upset. I can tell she's upset because she's not busy: she's sitting in the living room doing nothing, and when I kiss her hello I can tell she's been crying and she doesn't hug me to her saying How's my little man?

'What are you doing?' I ask her.

'Waiting for your dad to get home,' she answers in a frail little-girl voice that I've never heard her use before. 'Go on up to your room and play for a while, all right? Let me know if you get hungry.'

'Sure, Mom,' I say in my don't-worry-about-anything voice.

The minute I hear Dad's car pull into the driveway, I tiptoe over to the top of the staircase, crouch in the shadows and listen.

'Did you *see*, Randall?' says Mom in a fierce whisper.

'Yeah. Yeah, I saw…'

'It's *terrible!* Don't you think it's *terrible?* I don't know how a newspaper could even *publish* such photos!'

'Yeah, but…Listen, Tess…War's war…Aren't we having supper tonight?'

'War's war? What do you mean, *war's war?* This isn't war! This is a bunch of…a bunch of perverts…treating people like animals… How could they *do* such a thing?'

'Tess, all I can say is that when people are under pressure, or scared shitless, they're capable of doing just about anything.'

'How dare you…make up excuses…for this behaviour?'

I can hear she's brandishing the newspaper, maybe in his face.

'Listen, Tess, if you don't mind can we drop the subject? Do you think I really need to be screeched at the minute I get home from a fourteen-hour work day? Where the hell is supper? Or have we all decided to become anorexics like our son?'

I hear Mom fling herself onto the couch.

'I can't eat,' she says, her voice muffled because she must be sobbing into the cushions. Then she turns over and I can hear her clearly again: 'How can you be hungry after seeing photographs like that? It makes me sick, *sick,* SICK! The American army…'

'Don't you say one fucking word against the American army,' says Dad, striding into the kitchen and yanking open the fridge door.

The next morning while Mom is drying her hair with the electric hair dryer which I know means I've got a good ten minutes ahead of me, I get onto the Net and drink in the images of Abu Ghraib.

The guys are kneeling piled up on each other, it's like a bunch of circus acrobats except they're heavyset and completely naked, there's lots of naked Arab flesh which is neither black nor white but sort of golden-brown, and the U.S. soldiers male and female look like they're having a ball having their photos taken with all these naked Arabs and making fun of them and putting them on leashes and making them screw each other in the ass or hooking them up to electricity and it makes my penis very stiff but I don't touch it because I haven't got the time. I turn off the computer the same split second as Mom turns off her hair dryer and by the time she comes out of the bathroom I'm in my own room fastening the Velcro straps on my Nikes and ready to leave for playschool.

In playschool   I have to hold back   so no one will guess the truth   about my superintelligence   my super-plans   my superpowers

When I get home I go under the verandah with my Playmobil men and stack them in pyramids like at Abu Ghraib and hook them up to electricity and make them screw each other in the ass, panting and pushing while I laugh at them like Lynndie England.

I keep worrying about my dad not having had time to take part in the war yet and actually the war itself ended a year ago but President Bush says the American army is still needed to help Iraq handle its terrorists so there might still be a chance. Then Nick Berg gets his head chopped off. I learn this not from eavesdropping on my parents but in a very unexpected way—it turns up one morning on my good old sobbingweb, right next to the dead

37

lumps of Iraqi soldiers and the women being raped by dogs. 'Click here for the Nick Berg Beheading Video,' so I click. '*Warning: These are EXTREMELY GRAPHIC images!*' I'm not sure what graphic means but it probably means you can really see what's happening so I click again. You can see Nick Berg in an orange uniform sitting at a table with a bunch of Arabs, then one of them gets up with a long knife and stands behind him and slits his throat all the way through and holds his head up by the hair.

I must admit my eyes sort of pop out of my head when I see this, it's not like when C-3PO gets his head chopped off by a factory machine in *Attack of the Clones* and R2-D2 manages to put him together again which is a really funny scene. I don't dare ask Mom if God will be able to fix Nick Berg when he gets to heaven because I'm not supposed to know about all this.

'When are you going to join the army, Dad?'

My father mutes the TV which was only showing ads anyway, picks me up and sets me on his lap—face to face.

'You know what, Solly?' (I can smell the beer on his breath.)

'What?'

'Want me to tell you a secret?'

'Sure.'

'A *classified* secret?'

'Yes!'

'Okay, listen. At twenty-eight, I'm a bit old to start basic train-ing. But I don't *need* to join the army, because my company is doing a lot for the war effort as it is. Have no fear, Solly, I am *involved*. If everyone plays their part as enthusiastically as I'm playing mine, Arab terrorism will be history in a matter of months. Mark my words.'

Just then the baseball game comes on again; he grabs the remote control in one hand and his beer bottle in the other; the conversation is over.

It's getting hotter and hotter, the days are going by and pretty soon it will be time for my operation. Even if I've had long conversations with Mom about it and she's explained the whole process to me over and over again with the local anaesthesia, I can't say I'm exactly impatient to enter the clinic. But Mom will stay by my side from beginning to end so I'll be okay, I'll make her proud of me during the operation. If Schwarzenegger can take a scalpel and cut into his own flesh without batting an eyelash, I can grit my teeth and bear it. I'll feel no pain.

There's a big end-of-the-year party at my playschool. Mom bakes four dozen chocolate chip cookies and the place is hung with balloons and streamers as if it was everybody's birthday at once. It's funny to look at all the parents and think of them screwing together to make these children, except that lots of the kids have step-parents or else fathers who are sperm donors because their moms are lesbians like G.G., which Mom thinks I don't even know what that means.

Throughout the whole party I'm both a little boy showing his mother around and smiling modestly as the teacher Miss Milner compliments her on my excellent results, and a huge all-encompassing intelligence watching the scene from on high, looking down at these piddly little humans chatting together and sipping lemonade and munching on cookies and thinking they're so important. I can see that this playschool is a mere pinpoint on the map of California to say nothing of the United States, and the Earth itself is a mere pinpoint compared to the sun, I can keep on moving back and back until the Milky Way itself is nothing but a tiny speck in the distance…

Mom puts the big folder containing my drawings from the whole year into the trunk of the car. 'You're a fantastic artist, Solly—you know that?' she says as she buckles me into the back seat. 'Miss Milner says you're brighter than anyone else in the class…And Miss Milner says…'

My teacher's compliments have put Mom in a good mood; they mean her efforts are paying off, I'm exceptional already and we both know that this is *nothing* compared to what will come down later on. I just need to get over this little hurdle of the operation, it's the only thing that shakes me up a bit, and then I'll pick up my heroic destiny where I left off.

It's today. Today is the day. Mom gently shakes me awake and I can feel it's a different sort of day, my brain doesn't overflow with light and rush to fill the world, it just sort of cowers in a corner.

It's early—quarter of seven—but Dad has already left for work. He's propped a note against my cereal bowl: 'I'll be with you, kid—Stiff upper lip—Love, Dad,' and I think how everyone keeps saying this operation is nothing but adults don't tell children to keep a stiff upper lip for nothing so it must be *something*, the question is exactly what *kind* of something.

Mom and I don't say a single word as she drives me to the clinic. I can tell she's pretty tense herself, or at least impressed with the *somethingness* of the situation. Melanoma melanoma melanoma, I can hear the word going around in her head, a nice-sounding word for a horrible thing. 'Melanoma is one of the things, like snake venom,' she explained to me when I was about four, 'that can spread through the lymphatic system to the lymph glands. And from there to the rest of the body, which is called *metastasis*. And then if that happens you can die. Yes, my darling Solly. We don't know why God allows this in His plan of things, but even children can die of cancer.' But let's backtrack here: I'm not going to die, I'm not going to get metastasis or even melanoma because we're having what's known as preventive surgery, Dad says I should be grateful to my mother for her far-sightedness and I am, it's just that I don't like the idea of being cut into.

'Would you rather be put to sleep?'

'No!'

(*SOL's all-seeing consciousness must never be abolished.*)

The undressing. The feeling very small. My penis *really* tiny and shrivelled when I go to pee before the operation. Doctors and nurses speaking to me as if they knew me personally, which I resent. White plastic gloves and light blue surgical masks. They lie me down on my back and crank my bed up at an angle and turn my head to one side. I hate being manipulated this way, I hate people moving me around as if I were a monkey in a lab experiment. Now the anaesthesia, which is a word that means without feeling. A needle in Solomon's temple. Whole left side of head numb including left cheek. Mom flashes a smile at me from where she's standing on the far side of the room, but her eyes are full of fear.

'Nothing to it,' the doctor says. 'Piece of cake.'

He sinks a blade into my flesh. The nurse is there to staunch the flow of blood.

'I'm just gonna scrape out…a little more deeply here…make sure I've got the whole thing…You see? With my fingers in my nose, as the French say.'

The nurse snorts with laughter.

'I hope not!' says Mom.

'No, no, no,' says the doctor. 'It's just a manner of speaking. I learned it when I was studying in Paris, ages ago.'

'Well, those French have bad manners and I'd be grateful if you could refrain from using that sort of expression in front of my son.'

'No problem, Ma'am. Here, we're almost through.'

My blood is trickling down my neck, I can feel it, the nurse staunches it.

MY BLOOD   SOL'S BLOOD   flowing from his temple

a hole in my head

the wound is exactly where you put your finger to imitate shooting yourself

Dad told me about how G.G.'s long-ago husband committed suicide that way

his brains splattered all over the kitchen floor

    but my brain is staying inside

it can't come flowing out through the hole in my temple

it's thinking at top speed   to hang onto itself

keep everything in order   not let a single detail escape

The doctor has left the room. Mom is squeezing my hand and telling me how incredibly brave I've been and how I'm her little man and how proud of me she is. I try to smile at her but the whole left side of my face is frozen and I can only manage half a smile.

The day goes by and the feeling comes back and it's a bad feeling, aka *pain*. I don't talk about it. I refuse to complain. I can stand it. This is a test and I'm going to pass it with flying colours.

When supper comes the food is bland and soft so I can eat most of it, creamy mashed potatoes and yoghurt and applesauce. Dad arrives just as I'm finishing my dessert but it's as if he weren't really here, I can see through him, he's like a hologram of my father materialising in the clinic whereas he's really still light years away. I'm glad when he dematerialises again.

Mom spends the night on a cot in my room. The nurses bring me pills that take the edge off the pain so I can fall asleep. I have a block of solid dreamless sleep and when I wake up the pain's still there and I say nothing.

We go home later that day and Mom has detailed instructions from the nurse as to how to take care of my temple so it will heal. She explains to me about the dermis and the epidermis and skin cells dividing, it's a *good* thing when they divide quickly in an orderly way to repair an injured area like the one caused by my operation, but it's a *bad* thing when they divide quickly in a disorderly way which is known as cancer. She removes my bandages and dabs carefully at the wound with disinfectant and I tell her she's the nicest nurse in the world and she tells me I'm the patientest patient; I smile in a way that lets her know it costs me quite an effort to smile.

Day after day the pain is excruciating, which means like being crucified.

Four days after the operation, Mom calls Dad in while she's changing my bandage and he takes one look at my wound and I see him blanch and we realise this thing isn't getting better, it's getting worse, there's an infection. We don't know how, after all the disinfectant Mom's been pouring on it, but some sort of germ has gotten into the sore. Germs are like little microscopic animals that proliferate on living flesh and try to kill it and now there's an abscess.

'Pus,' Mom explains to me, 'is made up of cells which the germs have managed to destroy. There are various races of germs, just as there are various races of human beings.'

'Yeah, you've got some nasty terrorist cells attacking you there,' says Dad. 'We have to do a biopsy to see who's causing all the trouble, we don't know if it's the Shiites or...'

'Randall!' says Mom, interrupting him.

'Don't worry,' says Dad, 'we'll get the best of them.'

'Exterminate,' I say.

'Yeah, you betcha. We'll send in some armoured antibiotic tanks to take care of them.'

It turns out the doctor has to do a second operation.

This time he puts me out. Lights out. Sun down. Sol obliterated in the middle of the day. When I come to and see Mom bending over me, I have several long seconds of panic because I can't remember who I am. It's a terrible feeling, but at last I manage to swim back up to the surface.

This time I stay under surveillance in the clinic for an extra day and night. When they send us home, Mom's got a list of medicines to buy as long as her arm.

I feel lousy. The summer vacation is drifting away, July's already half over and I mostly stay in bed or wander around the house in a daze, I don't feel like getting onto any of the Google sites or rubbing myself because I'm not myself yet.

My head aches.

We go back to the clinic. Now Mom has to teach me a new word namely necrosis, which means that some of the skin tissue around my temple has actually died because the bacteria were so successful in attacking it.

'And now, darling,' she says, 'they're going to do a graft.'

'What's that?'

'Well, it means they'll replace that dead skin tissue, which is on a very visible part of your body, with living skin tissue from another, less visible part.'

'What part?'

'Your Highness's seat,' says Dad, trying to be light-hearted about it, but the truth of the matter is that they both look sick to their stomachs.

So the doctor puts me under once again and this time when I come to there's pain everywhere and my whole head is shaven and I'm running a fever. I have to spend a whole week recovering before they'll let me out of the clinic.

John Kerry is trying to beat George W. Bush in the race to the White House but we hardly pay any attention to the presidential campaign, my health is the only subject of conversation in the household. At grace and bedtime Mom prays for my recovery, Sunday mornings Dad stays home to look after me and Mom goes to church alone and prays and prays for me to get better again but I still feel lousy. Now Dad's furious with Mom for having set up this operation in the first place, and Mom's furious with Dad for having told his mother about it because apparently Grandma Sadie has gotten hysterical and now she's decided to travel all the way from Israel to visit us.

'Frankly, Randall,' says Mom, 'I must admit that I'm feeling very shaky myself right now, and I don't know how long I'll be able to live under the same roof as your mother, who puts me on edge even when I'm feeling A-1. How long does she plan to stay?'

'I'm not sure,' says Dad. 'I think she bought an open ticket.'

'You *think?* What does that mean? Did she buy an open ticket or didn't she?'

'Yeah, I think she said she did,' says Dad. 'What of it?'

'Oh dear Lord…'

Dad, who usually has problems with Grandma Sadie, suddenly rushes to her defence because someone else is attacking her.

'My mother is very well connected, Tess,' he says. 'She knows important people in the state of California. She'll be able to put us in touch with a good lawyer.'

'A lawyer?'

'Of course a lawyer! You think I'm just going to sit back and watch my son get butchered? I'm going to sue that doctor through the teeth. Fucking bastard. Fucking bastard.'

'Randall!'

'I'm sorry, Tess. It's just…I simply…can't stand it.'

And my father leaves the room because men should always be careful not to let anyone see them cry, even though crying is human as Schwarzenegger says in *Terminator II*.

I spend a lot of time sleeping and when I'm awake I feel completely blah. The prospect of Grandma Sadie's upcoming visit doesn't thrill me, either. I know she's counting on me to become the Great Genius none of the men in her life could be—neither her father who she actually never met, nor her husband who failed as a playwright and died young, nor her son who I once heard her call a spineless yuppy right to his face. I intend to live up to her expectations, I really do, but I wish she'd come to visit when I'm healthy instead of sick. Looking at me right now, it must be hard to believe that I'm the saviour of humanity.

Dad picks up Grandma Sadie at the airport in San Francisco and drives her all the way home with her wheelchair folded up in the trunk of the car along with several large suitcases that give all of us a sinking feeling as to how long she's planning to stay. Mom and I come out and stand on the front porch hand in hand to wait for them as Dad rolls her up the ramp, built especially as an addition to the house for his differently-abled mother, she's gotten even heavier since her last visit so the ramp creaks beneath her weight. The minute she gets into the kitchen she turns and beckons to me and I limp towards her, trying not to look too pitiful despite the bandages on my head and other bandages hidden beneath my pyjama bottoms.

'Solomon!' she screeches. 'Look! I've brought you a present!'

She scrounges around in her handbag and brings out something wrapped in tissue paper. When I unwrap it it's a kippa that's actually quite lovely, covered in black velvet and spangled with stars and spaceships stitched in gold thread and the words *Star Wars*.

'Try it on, Solomon. It used to belong to your dad. Remember, Randall? We gave it to you for your Bar Mitzvah, when you were all excited about the new *Star Wars* video game. Look, it's just like new! Isn't that incredible!'

'Could almost make you think I didn't wear it very often,' mutters Dad.

'Try it on, Solomon! See if it fits!'

'Excuse me, Ma,' says Mom, which always sounds weird to me when she calls Grandma Sadie Ma because of course she isn't her mother but it's just an affectionate term for her—'I know you mean well, but we're a Protestant family.'

'Try it on, try it on,' Grandma Sadie insists, paying no attention to my mother's objection so I'm not sure what I should do. I glance at Dad and he nods imperceptibly, after first making sure that Mom isn't looking in his direction, so I put the kippa on my head. It's way too big for me, but the up side is that it completely hides my bandages.

'Wonderful!' declares Grandma Sadie firmly. 'It fits you like a glove. This isn't poison,' she says then to my mother. 'It won't put Jewish ideas into his head. He can wear it when he feels like it, as a souvenir of his grandmother in Israel. All right?'

Mom looks down at her hands.

'Is that a yes?'

'I guess it's all right, if Randall thinks so,' whispers Mom.

'All right by me,' says Dad, relieved to be able to reconcile his mother and his wife in four little words. 'Now scoot off to bed, young'un, it's past your bedtime.'

I obey, so tired that I don't even eavesdrop on their conversation from the top of the stairs as I would normally have done were I in full possession of my powers.

From that day on the atmosphere in the house starts sizzling with bad electricity because Dad is away from sunup to sundown and these two women spend the whole day in each other's company and their conversation is full of short circuits. Now, in addition to taking care of me and doing all the shopping and cooking and housework, Mom has to see to the needs of her crippled Jewish orthodox mother-in-law including kosher food.

Sadie is certainly an imposing person in every way, I once heard Dad tell Mom that when he was little his mother belonged to Weight Watchers but after her car accident she gave up and just let herself become this huge and overbearing body that's really quite majestic in a way. Now she eats with a vengeance the way she does everything else. Her personality is imposing as well because she likes to express her opinions in no uncertain terms and loudly, so that even if I'm upstairs in my room I can hear bits and snatches of her hectoring whereas Mom's responses are totally inaudible.

'What a perfectly idiotic thing to do—whose idea was it, anyway?'

'How much did you pay for this so-called operation? What??? Say it again???'

...and so forth. The only thing Mom and Sadie have in common is their love for my father Randall, but it's definitely not the same love; the way they talk about him you wouldn't even think it was the same *person*.

And then there's me, of course.

Sadie's love for me takes the form of summoning me out to the verandah where she stations her wheelchair every morning at eight o'clock sharp and reading out loud to me from the Old Testament for two whole hours.

'You have to structure his days!' she hollers, when Mom suggests that two hours might be a bit long. 'You can't just let him wander around the house doing whatever he feels like when he feels like it, eating and napping and watching TV—that's a *terrible* regimen for a six-year-old! His mind will get all soft and flabby and by the time he goes back to school he'll have lost his headstart on the other children!'

Some of the Bible stories are boring to me so I just switch to another site in my brain and set my screensaver on *nod occasionally to show you're following.* Others are surprisingly filled with violence and rage, destruction and revenge, I especially like the one about

Samson getting so mad at Delilah for betraying him that he pushes at the columns of the temple until the whole building collapses and kills everybody in it including himself. 'Just like the human bombs in Israel these days!' I say, proud to show Grandma I know something about her country, but she snaps at me—'Not at all! It's not at *all* the same thing!'—and starts reading again.

After a couple of weeks she comes up with the idea of adding Hebrew lessons to my Bible reading, but Mom puts her foot down at this.

'I don't want my little boy speaking Hebrew,' she says.

'Why not?' says Grandma Sadie. 'It'll give him something to do and it's a beautiful language. Ask Randall—he loves it!'

'Randall?'

'Yes—remember? That guy you married?'

'Randall speaks *Hebrew*?'

'I must be dreaming,' says Grandma Sadie. 'Surely you know we lived in Haifa for a year when he was six?'

'Of course I do.'

'Surely you know he went to Hebrew Reali School there?'

'Yes…'

'And you think they taught classes in—what, Japanese? He passed his entrance exam in Hebrew after only *one month of tutoring* in New York! He was brilliant back then—just *brilliant*; I was proud as if to burst.'

'I see,' says Mom.

She's shaking with the emotion of this whole conversation because she knows Sadie blames her for Randall's not being famous yet and is always wondering how her brilliant son could have married a woman who never left the west coast of the United States, didn't go to university and can speak no foreign languages (whereas Sadie herself speaks two fluently and can get by in lots more), but luckily Mom's reflexes from her seminars on relaxation and human relationships kick in and she manages to keep her cool.

'Listen, Ma,' she says in an I'm-controlling-myself voice, 'I can see how learning Hebrew would have been useful to Randall at that point in time, but I must ask you to remember that you're a guest in our household, which is a Protestant, English-speaking household. When the time comes for Solly to study a foreign language, it will be up to his parents, not his grandparents, to decide which one. No offence, but I wanted to make sure that was clear.'

She turns on her heel and goes back into the house.

After a while it gets too hot out on the verandah so Grandma Sadie wheels herself into the house and starts talking to Mom again. The other one of her favourite things to hector people about is the subject of her book on the Second World War. She can rant and rave all day telling my mother statistics on this stuff that dates back to the middle of the twentieth century.

'I can't take it much longer,' Mom says to Dad one night in a trembly voice as they're getting ready for bed. 'Why can't she just leave the subject alone, why does she have to keep on drumming these facts of ancient history into my head?'

As usual, Dad does his best to patch things up and smooth things over between the two women. 'It's her specialty, Tess,' he tells her. 'She's one of the world authorities on the cradle aspect of Aryanisation. To us it may be ancient history, but to her it's bone deep; to her it's *yesterday*; it's *now*; it's *her mother*. Please try to understand...'

'Randall,' says Mom. 'I understand, but my kitchen's not a lecture hall. I've got a certain number of *other* things to think about right now, *in particular the health of OUR SON,* and I mean, I *can't* have my thoughts perpetually invaded by two hundred thousand Eastern European children kidnapped by the Nazis in the 1940s! Or those abominable *Lebensraum* centres or whatever they were called...'

'*Lebensborn,* not *Lebensraum.*'

'I don't give a—!!!'

Mom's swearwords are all the more powerful for being left unsaid. A huge silence follows this quarrel in their bedroom right next to my own and then I guess they fall asleep and I do too.

Mom says she's on the verge of having a nervous breakdown so Dad takes a day off work to drive me into San Francisco to see a new doctor and get a new diagnosis, and Grandma Sadie comes with us to give Mom a break.

The new doctor thinks I'm well on my way to recovery now but the scar on my temple is much more visible than the mole used to be and he doubts it will ever disappear completely.

This is a blow.

A conspicuous sign of imperfection on Sol's body: this is a blow.

On the way home I unbuckle my seat belt and lie down in the back seat and close my eyes.

Dear God...(I don't know what to say; I'm mad at him.)

Dear President Bush: I sincerely hope you'll be re-elected in November.

Dear Governor Schwarzenegger: I wish you'd come and rip out the heart of the doctor who did this to me. Dad's planning to sue him, sure, but it'll cost a fortune and take ages, it would be much better if you could just step in and take care of things in your usual swift way.

Dad and Grandma Sadie must think I've fallen asleep because they start talking in low voices up in the front seat so I prick up my ears. This is how I discover at long last, although it's classified information, exactly how my father is contributing to America's peacekeeping efforts in Iraq. I guess even when you get old at age twenty-eight you still can't help wanting your mom to be proud of you and feeling bad if she thinks you're a nebbish, which is a word she taught me that means a zero, a nothing, a weakling, in other words a spineless yuppy.

'Talon's going to change the face of modern warfare,' says Dad.

'Whose talent?' says Grandma Sadie.

'Not talent—Talon. The new warrior robot.'

'Warrior robots? Is *that* what you do for a living, Randall? You make warrior robots?'

'Oh, I don't actually build them myself. The main firm is on the East coast—in Waltham, Mass.—but they're hooked up to companies doing state-of-the-art research in robotics all over the world—Scotland, Switzerland, France—a number of them in Germany, as a matter of fact…Our company's one of the only ones in Silicon Valley to have been chosen to develop certain aspects of the technology.'

'I didn't ask you for a flow chart,' Grandma Sadie says sharply. 'Tell me about these Talon things.'

'The real acronym is SWORD, which stands for Special Weapons Observation Reconnaissance Detection systems—pretty neat, eh?'

'It depends what they *do.*'

'Well, Mother, they're pretty amazing,' says Dad. 'Like something

53

straight out of *Star Wars*. They've got all the advantages of human beings and none of the disadvantages.'

'Such as?'

'Such as, *A:* they don't die, which means they don't leave sobbing widows and orphans who'll need to receive pensions for the rest of their lives. You avoid the whole body bag syndrome, people getting upset about the number of American casualties.'

'I see.'

'*B:* They've got no physical or psychological needs, which also cuts expenses. You don't have to keep replenishing their supplies of food, drink, sex, and post-traumatic counselling. *C:* They're excellent warriors—mobile, relentless, accurate. They're equipped with cameras, so you see what they see, manipulate them at a distance with a joystick, order them to aim and fire. *D:* They're not jittery; they haven't got a girlfriend waiting for them back home; they don't give a hoot in hell about the enemy's humanity—or their own, for that matter...In a word, *they've got no feelings*—no anger, no fear, no pity, no remorse—which of course increases their efficiency as warriors.'

Now that he's gotten started, Dad seems as if he could run through the whole alphabet with his list of advantages but Grandma Sadie interrupts him.

'*Stop it!*' she hisses. Her voice is still whispering because she doesn't want to wake me but she sounds furious. '*Stop it!* Do you know what you're describing, Randall? Do you know what you're describing?'

Since Dad *does* know what he's describing, he gathers that Grandma's question must be rhetorical which means not really a question at all, so he waits for *her* to answer it. He doesn't have to wait long.

'The perfect Nazi, you're describing. The perfect, hard, steely, emotionless macho male. Rudolf Hoess, you're describing—the man who ran the gas chamber at Auschwitz. Get rid of feelings. Feelings are soft, female, disgusting. Don't think of the enemy as human, think of them as vermin, and of yourself as a machine. Concentrate on your orders; *be* your orders—kill, kill, kill.'

'I'm afraid that's not just the Nazis, Mom—that's basic military training. Every soldier in the world has been inculcated with that message, from Gilgamesh to Lynndie England. Do you think your precious Tzahal is taught otherwise? Do you think that when Sharon inspects his troops he tells them, "Now don't forget, ladies and gentlemen: the Palestinians are human beings just like yourselves, so when you drop a bomb on Ramallah, be sure to have a loving thought for each and every one of your victims, be they man, woman or child"…'

'*Stop* it with Tzahal, Randall! A long time ago we agreed that subject was off limits between us. But *robots*!'

My heart is tingling like a snare drum. I'm thrilled at the idea my Dad is helping to send robot soldiers out to kill our enemies in Iraq. When he said he was *involved,* I had no idea what a front-line high-tech top-level involvement he meant. Just the thought of those weaponised robots shooting Arabs dead and standing there oblivious to their bloody twitchings in the sand makes my penis harden for the first time in months. I pull the blanket over my body and gently rub myself which means I'm finally on my way to recovery, and then I fall asleep.

The robots are stealing children from households all over the city and taking our brains out to see how they work, the hospital is full of children whose skulls are empty because our brains have been removed, but we've been hooked up to machines to keep our bodies alive. Even though she knows I'll never be able to think again, Mom comes to visit me in the hospital every day. I can see her and recognise her but I can't talk to her. For some reason I don't find this upsetting; it's okay with me.

When I wake up again we're almost home and Dad has come full circle to the beginning of the conversation.

'Santa Clara will be hosting a humungous international robotics conference in October,' he says. 'My company's sending me to Europe next month for some preliminary meetings.'

'Where in Europe?' asks Grandma Sadie, as Dad pulls into our driveway and parks.

'All the places I mentioned—France, Switzerland, Germany…'

'You'll be in Germany in August?' says Sadie.

'Yeah, I've got three different meetings there—Frankfurt, Chemnitz and Munich.'

'You'll be in *Munich* in August?' Grandma says, and Dad falls silent because he realises this is another rhetorical question. He switches the motor off and for a while all you can hear are birds chirping and the faraway bark of a dog.

'You know what, Randall?' says Grandma Sadie after a long pause. '*You know what?* The whole family is going to come and join you in Munich.'

'I don't—'

'Yes.'

'I don't get it, Mother.'

'Yes. It's the perfect idea. The perfect idea. Listen. We'll take my mother with us.'

'You must be—'

'Yes, we'll take Erra with us. Because her sister, her older sister Greta who lives near Munich, happens to be dying. She wrote me a letter saying she'd give anything to see my mother again. The whole trip will be on me.'

'Forgive me for saying so, but I think you've gone completely off your rocker. You'll never convince your mother to come. Not only has she not set foot in Germany since she left sixty years ago (it's the only country in Europe where she *never once* gave a concert)—not only has she been out of touch with this so-called sister of hers for all that time…She hasn't even seen *you* in fifteen years!'

'Fourteen.'

'Fourteen, right. OK. Thanks but no thanks, Mother. This sort of family psychodrama is definitely not for me.'

'But just think, Randall. Think about it! It'll do Tessa a world of good to get away; she's never set foot outside of the United States of America. And Solomon! Instead of moping around for the rest of the summer until his hair grows back and school starts up, it'll be an *adventure* for him! It'll take his mind off all these useless trials and tribulations you've put him through. And Greta… Greta helped me with my research, Randall. I owe her a lot; I've kept in touch with her these twenty-odd years…She's *dying*, she has cancer and she's *dying* and her most fervent wish is to see her only sister one more time before she dies…And as for you, you'll be in Munich anyway, so where's the problem? I ask you, where's the problem?'

The household goes all topsy-turvy with Grandma Sadie's idea.

Over breakfast the next day which is a Saturday we take a vote: Mom and I vote *yes* and Dad votes *no;* that makes it three to one, so even if G.G. votes *no* the *yesses* will be in the majority.

'That doesn't matter!' Dad points out. 'If Erra votes no, she *won't come*, which would make the trip pointless for the rest of you.'

'No it wouldn't!' say Mom and I at the same time.

'We'd still get to see Germany,' Mom adds, 'and meet your grandma's sister. It's not every day you learn you've got relatives in Europe.'

'There's only one way to settle it, Randall,' says Grandma Sadie. 'Call Erra.'

'*You* call her. It's your idea; you call her.'

'That's ridiculous. It's been so long since I spoke to her she wouldn't even recognise my voice.'

'Listen, Mom. If you want to take your mother to Munich, you're going to have to speak to her. You might as well start now and get it over with.'

'Come on, Ran, you'll do a better job of convincing her. You and Erra have always been so close.'

'But I don't *want* to convince her! *You're* the one who wants to convince her!'

'All right, okay…Anyway, it's too early right now, because of the time difference. It's only six a.m. in New York.'

'Wrong again—it's three hours *later* in New York, not three hours earlier. That makes it twelve noon. The perfect time to call.'

'Oh, for heaven's sake,' says Grandma Sadie, blushing to the roots of her wig. 'All right, already.'

She wheels herself down the hall to the guest room and shuts the door so she can make the phone call without our hearing it; all we can hear is the sound of her voice which isn't nearly as shrill as usual. We don't want to seem like we're straining to catch what she's saying, so Mom gets up and murmurs, 'Could you help me clear away the breakfast things, Randall?' and Dad sort of jumps up nervously and says 'Sure.'

'Did you want any more milk, darling?' Mom asks me and I say 'No thank you,' so she pours my whole glass of milk down the drain even though I only took one sip out of it because you never know, that little sip I took might have put germs on the glass and after all that's happened with germs recently it's better to be safe than sorry.

'Would you like to try to do a Big Job, sweet?' says Mom by which she means poop, but just as I'm padding obediently towards the bathroom Grandma Sadie rolls out of her bedroom and blocks my way with her wheelchair. She just sits there with her eyes glazed, saying nothing. She looks stunned.

'So?' says Dad, flipping up the dishwasher door a little brutally. 'What happened? How did Erra vote?'

Grandma Sadie closes her eyes and opens them again and says, in the softest voice I ever heard her use: 'Yes. She voted *yes*.'

Mom and I start cheering—'Hooray, hooray!'—and Dad stands there stock-still in the middle of the kitchen murmuring 'You must be joking, you must be joking' under his breath.

A mere three weeks later we're in the plane.

a million times   in computer games   in movies
     on the Net   or with my friends' Game Boys and Play
   Stations,   I've gone zooming through space
     plunging   soaring
whirling effortlessly amidst the galaxies
making spaceships explode at the touch of a button

feeling the brief scarlet light of their destruction reflected on my face…

but actual flight is an unpleasant surprise to me

The rising high whine of the engines and the plane's droning vibration in my entrails scare me to death. I squeeze Mom's hand until she says 'I'm sorry darling but you're hurting me,' and takes it away. Then I really panic because we go into take-off and I feel squashed and flattened against my seat and my head begins to pound. All around me people are behaving as if nothing was happening, they're reading and chatting and looking out the window whereas there's a scream inside me struggling to get out. I freeze my whole body to lock it inside but it's tearing my chest apart, flying is *torture*, my stomach heaves, I'm going to be sick, *Mom, Mom, how can you allow this to be done to me?* as Jesus also couldn't help wondering when they nailed him to the Cross, 'Father, Father, why hast thou forsaken me?'

'Oops—here, sweet,' says Mom. She pulls a white bag out of the seat pocket in front of her, opens it and holds it under my mouth. I'm shocked. So people know in advance that flying can make you throw up and they just take it for granted and put a paper bag there for you to throw up in? Vomiting is the exact opposite of what's supposed to happen to food when it enters your stomach. Vomiting is *chaos*, like the cosmos before God started taking an interest in it. I retch and tremble and discover exactly the experience of *cold sweat* but I can't throw up because I didn't have anything for breakfast. Mom blows gently on my forehead and after a while the worst symptoms go away but I can't believe I have to go through this *three more times*—we're stopping off in

New York so G.G. can join us on the same flight, which means there will be *four take-offs* in all, two on the way to Germany and two on the way home.

The trip is a complete nightmare and I don't like being seen in public grabbing my mother's hand in fear every time there's a bit of turbulence. I just wish it would end. I just wish the plane, with its deafening noise and its bumpiness and its hundreds of passengers smelling of body odour and bad breath and its screaming babies and its obese German ladies standing in line to pee and its stewardesses with wrinkles around their eyes when they smile—I wish *all this would vanish* instantly when I snap my fingers and we could just be on the ground in Germany.

In New York the scene of mother and daughter getting reunited after so many years isn't like it would have been on TV, complete with hugs and sighs and tearful explanations. It happens inside the plane itself because for us New York is just a stopover and we're not allowed to get off, also because of Grandma Sadie's legs being paralysed she can't get up when she sees her mother standing there in the doorway with her halo of white hair. She sticks up her arm to wave and G.G. sees us and comes down the aisle and greets us one after the other—giving us the same peck on the cheek whether it's been four months or fourteen years since she last saw us. Then she continues on to her seat which is far away in the back of the plane and the nightmare of take-off starts all over again.

Once we're up above the clouds the problem shifts from fear to boredom because there's nothing to do. Mom has checked the movie program and decided I'm too young to see *Bridget Jones's Diary*, though I doubt it gets as graphic as the Abu Ghraib or Force Fucking sites but I keep these thoughts in my brain so she won't be traumatised. She herself is reading a book about all the interesting places to visit in Munich and the surrounding area.

Grandma Sadie ordered a kosher meal in advance, which to tell the truth I'm not sure what that means except that it's for Jewish people. Mom says grace very softly and eats everything on her tray because she says it's a free meal so you might as well take advantage of it, plus this is her first transatlantic flight and she's filled with excitement. Of course the meal's impossible for me, but since Dad's already in Europe and can't criticise her Mom has brought along a bag full of soft nibblies for me, so whenever I feel hungry I can just slip my hand into the bag and pull something out, peanut butter sandwiches, bits of cheese, a banana, I swish them, melt them against my gums, liquefy and control them, hoping against hope that they'll move slowly through my digestive tract and download into well-formed poop, not make the whole system block and come spewing up again as vomit.

As we fly over the Atlantic Ocean during the night, Mom has to get up twice to help Grandma Sadie go to the bathroom. It's a whole expedition.

When we land in Munich the air is thick with words I can't understand. I find it offensive and stifling so I cling to Mom's arm and listen to her and Grandma Sadie with all my might, I'm still all-powerful but for the time being in this humungous modern airport I have to go on behaving like a normal little boy and look disorientated, which I do. When we finally come through the sliding glass doors Dad is waiting for us with a big smile glued to his face, which I can tell means he's dreading the next few days of his life. Dragging a suitcase in one hand and pushing his mother's wheelchair with the other, listening to his wife with one ear and his mother with the other, all the while making sure that his beloved grandmother won't go astray and keeping an eye on his young son, he leads us to the car he just rented at the airport.

I settle into the back seat between Mom and G.G., Grandma Sadie sits up front with the map in her lap because Dad can't read the road signs.

'Quick—what do I do here—go left?'

'Right! Right! Right!' shrieks Grandma Sadie who speaks fluent German.

'Shit,' says Dad, swerving violently to the right at the last possible second, and Mom says:

'Randall! What language is *that?*' but her joke doesn't go over very well.

'*Shit!*' Dad repeats. 'You wanna take the wheel, Tessie?'

Mom cringes and turns crimson.

I don't like the road signs being in German, either. They feel like doors slamming in my face one after the other and I refuse to ask Grandma Sadie what they mean, I don't want ever to admit to any lack of knowledge and by the time I grow up everyone in the world will speak English or if they don't that's one of the laws I'll pass when I'm in power to make sure they do. The foreignness of this country makes my skin crawl and my scar is still ugly even if I hide it with the kippa, I try to shine up my tarnished self, polish my medals, remind myself that I'm the most brilliant six-year-old in the entire world, it's not easy in this crowded car with all the bad vibes between the adults but at least Mom squeezes my hand in an encouraging way.

Finally we reach the city of Munich itself and head for our hotel and now, in a very loud voice that fills the entire car, Grandma

Sadie is hectoring us about which buildings were built when and which neighbourhoods were reduced to rubble by Allied bombing which is hard to believe, everything looks so clean and modern. I see G.G.'s hands moving, she keeps sort of clasping and unclasping them and twisting her fingers around each other and I realise she hasn't said a word since we set foot on her native soil. I look at her out of the corner of my eye. She's staring straight ahead of her with a sort of anguished look on her face and it seems like she's turned into an old old lady in one fell swoop.

'Do you recognise anything?' Grandma Sadie stops running off at the mouth long enough to ask.

She can only be talking to her mother because no one else in the car could recognise anything in Munich having never been here before, but G.G. doesn't answer. She just keeps staring straight ahead and twisting her thin fingers around each other and looking ancient.

It's the first time I've ever stayed in a hotel and I don't like it because Grandma Sadie is trying to be economical and even though the whole trip was her idea in the first place she can't help reminding us that it's costing her a fortune, so the hotel is actually pretty tacky and all three of us have to sleep together in the same bedroom which we're not used to. Grandma Sadie and G.G. also share a room, which must be really something but I don't want to know what. We have a real bummer of a meal in the hotel restaurant where the menu says that lots of dishes are the *worst*. Even if it's spelled *wurst* and according to Sadie means sausages (which makes Mom laugh), it spoils my appetite and all I can eat is a slice of white bread with the crusts cut off. Grandma adds that when you want to say I don't care a fig in German you say I don't care a sausage, which makes even Dad laugh but it seems pretty idiotic to me, how could you possibly care a sausage?

Then Grandma Sadie turns to G.G. (who still hasn't said a word except to order her meal) and says 'Mommy'—which is a strange word to be coming out of the mouth of an old lady like Grandma Sadie but she's trying to be ingratiating with her mother and get her to be her usual self again because it's impossible not to notice how silent she's grown—'Mommy, do you remember that song you taught me once about Johnny Burbeck? The guy who fell into his own sausage machine and got ground to sausage meat? How did it go?'

'Please!' says Mom, worried that such a song might upset me or my stomach.

Anyway Erra doesn't answer, she's taking small sips from a glass of beer and just staring at the tablecloth and no one knows what's the matter with her.

'And then you asked me, What's a wiener—remember?'
Still no answer.

'What's a wiener, Solly?' asks Grandma Sadie, turning to me.
'I don't know,' I say.

'It's a hot dog,' says Dad, with a big grin on his face as if he knew what the punch line was going to be.

'No, silly, it's a person from Vienna!' says Grandma Sadie and the two of them burst out laughing and Grandma Sadie says, 'What's a hamburger, Solly?'

'The thing you buy at McDonald's,' I say lamely.

'No, silly, it's a person from Hamburg!'

Again she and Dad laugh their heads off.

'And then there was…Ah, help me, Randall…What was the third one?'

Luckily Dad can't remember the third one, so that subject of conversation peters out.

G.G. doesn't say a word all evening.

I sleep like a log.

More fuss in the morning, because they only have cold hard-boiled eggs in this cruddy hotel and I like mine warm and soft. Mom goes to the kitchen to reason with the personnel but since she doesn't speak German she can't get her point across so she asks Grandma Sadie to come and translate for her and Sadie who has already begun breakfast says in a loud voice while still shovelling food into her own mouth, 'Quit spoiling your son, Tessa! If he's hungry he'll eat any kind of egg. If he's not hungry there's no point in kvetching.'

Mom comes back to me shrugging her shoulders with apology and I'm so furious with these people for humiliating her that I could practically cook my egg myself.

Unfortunately G.G.'s long-lost sister who is at death's doorstep doesn't live in the city of Munich itself, she still lives in the little town they grew up in which is two hours away by car. My heart sinks.

'That's endless, Mom!' I whine.

'We don't have much choice in the matter, sweet,' she answers.

'Two hours is what it takes me to drive in to work every morning,' says Dad.

'You can't compare, Randall,' says Mom. 'It feels much longer to a child.'

'You're wrong about that,' says Dad. 'To me it's endless, too.'

We go back to our same seats as yesterday, G.G. to my left and Mom to my right in the back. It takes us ages to get out of the city but finally we're driving through green fields.

'We're heading straight east towards the Austrian border,' says Grandma Sadie. 'Berchtesgaden is in the Alps just south of here— you know, the so-called Bavarian Redoubt, Hitler's favourite retreat. He and his cronies had these incredible underground warrens built for themselves in the mountain. They were filled to bursting with champagne, cigars, specialty foods and clothing— enough to hold out for decades!…Now they're turning the whole thing into a luxury hotel.'

'So we're just a stone's throw from where Governor Schwarzenegger was born, in Austria!' says Mom, delighted at this chance to prove that she's been studying the maps.

'Well, I guess you could call it a stone's throw—if you're a giant!' says Grandma Sadie drily. 'Schwarzenegger was born near Graz, about a hundred and fifty miles southeast of here.'

'Ah! Good thing there's *some*body in the car who knows every-thing!' says Dad.

'No, no, Tessa's remark was relevant,' says Grandma Sadie concili-atingly. 'Schwarzenegger's family had strong Nazi leanings.'

Mom doesn't want to get Sadie started on *that* subject, though, so she turns to G.G. and says, 'Must be a weird feeling for you to be travelling through this landscape, eh?'—and then, in a whisper— 'Oops! She's asleep!'

G.G.'s head is tipped back and her mouth has fallen open and she's snoring a bit. I can't get rid of the feeling that she's getting older by the minute. Seen close up like this her skin is like white transparent parchment covered with a million tiny lines and she's so thin, so very thin and small, I never noticed how small she was before, she looks like a ghost or a dead sparrow, what if she's dead? No, she's snoring so she can't be dead, but I move away from her and cling to my mother's arm, please God I don't want for my mother ever to get old, please God keep her always young and beautiful—

In my head everything feels strange   sort of floaty and dissolving   as if I weren't really here   no one's paying any attention to me   we drive and drive

When I ask how much farther, Mom's advice sounds like something straight out of her Buddhist yoga class: 'Don't think about getting there, sweetheart. Tell yourself you *are* there. This is a real moment of your real life! Drink it in! Look at the beautiful scenery!'

I force myself to look. Rolling pastures. Green meadows. Cows, tractors, barns and farmhouses. More rolling pastures. More cows and barns. It all seems sort of miniature, like one of those dumb little farms you sometimes see in zoos to familiarise city children with the country. Even the highway feels small compared to highways in California. I take a deep breath and squeeze my knees with both hands to make sure I'm there.

So far this trip is a major drag.

G.G. wakes up just as we're entering the town she used to live in as a child. She wakes up the same way I do—snapping out of sleep, clicking into wakefulness—instantly alert and watchful, no tiredness in her eyes.

Somehow the whole car seems to have caught her silence. No one says anything. Ten immobile lips. My father drives very slowly towards the centre of the town.

Suddenly Grandma Sadie does something unexpected—she

sticks her hand into the back seat and takes G.G.'s hand. Even more unexpected is that G.G. takes *her* hand and strokes it gently.

She's the one who says, 'Here, Randall. You can turn left here and park. Yes. It's that building right over there.'

We go through the usual rigmarole, hoisting the wheelchair out of the trunk, opening it up, helping Grandma Sadie into it, locking the car doors, the whole bit. People in the street stare at us as if we were a circus act and I hate seeing how conspicuous we are, this oddball collection of English-speakers including a cripple in a wig and a wispy white-haired witch and a little boy with a *Star Wars* kippa on his head. I wish I could zap their eyes with a laser beam to force them to look away from us but at long last we find ourselves inside the building.

The corridor seems pitch dark after the brightness of outside, but Grandma Sadie propels herself down it, leading the way. As Mom and I follow, holding hands, Mom bends down and says to me in a whisper, 'Maybe you should take your hat off, sweet.' Bringing up the rear, G.G. is clinging to Dad's arm which she wouldn't normally do but today she's walking slowly, so slowly that they drag a long way behind, and eventually she stops.

'What's the matter?' yells Sadie, having now reached the elevator at the far end of the hall.

'Her heart's beating too fast,' Dad calls back. 'She's going to take a nitro. Can you wait a minute?'

'Of course we can wait a minute,' says Grandma Sadie. 'So we'll wait a minute.'

G.G. draws a little bottle of medicine from her bag, shakes a couple of pills into the palm of her hand, claps her palm to her open mouth and waits. After a moment she nods and clutches onto my father's arm again.

We're gathered in front of a door marked *3W* and Grandma Sadie—after looking intently at each of us to make this moment seem even more impressive than it already is—leans heavily on the doorbell.

A few seconds later we hear a bunch of locks being turned and a massive female figure appears, silhouetted in the doorway. Grandma Sadie speaks to her in German and she replies in German and I think I'll die if I have to spend this whole afternoon listening to German but then Grandma Sadie translates: 'She says today is her nurse's afternoon off so unfortunately she's alone. Her illness prevents her from giving us the hospitality she would want, but lunch is ready and waiting on the table. This is Greta,' she adds, which is totally unnecessary.

Again Greta says something in German but suddenly G.G.'s voice rings out loud and clear: 'Today,' she says, 'communication will be in English.'

Releasing my father's arm, she steps forward theatrically and all of us move aside.

The two aged sisters are now standing staring at each other, about two feet apart. They don't look alike, that's for sure. Greta has coarse features, deep lines that cut her pudgy cheeks and chin into reddish slices, long grey hair twisted into a braid, a full body that sways and ripples under her hot-pink sweatsuit as she steps forward, holding her arms out to G.G.

'Kristina!' she breathes—which name instead of Erra is certainly a surprise to me, but since no one else bats an eyelash I guess it must be G.G.'s old name from back when she was German.

'Kristina!' she repeats, with tears glittering in her eyes that are pretty much buried in the fat of her face.

Instead of rushing into Greta's outstretched arms, G.G. takes her firmly by the wrists and says in a fierce English whisper: 'Let us please go inside now.'

'Yes, of course,' says Greta with an accent. 'Forgive me. Please come in, all of you, come in. Take off your shoes, if you please, there is much dust in the streets.'

Grandma Sadie completes the introductions and Greta shakes hands with each of us in turn. When she sees the scar on my temple, her eyebrows crinkle together in a W.

'Is an accident?' she asks with a gesture towards her own temple.

'Oh, it's nothing,' say the four adults at the same time, which makes them burst out laughing, also at the same time, which makes them laugh even harder, but personally I fail to see anything funny.

The table is spread with dozens of dishes I can't eat, different kinds of sliced cold cuts with splotches of fat in or around them, pickles and radishes, devilled eggs, stinky cheeses, potato salad with onions, hard black bread…Luckily Mom caught sight of a box of Kellogg's cornflakes as we passed through the kitchen and she asks Greta if I could possibly have a bowl of that, knowing that Dad won't dare get on her case about my eating habits in front of a stranger.

Mom suggests we all join hands and during grace she thanks God for this miraculous reunion of two sisters after six decades of separation. No one seems very thrilled about it though, not even Grandma Sadie who dragged us all here, and when no one applauds or kisses me after grace I start thinking this whole trip is nothing but a big mistake. I eat my cornflakes one by one, as slowly as I can because Mom has forbidden me to leave the table: 'We're not in our own home,' she told me, 'so you've got to be on your best behaviour, sweet.' My eyes flit and fly. Being in this living/dining room is like being inside a little girl's doll's house, it's completely stifling with all the furniture and knick-knacks, embroidered cushions, doilies, cut-glass bowls, statuettes, flower-patterned wallpaper, framed photos and pictures on the wall, every inch of space occupied and decorated and no breathing space anywhere, I wish I could turn into a Teenage Mutant Ninja Turtle and kick smack slice and dice my way out of here—no, Superman would be even better, I'd just raise my arm and rocket up, up and away, ripping through the roof and bursting straight into the clear blue sky. Oxygen! Oxygen!

'So you've kept the place,' says G.G.

'Yes,' says Greta. 'I have raised my children here.'

A silence. We gather that G.G. has no questions to ask about these children.

'I see they closed the school,' she says after a while.

'Oh! very many years ago. The whole place is only residential since—in the seventies, I think. A little time after Mama's death.'

This, too, meets with a stony silence from G.G. Why did she come to Germany? I'm beginning to wonder. If she didn't want to see her sister and reminisce about the past, why did she vote *yes* in the first place? Nothing Greta has to say about their family seems to interest her.

'I found out who denounced us to that Agency, the one who sent the American lady Miss Mulyk to take you away…It was our neighbour—Mrs Webern, you remember her? Her husband was a communist…'

No response from G.G.

'Papa came back in 1946,' Greta continues, and Grandma Sadie nods energetically to encourage her to go on with her story and pay no attention to G.G.'s rude behaviour, 'after a year of being prisoner of the Russians. He cried all night when Mama told him you and Johann were gone forever. He was a teacher here again, and then the school principal, and finally the town mayor in the sixties until his retirement. But Grandfather never came back from the…from the…you know. That…hospital.'

I listen hard to every word this fat pink woman says and stash it carefully away in a corner of my brain for future reference because nothing must escape my knowledge of the universe but for the time being I have no idea what she's talking about and meanwhile the person she's talking *to* namely G.G. is ignoring her, in fact now she's doing something fairly shocking which is lighting up a cigar in the middle of a meal, but even Mom can't quite get up the nerve to tell her to put it out because this isn't our home.

A silence happens, where my father accidentally makes a slight burp because of all the German beer he's been putting away since we got here, and I actually see my mother kick him under the table for his uncouth behaviour.

'I followed your career, Kristina,' says Greta, hoping this new subject might somehow melt her sister's ice. 'I have I think a complete collection of your records—look!'

She gestures towards her CD player and everyone but G.G. turns their head. After another silence, Grandma Sadie joins in the conversation to lighten up the atmosphere a bit.

'How unkind of you, Greta,' she says in a teasing sort of voice, 'to torture me with all these delicious-looking cold cuts made from pork!'

73

'Oh my heaven,' Greta exclaims. 'This was not on purpose!'

'No, no, I'm only joking. There's more than enough for me to eat,' says Grandma Sadie, heaping a second mountain of potato salad onto her plate.

'You would like a little more leberwurst, Kristina?' says Greta and G.G. declines, waving her cigar in the air and saying 'I'm fine' so Greta says in a loud voice, trying to make us laugh, 'Can you *believe* this skinny thing once dreamed to be the Fat Lady in the circus?' and Mom and Dad laugh politely although they've heard this story a hundred countless times already and so have I, and Grandma Sadie says with her mouth full, 'I could *almost* apply for that job now, hey?' At this everyone laughs a bit and, looking at massive impressive Sadie, I must say it's hard to believe she came out of little elf-like Erra.

'The clock is gone?' G.G. says suddenly. 'There used to be the most beautiful clock…right over there…'

Yet another silence happens. Mom and I look at each other because this silence feels different from the others.

'Don't you remember?' says Greta in a low voice, as if she couldn't believe her ears. 'Grandfather broke it…'

'Ah…he broke it? No, I'd forgotten that.'

'How could you…how…it was the day he broke everything… the day…You mean you don't…?'

'No, I'm sorry. I guess I've lived too many other lives in the meantime. My memories of this one are…er…sketchy, to say the least. Also, don't forget I'm younger than you. You were—ten, weren't you? at the end of the war; I was only six and a half. That makes a big difference.'

'Yes, this is true,' says Greta. Pushing her plate away, she heaves herself to her feet. 'Please, Tessa,' she says to Mom, 'would you mind to make the coffee for your family? I must now lie down for a little while.'

She wavers. Takes two steps, then stops and wavers again. We don't know what to do. Sadie can't help her and the rest of us don't dare to touch her because she's a stranger to us. At last Erra rises slowly from her chair.

'Let me help you, Greta,' she says—and the two old women hobble out of the room together.

'What exquisite china!' exclaims Mom, carefully lifting tiny flowered cups and saucers down from the kitchen cupboard.

'Yes, aren't they delicate?' says Sadie. 'Made in Dresden, of course.'

They go on like this. I don't know how women don't drive themselves nuts with their constant chirping and twittering about *delicate this* and *sweet that* and *exquisite the other* but since I don't have to stay at the table during coffee I move off down the hallway, looking for a bathroom in which to download.

My poop is perfect. Missile-shaped. Firm without being hard. Boy, I think, pushing it out, do I ever miss the Net. Do I ever miss Google! I wonder if anyone's even *heard* of the Internet in this little hick town.

As I head back towards the dining room, padding down the hall in my sock feet, I glance at my electronic watch and see that luckily it's already three-fifteen. Mom said we'd be leaving at around four, which means that in just half an hour I can start tugging at her sleeve and pretending to be indignant: *You said so…you promised me…*

Just as I'm imagining my own voice saying these words, I hear G.G. saying them in exactly the same indignant tone of voice: 'You said so! You promised me!'

Greta answers something to her in German.

The door to the bedroom has been left ajar, and when I peek in to see what's going on I can't believe my eyes: the two old women are fighting over a doll! G.G. is hugging it in her arms—a stupid old doll in a red velvet dress—and her face is twisted with rage.

'She's *mine!*' she hisses. '*Always* she was mine. But apart from that—even if she *hadn't* been mine—you *promised*, Greta!'

Again, Greta answers her in German. She sounds completely exhausted. She goes over to her bed and falls onto it, so heavily that the springs creak. She sighs once and then doesn't move.

Still holding the doll in her arms, G.G. comes over to the foot of the bed. She stands there looking down at her sister for a long time, but unfortunately she now has her back to me so I can't see the expression on her face.

II

Randall, 1982

This spring I felt the shape of a year for the first time. When the leaves started coming out on the trees, I acutely remembered them coming out last spring and I thought to myself in awe: *so that is a year.*

Each season has its games you can lose yourself in. Springtime is marbles, as soon as the pavement is dry enough to play. Flicking them hard until my third fingernail is bruised. The satisfying click of their collision. Tag in the courtyard with other kids from the building. Climbing the jungle gym in the playground. Hanging from my knees on the parallel bars. Swinging hand over hand on the bars and finding I can make it from one end to the other, my arms are strong enough now and won't desert me like they did last year, when about halfway across I'd suddenly go all weak and have to give up and drop to the ground. Summer is playing softball with Dad up in Central Park. I throw and throw and throw the ball until my shoulder aches, and he catches it, sometimes. My dad's not particularly athletic so he misses the ball fairly often and when he misses it he doesn't run like mad to pick it up the way some dads do, he just sort of amble-jogs over to where the ball is lying so I get bored a bit but at least he looks like he's having fun. Then it's his turn to throw and my turn to have the glove which is quite a bit too big for me but when I start school in the fall they're going to buy me a glove my own size. The second the ball smacks against the fat leather palm I close the huge padded fingers quick as a wink and I've got that ball and I say 'You're out!' When I get tired we go over to the baseball diamond, I hook my fingers into the wire fence and hike myself up and watch the big guys playing hardball. I have to stay behind the wire fence because Mom's afraid I'm going to get the ball in the teeth which is a rather strange thing to be afraid of but I can understand her to the extent that I've already lost my baby teeth up in front so these incisors are my last stand. You lose the second set, you're done for.

Fall is the huge floaty piles of dead leaves you can run through and roll around in like a crackling crunching cushion.

Winter is snowball fights—the icy sharp delightful pain of getting a snowball right at the nape of your neck and feeling the water start to trickle down your back under your clothes. Leaping on the other guys, rubbing their faces in the snow, panting, jostling, wrestling, pounding. Making snowmen. Burying someone, or having them bury you, in the snow. Tobogganing in the Catskills. The whoosh of the toboggan when it gets going real fast and the wind whistles in your ears and you hit a patch of ice and the wood of the toboggan screams and you think you might get hurt but you don't, all you do is turn violently over into a snowdrift. The strong thud of all the bodies clumped together when the toboggan comes to an abrupt halt. You get to your feet groggy with relief and stagger and laugh.

★

I'd always rather be playing than doing anything else because you can lose yourself completely. The rest of the time you have to worry about how well you're doing.

One thing I know is I'll never draw people without stomachs again. Last spring I brought a whole slew of drawings home from kindergarten, I was really proud of them but when I showed them to Mom she said 'But Randall, where are the stomachs? You forgot to draw the stomachs!' and I looked at the drawings and saw that she was right, everybody's arms and legs sprouted directly out of their heads, so the week after that I did another batch of drawings and on Friday I brought them home but just as I was about to take them out of my satchel I realised—Oh, no! I forgot to draw the stomachs *again!* I couldn't believe I'd made exactly the same mistake. I was really disappointed in myself and I didn't even show them to Mom because I was afraid she'd think I was stupid.

It's not that your parents don't love you the way you are, it's just that when you're a little kid you've got an awful lot to learn, and maybe (*maybe*) the more you learn the more they'll love you and maybe when you come home with a college diploma you won't have to worry about it anymore. Not everybody gets to go to college like Mom and Dad who met each other at Bernard Baruch where Dad was playwright-in-residence and Mom was studying history as usual but she also joined the theatre club and they put on the play of *Alice Through the Looking Glass* where Mom played the Dormouse and Dad played Tweedledum. I have no difficulty picturing Dad as Tweedledum because he's like that, sort of roly-poly and amusing, but it's almost impossible for me to picture Mom as the Dormouse. The Queen of Hearts yes, giving everyone orders in a no-nonsense voice and arbitrarily shouting 'Off with his head!' whenever it takes her fancy—but my tense, hyper mother as the lazy drowsy distracted rodent who keeps drifting off and has to be moved around from saucer to saucer by the Mad Hatter and the March Hare…incredible. Anyway that actually *is* how they first met and fell in love. It's really strange to think about your parents falling in love with each other, I've talked about it with kids at school and whenever I go over to a friend's place and meet his parents I try to imagine those two individuals falling in love, with some parents I can do it but not with my own. My dad is *so* laid back and my mom is *so* stressed-out, what did they ever see in each other? What did they think their marriage would be like? How did they think they could get along?

They don't, that's for sure. They fight almost every day these days and one of their favourite subjects to fight about is Jewishness. Mom is much more interested in it than Dad which is ironic because Dad is the one who was born a Jew whereas Mom was born a Goy. She insisted on converting when she married Dad. Dad doesn't give a damn about religion but he loved her so much that he agreed to the ceremony which means I'm Jewish too because Jewishness comes from your mother even if she was born a Goy. In exchange for letting her convert Dad got to name me, and now they fight about that because he named me Randall after one of his friends who died, but Mom says it's no name for a Jewish boy whereas Dad (whose own name is Aron) says that given the way Jews have been treated over the past couple of thousand years there's no point in Jewish kids calling attention to themselves just now, they might as well keep a low profile for the next few millennia while they wait to see which way the wind is going to blow. Mom says that in Israel Jews aren't hiding anymore, everyone is proud to have a Jewish name, and Dad says he has no more wish to go back to Israel than to go back to being a caveman. 'That's even more authentic isn't it?' he says. 'Why stop at 4000 B.C.? What was wrong with 40,000 B.C.? We could go even farther than that, we could shrivel up into molluscs and and plop back into the ocean where we came from. People used to get along fine back then, I remember, there were the most delightful cocktail parties…' and Mom stomps out of the room because Jews shouldn't eat shellfish. That's just an example of one of their fights.

Mom has to give a lecture tonight and she's getting ready for it sitting at her dressing-table in her and Dad's bedroom. She doesn't know I'm watching her because I'm lying on my stomach in the hallway pretending to play with my Dinky toys. First she puts on red lipstick and rolls her lips together, then she leans forward and studies her teeth to make sure they're bright and white without a speck of lipstick on them. She pats her hair and nods, walks across the room to get her sheaf of papers, comes back, sits down, picks up her hairbrush to use it as a microphone, clears her throat, smiles at herself in the mirror and begins. 'Ladies and gentlemen,' she says, but then she's not happy with the sound of her voice so she says 'Shit' and hits her own mouth which gets lipstick on the back of her hairbrush and she says 'Shit' even louder. She wipes the hairbrush with a Kleenex and starts over again saying 'Ladies and gentlemen' again in a different tone of voice, 'I'm glad to see so many people here tonight…' and then she just mumbles, reading her paper and glancing up at the mirror as if her reflection was the audience, checking her watch every now and then to see how much time she's got left to talk. I can't hear what she's saying but as she turns the pages she gets more and more het up and this worries me so I roll my Dinky toys down the hall for a while to be out of earshot but when I come back she's still at it and she looks more upset than ever. Finally she runs to the bathroom and opens the medicine cabinet and gulps down some pills and I can see her gripping the edge of the sink and looking at herself in *that* mirror and then she literally slaps her own face, just once with each hand on each cheek but really hard, I wish she wouldn't so I say 'Mo-o-om…' in a real whimpery tone of voice and she jumps and whirls around with an accusing look on her face but I repeat, very whiningly, 'Mo-o-o-m…I've got a stomach ache.' So she comes over and says 'Poor baby,' which I like the sound of, 'why don't you go lie down? I'll tell your father to make you some herbal tea—I have to be out of that door in less than thirty seconds.'

Once in a dream I went up to Mom where she was sitting working at her desk and I tugged on her sleeve to get her attention but she didn't even turn her head towards me, she just said in a stony voice, 'No. Go away, do you hear? I didn't want you. Don't ever bother me again,' but in real life she's never spoken to me that way.

I've always seen more of my father than my mother, which isn't typical. Dad is an excellent cook and fortunately he works at home because his own job is to be a playwright. Sometimes his plays get produced but so far none of them has been a big hit, I'm sure it will happen some day and his talent will be recognised at last although admittedly he's getting sort of old, he's going on forty already whereas Mom is only twenty-six. She gives lectures on evil in universities all around the country. Admittedly evil is a strange specialty to have and I don't know how to explain it so when my friends' mothers ask me what my mom does I just say she teaches History and is also working on a doctorate. That shuts them up even though I don't know exactly what it means because she's not planning to be a doctor.

Anyway she's the breadwinner in the family and this is unusual too and the result is that Dad and I are often alone together. I miss Mom when she's off on a trip but it's also fun because Dad and I do lots of stuff she'd be against, with a gentlemen's agreement, as Dad calls it, to keep it a secret between the two of us. We shower when we feel like it, keep irregular hours, sometimes watch TV while we're having supper, drink Coke and spurt ketchup all over our food, not to mention things that can give you cancer like monosodium glutamate which is forbidden now even in Chinese restaurants.

I can smell breakfast cooking and even though the smell is *wonderful* it fills me with dread because it means another fight for sure. Dad's making bacon and eggs and Mom prefers for us to respect the Jewish custom of not eating stuff that comes from pigs. She has nothing personal against pigs and in fact when she was a little girl she thought the United States sent thousands of pigs to invade Cuba which wasn't really the case so now it makes her laugh, but still she feels strongly about trying to stick to the rules of kosher cooking whereas Dad always prefers to make up his own rules.

Dad has this joke about a poor man who used to sit on a bench out in front of a greasy spoon every morning because he couldn't afford to buy himself breakfast but he just loved the smell of bacon frying so he'd sit there and breathe it in to his heart's content. But the restaurant owner noticed this and after a while it started getting on his nerves so he came outside with a tin plate and said, 'You have to pay me for all the pleasure you've been getting out of my bacon.' The poor man fished a coin out of his pocket and dropped it in the plate where it made a ringing sound, then he picked it up again and put it back in his pocket. 'That's not what I call payment!' said the restaurant owner and the poor man just smiled at him and said, 'Seems fair to me—I get the smell of your cooking, you get the sound of my money!'

Dad's got another joke where this poor man is begging in front of Katz's delicatessen down on Houston Street and this big fat businessman takes pity on him because he seems so miserable, so he drops a five-dollar bill into the guy's hat. But then a few minutes later the fat businessman walks past the deli again and sees the poor man inside, stuffing himself on smoked salmon and cream and he can't believe his eyes. He goes into the deli and says to the man 'What are you doing? I give you five bucks and you splurge it all at once on smoked salmon and cream?' And the poor man looks up at him and says (it's really great the way Dad imitates his voice), 'I can't eat smoked salmon and cream when I'm broke, I can't eat smoked salmon and cream when I have money—*when can I eat smoked salmon and cream?*' Every time Dad tells this joke it cracks him up but Mom doesn't laugh at all and I can tell that deep down she agrees with the fat businessman, namely that you shouldn't waste money.

I come out of my bedroom and sure enough, Mom is sitting at the breakfast table with a look on her face like the Golem she sometimes tells me about.

'Some bacon and eggs, Randall?' says Dad and I say 'Sure' right off the bat because there are two arguments in favour of that answer, firstly my stomach is longing for it and secondly I'll be making Dad happy, whereas there's only one argument in favour of the opposite answer, namely making Mom happy. Better still would be not having to feel torn apart the minute I get out of bed in the morning.

'You're turning our son into a pig,' Mom mutters as Dad dishes the food onto my plate, which also reminds me of the Queen of Hearts who turned the baby in Alice's arms into a pig. Maybe real mothers sometimes look down at the squirmy shitty little animals in their arms and wonder: Where the hell did *this* come from? Maybe Mom wondered that when I was a baby and she couldn't help being disgusted with me.

'Oh, come off it, Sadie,' says Dad in a friendly, guffawing sort of voice as if she couldn't mean it seriously—he doesn't enjoy fighting as much as she does and I've never once heard him raise his voice.

'Did you wash your hands and face?' Mom asks me and I say 'Yes' because I definitely don't want those scrambled eggs to get cold. 'Show me your hands,' she says and as I hold them out to her, palms up, my heart sinks because maybe she'll be able to see that I'm telling a lie and haven't actually washed my hands since bedtime last night, though how they could have gotten dirty while I was sleeping I don't know. She takes my hands in hers and turns them over.

'Randall. You've been chewing your nails again.'

'Sadie, let the kid have his breakfast—his nails will grow back.'

'His nails will grow back!' says Mom, turning to Dad in indignation, which at least gives me the chance to sit down and get some

food into my mouth. *'His nails will grow back!!'*

'Let me warm up your coffee, Sexy Sadie,' Dad says, which (translated) means that this is not at all a good beginning to a perfect summer's day in early July 1982 and perhaps we should start all over again, what do you think?

Mom holds out her cup and accepts the coffee and even says thank you because she doesn't want to set a bad example for me.

'So what are your plans for the day, Randall?' she asks me and in a flash I wonder silently to myself: doesn't she remember what it was like to be a little girl on summer vacation and have no plans at all apart from playing and hanging out with friends and revelling in the luscious liberty of the endless days?

But before I can answer her Dad comes to the rescue: 'Oh, don't worry about him,' he says in a bantering tone of voice, 'he's got a full schedule of Bible study and reading classes and athletic work-out—that's from nine to ten a.m.—and then—'

'Spare me, Aron,' says Mom. 'If you could just spare me *one out of ten* demonstrations of your irresistible sense of humour, I'd be satisfied.'

She pushes her chair back from the table then and it makes a loud noise as it scrapes the floor. I don't want her to leave in a bad mood so I say, placatingly but vaguely, 'No, Mom, don't worry. I've got lots of stuff to do. I have to clean up my room and in the afternoon I'm invited over to Barry's to play.'

'Well that's good,' says Mom from the entryway where she's checking out her appearance in the full-length mirror, 'because I wouldn't want you out of doors, they say it'll be hitting ninety-five this afternoon.'

I pick up the last tiny crisp salty fragment of bacon on my fingertip and slip it into my mouth and lick my finger but even though her back is turned she sees me do this in the mirror and says 'Don't eat with your fingers!' but she says it automatically because she's concentrating on her appearance now, sort of hitting her bangs over and over again to make them fall into place correctly. She won't leave the apartment until her appearance in the mirror meets with her approval which sometimes takes quite a long time which I don't understand; everyone thinks my mother is very beautiful except my mother herself. Now she's checking her profile to make sure that her stomach isn't sticking out; she's always worried about being too fat which she isn't, as Dad says she's simply curvaceous and I completely agree. Now she's hitting her hair again. Ah, at last—'Okay, you guys, be good. See you later.' She doesn't even blow us a kiss as she goes out the door.

I can feel Dad give a little sigh of relief even though it doesn't make any noise at all. The truth is that the atmosphere relaxes every time my mother leaves a room and tenses up every time she enters one—I'm simply stating the facts. My mother is really a very nice person, I truly *love* her and I just wish I could figure out what to do to make her more relaxed and happy and I think Dad feels exactly the same way. Our eyes meet for a second over the breakfast table to say this and then Dad gets up and starts clearing the dishes away and whistling under his breath and I go back to my bedroom to get dressed.

Dad says she's hard on everyone but especially hard on herself and it's because she has a goal of Excellence, so all we can do is try our best to be Excellent and not worry about it too much. At least I'm making progress and now I'll never forget to draw people's stomachs again.

I make my bed and put my little teddy bear named Marvin on my pillow where he belongs. Once Mom actually threw him out. I found him in the wastebasket under my desk when I got home from kindergarten and I couldn't believe my eyes. 'Who threw Marvin away?' I bawled, sobbing with rage and also with the sense of loss I would have had if I hadn't found him in time. 'Who threw Marvin away?' That day Mom was contrite, she put her arms around me and apologised, saying it was because he was so old and banged up. 'But that's what I *love* about him!' I said, continuing to sob because, though I was definitely feeling better thanks to her apology, I was also enjoying the unusual sensation of having the upper hand in a confrontation with my mother. I held the teddy bear out in front of me with both hands until she apologised again. What I'd said was true, though—I love Marvin not despite but *because* of the fact that he's a banged-up old bear, because the cymbals he used to carry in his front paws are broken off and so is the key in his back which you could wind up to make him march, and one of his golden-brown marble eyes is marred and bleary so he looks half blind. But what I love more than anything about Marvin is probably the real reason for Mom's throwing him out, namely that he used to be my Grandma Erra's toy when she was a little girl.

Grandma Erra is another bone of contention between my two parents and a sensitive subject in the household in general: Dad and I are crazy about her whereas Mom has mixed feelings which is an understatement. We've got all her records and people are always impressed when I tell them that Erra the famous singer is actually my own grandmother. It's true that looking at her it's hard to believe she's a grandmother, especially when she's on stage with the make-up and lighting and from a distance. She's only forty-four years old and looks younger because she's thin and lithe and lively and the funny thing is that when she was little she wanted to be the Fat Lady in the circus when she grew up. On stage she looks like a waif or a weightless fairy and the sounds that come out of her are totally eerie and unique. She's got a whole group of singers and instrumentalists that she's in charge of, they all rehearse and travel and perform together but the other musicians are basically back-up and when push comes to shove Erra is alone at centre stage with her wispy blond hair shining like a fairy crown in the spotlight and thousands of eyes riveted to her and thousands of ears following the wild wailing meanders of her voice.

I feel a special connection to Grandma Erra because the two of us have identical round brown birthmarks. Hers is on the inside of her left elbow and mine's at the base of my neck or rather halfway between my neck and my left shoulder. One day when I was spending a weekend at her place which is a loft down on the Bowery we compared our birthmarks and she told me hers helped her to sing so I told her mine kept me company, I said it was like a furry little bat perched on my shoulder and that it whispered advice into my ear whenever I needed it and she clapped her hands and said 'That's great, Randall—promise me you'll never lose contact with that bat!' So I promised her.

She's so *warm*.

I don't know exactly what Mom has against Grandma Erra, unless maybe she's jealous of her fame and success and the fact that everyone admires her so much. I think she thinks her mother is a dreamer and I once heard her call her a reverse ostrich, in the sense that she's got her head not in the sand but in the clouds, and refuses to deal with the nitty-gritty problems of people down on earth. Mom keeps up with all the wars and famines in the world for instance whereas Grandma Erra doesn't even have TV. Also Mom thinks her mother is immoral because she's slept with so many people. It's exciting in my opinion to be so immoral. Mom never even met her real father, which was quite unusual in those days, so when you come right down to it she's a bastard except you're not supposed to say bastard you're supposed to say illegitimate child. For a while she had a stepdad she really liked named Peter who used to take her to Katz's every Sunday which was right around the corner from where they lived, but then this guy named Janek came along and Grandma Erra decided to live with him instead so she threw Peter out on his ear and Mom was crestfallen. She couldn't *stand* her new stepfather Janek because he never paid attention to her and spoke almost no English and also he chewed his nails and gritted his teeth and sometimes locked himself away in silence for days on end, drinking gin and staring at the wall. Finally he ended up committing suicide right in their very kitchen, which is absolutely incredible. Luckily Mom who was ten years old at the time was away at school and didn't see his blood and brains splattered all over the kitchen tiling. After that they moved onto the Bowery a few blocks away and since then Erra has had all sorts of boyfriends and nowadays she's living with a woman, which is something that happens called homosexuality. Mom finds it too unstable for a little boy so she won't let me stay overnight at Grandma Erra's anymore.

I spend the whole morning watching TV which I know would make Mom mad but Dad lets me; he says intelligent people have to know all about the world's stupidity so I can watch TV but we keep it a secret between us. This morning is pretty good with 'Garfield' and 'G.I. Joe' and especially 'Spider-Man' which is my favourite; sometimes Dad comes and watches it with me and it makes him laugh because it dates all the way back to when he was a teenager and he used to read it in comic books.

After lunch it gets baking hot in the apartment and Dad suggests we take a dip in the neighbourhood pool so we put on our swimming trunks under our clothes and·go down into the street. It feels like we just walked into an oven and there's a smell of melting tar in the air. I like holding Dad's hand when we cross the street together, in a year or two I'll be too big to hold it so I want to be sure to enjoy it while it lasts.

The pool is a total pandemonium of about a thousand kids of all colours and sizes splashing around and yelling with their voices bouncing off the walls, it scares me a bit but Dad picks me up in his arms as we go into the water and then I'm fine. He takes me down to the almost deep end and lets me dive off his shoulders a few times until the lifeguard blows the whistle and tells us to stop because it's against the rules. One thing I like about Dad is that he doesn't obey rules too closely. You should always play *with* and not *according to* the rules, he says, because a life with no danger in it is not a life. Eventually he hoists himself out of the pool, all dripping with his hair plastered to his slightly bald head and his skin white and flabby making him look rather unattractive compared to some of the other younger darker sleeker dads, but I don't care because he's the best father in the world. He puts a towel around his shoulders and sits down with his hands folded on his friendly pot as he calls it, which is his stomach, and watches me as I fool around by myself in the shallow end. I don't know how to swim yet but I have a thing I like which is jumping up and down, plunging to a crouch under the water while breathing out through my nose and mouth, then leaping up in the air and breathing in, then plunging down again—I really get into the sound of the water in my ears and the rhythm and weightlessness and mindlessness of the movement, I could go on doing it for hours but after a while Dad comes and catches me in his arms and says it's time for him to get back to work.

He drops me off at Barry's which is just two blocks away and I play there for the rest of the afternoon. Barry's got all sorts of war games, GI-Joes and Masters of the Universe and some very authentic-looking machine guns which are fun to fool around with. Barry's mom is always nice to me because she's a fan of Erra's, so for our snack in addition to a bowl of Cheerios she lets us have some lemon Jell-O powder and lick it right out of the palm of our hands which Mom would never do because she says it's nothing but chemicals that give you cancer. Dad picks me up at six and we do food shopping on the way home, he buys some whitefish and then a bottle of white wine to go with it and hopefully put Mom in a good mood. But when Mom comes home at seven from her day of doing research it doesn't look as if any amount or colour of wine would do the trick. I go off into my room and start playing war with my Playmobil characters because I'm not allowed to have soldiers because Mom is against war and doesn't want me to turn into a violent macho male like most men are.

'People don't *know* about this, Aron,' I hear her say from afar in a voice filled with emotion that scares me. 'They know about the camps but they don't know about this.' And then I can't hear what Dad answers and then she says 'Over *two hundred thousand children!* Kidnapped! Stolen! Torn away from their families in Eastern Europe…' and I start feeling really nervous. My little bat-birthmark suggests making exploding noises with my mouth and turning my Legos into helicopters and bombers and ground-air missiles to drown out the sound of my mother's voice so I do it and it works.

When Dad calls me for supper, Mom is sitting with her elbows propped on the table holding her head in her hands as if it weighed a ton, and Dad is taking off his apron. He brings a candle over and says in a half-joking sort of way, 'Sadie, it's Friday night—would you like to light the Sabbath candle?' but Mom sits up suddenly and her hand flies up all by itself and knocks the candle to the floor. 'If you can't follow the tradition,' she says, 'the least you can do is refrain from mocking it!' I don't think she broke the candle on purpose but anyway it breaks and Dad picks up the two pieces and puts them in the garbage can without a word.

As we're eating the whitefish which Dad has filleted for me because I'm scared of getting a fishbone stuck in my throat and choking to death, Mom turns to me and says 'Randall' in a way that makes me wish I were back at Barry's place licking lemon Jell-O out of my palm without a care in the world.

'Yes, Mom?'

'Randall, I'm going to have to go away for a while. To Germany. I know it must seem to you like I'm away an awful lot…but the documents I need for my thesis are almost all in Germany, that's how it is.'

'Sadie,' says Dad, 'the kid doesn't know what you're talking about. He wouldn't be able to find Germany on a map.'

'Well it's time he *learned* where Germany is because he's got German blood in his veins! Did you know that, Randall? Did you know that your Grandma Erra was *born* in Germany?'

'No,' I whisper. 'I thought she was born in Canada.'

'She *grew up* in Canada,' says Mom, 'and she never talks about the first years of her life but the fact is that they were spent in Germany. Listen, darling, it's important to me to find out as much as I can about this. It's for your sake, too, you know? I mean, how can we build a future together if we don't know the truth about our past, right?'

'For Christ's sake, Sadie, the kid is *six years old*.'

'Okay, okay,' says Mommy, in a surprisingly low voice. 'It's just that…I have lots of questions about this particular fragment of our past. *Lots* of questions…And Grandma Erra herself…either cannot or will not answer them. So…I have to go to Germany.'

'You already said that,' Dad points out.

'I know, Aron,' says Mom, still without raising her voice. 'The reason I'm repeating myself is that I've left out the most important thing…and the reason I've left out the most important thing is that it makes my head absolutely spin. I received a letter today… from Erra's *sister*. She says that if I come to see her in Munich she'll tell me everything she knows.'

A heavy silence follows this declaration. I glance up at Dad and he looks desperate, plus he's left most of his meal in his plate which almost never happens.

The conversation has made everyone uncomfortable, and as I'm sort of sidling back to my room, trying not to draw attention to myself, I hear Dad saying to Mom, 'You're so obsessed with the suffering of those children forty years ago that you can't even see your own son suffering right next to you. *Drop it*, Sadie. Can't you just *drop the whole thing?*'

'*No I can't,*' says Mom. 'Don't you understand? This…evil…isn't some sort of abstract *concept* to me. It has to do with *my own mother!* Getting her to talk about her early childhood is like pulling teeth. It took her fifteen years to admit that Janek was stolen, not adopted, twenty years to cough up the name of her German family and the town they lived in; I need to know more about it, surely you can understand that? I need to know who my own grandparents were! If they were given a little Polish boy to replace their dead son, they must have been Nazis or at least in the good graces of the Nazis. *I need to know!'*

I close the door and pick up my Playmobil and Lego war where I left off.

My parents do the dishes and when it gets to be my bedtime Dad comes in and tries to help me forget the discomfort by giving me a paddle-whacking. This means that I lie down on my stomach in my pyjamas and he goes up and down the entire length of my body whacking me rhythmically with the flat of his palms and singing at the top of his lungs. Tonight he sings the song where the words sound like gibberish the first time you hear them:

Ooooooh, mayrezidotes and dozidotes and liddlamzidivy,
A kiddlidivy too wouldn't you—oo? A kiddlidivy too wouldn't you?

It just sounds like complete gibberish but then the song goes on to explain:

If the words sound queer
and funny to the ear
A little bit jumbled and jivy,
It's: Mares—eat—oats, and does—eat—oats, and little lambs eat ivy!
Oh…

Then he sings it fast again and this time you can understand it all, including the last line, *a kid will eat ivy, too, wouldn't you?* I often wish that grown-ups would sit down and explain everything to me slowly the way this song does.

As usual Dad's paddle-whacking makes me scream with laughter and I beg for more but just then Mom comes in and says it's too much excitement right before bedtime and I need to calm down. So Dad gives me a big hug and a kiss on the forehead and Mom sits down on the bed next to me to tell me a story which I also like. When she was my age she knew how to read but I haven't learned yet so I have to wait for someone to read to me, it's another example of my never being good enough, even though I try. Tonight she tells me the story of Little Black Sambo which she doesn't even need the book for because she still knows it off by heart from when she was little. I've pretty much memorised it too which is another way of saying learned by heart and I get to say all the words Little Black Sambo says: 'Oh! Please, Mr Tiger, don't eat me up, and I'll give you my beautiful little Red Coat,' and so on, all the way to where the tigers have melted into a puddle of butter and Sambo says 'Oh! What lovely melted butter! I'll take that home to Black Mumbo' (who is his mother) 'for her to cook with,' and then Black Mumbo makes pancakes and Little Black Sambo eats a hundred and sixty-nine of them because he's *really hungry*. When the story is over Mom puts her arms around me and rocks me gently, sort of humming under her breath, and the skin of her arms is very soft but the way she holds me isn't.

On the morning of her departure for Germany I wake up early, it's only six-thirty. I like knowing how to tell time which I learned only last spring in kindergarten. Dad's got a joke which goes, 'Why did the little moron throw the clock out the window? He wanted to see time fly.' It's a pretty good joke but at the same time I'm seriously worried about time flying. Mom says the older you get the faster it goes and I'm afraid that if I'm not careful my whole life will just rush past me in one fell swoop and I'll wake up inside my coffin and it will be all over without my having had time to appreciate it. I know that dead people don't actually wake up and *realise* they're inside their coffins under the ground but still, it's a frightening thought to think they've been put there, like Grandad when we went to his funeral in Long Island. I found it appalling that my own father's father was really and truly inside that box and everyone seemed to take it for granted that this was okay, this was the way these things were done. The grave-diggers put the coffin on some ropes and tied the ropes around the coffin and hoisted it up and swung it over the grave and lowered it down until it hit the bottom and then they untied the ropes again and jerked them back up out of the grave. I mean, they were leaving a whole human *person* down in that hole but they wouldn't want to waste a couple of good *ropes*, right? I could see they were completely used to this, they did it every day and it was just a job to them whereas to me the person they were putting into the ground was my one and only grandfather (since Mom never met her dad) and I was never going to see him again and that's when I really understood the meaning of the word *never*.

I glance at the clock and see that while I've been lying here thinking about death, exactly three minutes have gone by.

After Grandpa died, Grandma had to sell their house in Long Island. That house used to be one of my favourite places to visit, with lots of nooks and crannies and closets and pantries, but Grandma said she couldn't run it all by herself so she went to live in a home with other old folks. Now there's no place for all the cousins to get together and play hide-and-seek like we used to do at their house, you can't play hide-and-seek in an apartment in Manhattan. Once I hid scrunched down in a big cardboard box in the basement and when my cousins came downstairs I heard them calling me—'Randall! Randall!'—but it was such a good hiding place that they didn't find me at all, and after a while they gave up and went outside to play Frisbee and forgot all about me. Meanwhile I just stayed there and waited and waited and by the time I finally came out I was cold and stiff all over and when my cousins saw me they didn't even say 'Where *were* you? We looked all *over* for you!' and I felt hurt that they hadn't missed me and I thought to myself, that must be what it's like when you're dead, life just goes on without you.

Now it's seven o'clock and I hear Mom's alarm clock ringing so I have the right to go into their bedroom if I want to, which I do. I come slinking in very quietly on my hands and knees and press up against the foot of the bed where they can't see me. Their blanket is lying in a heap on the floor, they've got just a sheet on over their bodies and their four feet are sticking out over the edge of the mattress. Dad's feet are huge and a bit dirty underneath because he likes to walk around the apartment in his bare feet and what fascinates me especially is the thick yellow skin around the edges of his heels, which when you touch it feels like wood instead of skin. Mom's feet are cleaner but she's got bony bumps called bunions at the base of her big toes which aren't attractive either. On the whole I find adult feet quite ugly and I must say that's one of the things about growing up which I'm *not* looking forward to, is watching my feet grow gradually uglier as the years go by.

I tickle the thick yellow skin on Dad's left heel very lightly with my baby fingernail—so lightly that he can't feel it at first. Then I move slowly towards the instep—ah, that's got him! But since he still doesn't know I'm in the room, he thinks a fly must have lit on his foot by accident so he just kicks to shake it off. Then I really tickle him in earnest and he shoots up to a sitting position with a yowl. 'What the *hell*—?' says Mom because in sitting up Dad pulled the sheet off her body and now she sees me and her whole chest is bare with her breasts hanging right out there in the open, so she turns over violently in the bed and grabs her nightgown.

When I was a little kid Mom and I used to have baths together and she wasn't shy at all about her breasts, she'd even let me play with them. But a while ago they became off limits to me and now only Dad gets to see them apart from Mom herself of course. (Was there one particular *day* when I got too old to see my mother's breasts? How did she decide exactly *what day* it should be?) It's a funny thing about women's breasts, when you're first born you spend hours a day nuzzling and guzzling there, then little by little you get pushed away and the day comes when you're not even allowed to see them anymore. But on TV and in the movies women are always showing off their breasts, all except the nipples, as if the nipples contained some sacred secret, which they don't, most of the time they haven't even got milk in them. As to what's between their legs, Mom always kept her panties on in the bathtub so I've never seen that part of a woman's body except on statues in parks where they have nothing at all, so I asked Dad about it and he said there's lots of interesting things down there, they just don't stick out the way ours do.

Mom goes into the kitchen to make coffee and Dad and I go pee together in the bathroom. We stand side by side at the toilet bowl and aim our two yellow arcs so that they meet and mix in the clear water and I find it really interesting how at first you can still see the separation between yellow and clear but in a few seconds it's the same colour all over, light yellow. I'm good at aiming now whereas when I was little I'd get drops of pee on the floor almost every time and Mom would make me clean it up with a sponge and rinse out the sponge under the tap and it made me sick to think I was actually touching my pee with my own bare hands.

Mom's plane doesn't take off until seven p.m. but I know our whole day will be coloured with the idea of it. As she drinks her coffee her eyes are all jumpy with suitcases and passports and visas and maps and I can see there's no room in there for me.

'Can you believe it, Aron? In less than twenty-four hours I'll be in Germany. It's *insane!* Hm, hm, hm, let's see. A list. That's what I need to do, is make a list. Always remember, Randall, when you feel overwhelmed, make a list. Take a long, hard look at your obligations and get them down on paper in descending order of importance. You should start with the biggest job, the hardest job, the one you feel like doing *least*. That's called taking the bull by the horns.'

'I never get *past* that stage,' says Dad, 'because the bull always gores me and the crowd leaps to its feet, cheering, and all I can do is lie there in the dust and bleed to death.'

'Aron!'

'No, your mother's right, Ran. Do not do today what can be put off until tomorrow.'

'It's the other way around!' I say, laughing. 'Do not put off until tomorrow…'

'Oh? Sorry…For some reason I always get that proverb wrong.

So what's your bull, Sadie?'

'Huh?'

'The one you've decided to grab by the horns today?'

'Ah…packing my suitcase. That's my number one priority, getting packed.'

She goes into their bedroom after breakfast and as Dad does the dishes we hear her talking to herself, she's taking clothes out of the closet and laying them out on the bed and appraising them, saying 'Now let's see, let's see, this is getting a bit tight around the waist, this sweater doesn't match these pants, should I bring two skirts or three, I wonder if they sell pantyhose in Germany'—all of which would be fine and dandy except that we can also hear a *second* voice in between these comments saying 'What did you buy it for, stupid?' and 'Whose fault do you think that is?' and 'Scared to get on the scale now, aren't you?' and 'How long do you think it will take you to figure *that* out?' After a while Dad goes over and gently closes the door to their bedroom because it's a little bit upsetting to hear your own mother talking to herself in two different voices like that.

Usually when Mom travels she's gone for two or three days, a week at the most. This time it will be for a *fortnight* which Dad told me is short for fourteen nights. I'm starting to miss her already with an ache in my stomach. I wonder if she misses me too when she wakes up in a faraway hotel room. Does she wonder what I'm doing while she's gone?

The days tick by and despite missing my mother I would say I'm having a fairly good summer.

Mom calls long distance and I answer the phone, she says 'Hi, sweetie' and a couple of other things to me but I can tell she's impatient to get our conversation over with because the call costs money and basically she wants to talk to Dad. They talk for quite a long time and even if Dad doesn't raise his voice I can tell he doesn't like what he's hearing, which makes me have to go to the bathroom with diarrhoea. Afterwards he tells me that Mom is all revved up about what she learned from Grandma Erra's sister in Munich.

The very next day Grandma Erra herself calls, which makes me feel guilty even though I'm not the one who's prying into her past. She's surprised when I tell her that Mom is out of town, which for sure means that Mom didn't tell her she was going off to meet her sister in Germany. I realise this at once so I say I think she's on a lecture tour.

'A lecture tour in the middle of the summer?' says Erra. 'That's impossible, all the universities are closed.'

'Maybe it's in the Southern Hemisphere,' I say, both to show off what I've learned about the seasons and to keep things sounding logical.

Erra shrieks with laughter, and then she says, 'Well, what would you say to the four of us having a picnic together next Sunday?' When she says *the four of us* I realise it means I'm going to meet her girlfriend at long last—yet another secret which Dad and I will have to keep buried in our gentlemen's agreement.

On Saturday Dad comes home with his arms full of bags from the supermarket and on Sunday he spends the whole morning getting the picnic ready, but just as he's packing everything into the basket it starts to rain. Not a few droplets or a refreshing summer shower that leaves the sky washed bright blue afterwards—no, a real deluge thrashing down from stubborn steel-grey clouds that look as if they've come to stay. I feel glum because it's clear that sitting on a blanket on the grass in Central Park is going to be out of the question for the foreseeable future, whereas I was truly looking forward to it. Dad calls Grandma Erra and says, 'God seems to have other plans for the day,' but then she says something I can't hear and he answers: 'Terrific. We'll be ringing your doorbell in an hour.'

Turning to me he says, 'We'll have the picnic on the Bowery.'

By the time we get there we're streaming wet and Grandma Erra and her friend come at us with towels, rubbing our heads until we're frizzy and dizzy and the rainstorm has become a dramatic element of the day, an enemy like a dragon from whose clutches we've managed to escape with our picnic safe and dry. A tablecloth has been spread right on the floor in the main loft space, and set with cardboard plates and plastic cutlery as though the cupboards weren't full of real dishes and silverware. Erra's girlfriend (whose name is Mercedes as if she were a fancy car) is small with dark hair and dark eyes because she comes from Mexico, and when she shakes my hand and says 'Good to meet you, Randall!' it makes me feel as if she meant it.

Grandma Erra sweeps me up into her arms which are stronger than they look and kisses me on the forehead, the nose, the chin and both cheeks, smiling into my eyes between kisses. She's got sapphire-blue eyes which you can see wrinkles around close up, and her hair is almost all white now with just a few strands of yellow left. 'My little man,' she says, 'it's been far too long, hasn't it?' and I say 'Yes.'

So we sit on the floor, each of us on one side of the tablecloth, and I must say that for old ladies in their mid-forties Erra and Mercedes are much better at sitting cross-legged than my dad who just turned forty; after a while the cramps in his legs get so bad that he has to fetch himself a cushion. Not only is the food scrumptious but there's a special feeling in the room as if we were all actors in a play, because of the dark grey sky outside like an ancient castle and the rain lashing against the windowpanes like a dragon's tail. Mercedes lights two candles which makes it even more theatrical, and when we finish eating, Grandma Erra uses one of the candles to light a thin cigar.

'So my daughter has gone gallivanting off to the Southern Hemisphere, has she?' she says with a small ironic smile.

'The *Southern Hemisphere?*' says Dad and I blush and look at him urgently so he'll understand why I told that white lie. 'Oh... Randall must have gotten mixed up. She's in the *South*, is what he meant. The South of Germany, actually. Doing research.'

'Search, re-search and re-re-search,' sighs Erra. 'I wonder if she'll ever actually find anything.'

Mercedes giggles, then puts a hand to her mouth because I'm there and she shouldn't make fun of my mother in front of me.

'Germany! God, if I'd known it would turn into such an obsession...' says Erra. 'Strange profession, don't you think, Aron? Meddling in other people's lives?'

'Oh I don't know,' says Dad. 'My own profession is worse: I *steal* from other people's lives to create my characters. People who live in glass houses shouldn't stow thrones.'

'Throw stones, Dad!' I say, correcting him, though I know he made the mistake on purpose.

'No, it's not the same thing,' Grandma Erra says. 'You're an artist.'

Still with the thin cigar between her teeth and a spiral of smoke going upward that makes her squint, she walks over to the piano in a corner of the loft.

'Come here, Randall,' she says, and I obey with pleasure. 'Let's make a little music together.'

'I don't know how to play,' I say.

She picks me up, sets me on the piano stool, and smooths my hair which must still be tousled from the towelling.

'That furry little bat on your shoulder will help you, won't he? What I need is for you to stay down here in the low register…and play only black notes—but *softly, very softly*, okay? And *listen* to what you're playing until you like it.'

Dad and Mercedes are completely quiet at the far end of the room. As the saying goes, you could hear a pin drop. Using both hands, I play some black notes softly and slowly. Grandma Erra stands close to me, listening and nodding, she stubs out her cigar and a few seconds later I hear a low hum coming from her chest. Then when I keep on playing she responds to each of my notes with a note of her own, either in harmony or disharmony, and it's as if we were walking slowly through the woods together and hiding behind trees. My fingers gradually gain speed and so does her voice but we go on respecting the rule about *softly*, so it's as if we were tap-dancing together in the snow.

After a while it feels like a right time to stop, both of us stop at the same instant and Dad and Mercedes clap for us—but *softly*, so softly you can't hear them, which makes us laugh. Grandma Erra spins the piano stool around and lifts me off it, clasping me in her arms.

'You see?' she says. 'You played!'

She carries me back across the room, holding me effortlessly on one hip.

'I thought I heard some words in there,' says Dad. 'At least a syllable or two, every now and then…You wouldn't be turning human on us, would you Erra?'

'I've always been human!' laughs Grandma Erra. 'But it's true I've started using words in my singing…thanks to Mercedes. She's a word magician.'

'Are you?' I ask her as Grandma Erra sets me down in an armchair.

'The magic isn't in me,' Mercedes says, 'it isn't in people, it's in what happens *between* people. Learning to use it is mostly a matter of concentration.'

'I've got a major concentration problem,' says Dad.

'Shhh…' says Mercedes, putting her finger to her lips and lowering her voice to a husky whisper. 'Sometimes if you just shut your eyes and listen very closely, the magic will happen. Ready, Randall?'

'Ready.'

'Okay. There's a soft white cloud in your brain, like a ball of cotton…Can you see it?'

'Yeah.'

'There's a string coming out of the cloud, isn't there? You pull gently on the string and it's got lots of small coloured ribbons on it, like the tail of a kite…so you keep on pulling gently…the ribbons are all stitched together…they're words, the ribbons are words—and look, look what they bring to you from the far side of the cloud!'

I open my eyes but Mercedes says, smiling, 'No, no, when I say *look* I mean inwardly. To look inwardly, you have to keep your eyes closed. Okay…now the magic will happen, the images will move from my brain into yours and you'll start seeing everything I say.'

She goes on talking in a low voice with pauses between every word: 'Here is…a dead crow…Here is…a fairy with iridescent wings…Here is…a bowl of porridge…Can you see them, Randall?'

I nod because I really can. The silence is strong and long so I can really go into it, I see one of the motionless crow's eyes, half open and glazed over, and the diamond tiara nestled in the fairy's golden hair, and the steam rising from the bowl of hot cereal that Dad sometimes makes for breakfast in the wintertime, with brown sugar and cream on it and even raisins sometimes, luscious.

When I open my eyes again the three adults are smiling at me.

'It goes on all the time,' Mercedes tells me. 'The magic part is just being aware of it.'

'Are you a poet?' Dad asks her, which makes her burst into the loveliest laughter I've ever heard, like a million droplets of water scattered glittering into the air around us.

'No,' she says. 'I'm a therapist. I do image therapy'—and even though I'm not sure what that means it sounds like a very pleasant thing to do with her.

'A fascinating demonstration,' says Dad, lighting up a cigarette which we both know Mom wouldn't approve of. 'But plays are a whole different ballgame. You can't write a play about a dead crow or an iridescent fairy or a bowl of porridge, you have to somehow bring them all together.'

'Not only that,' says Grandma Erra, 'but Mercedes' magic only works among users of the same language. If she'd said *cuervo muerto* instead of *dead crow*, Randall would have seen nothing. That's why I've always preferred pure voice. Everyone can understand the voice—my singing is utterly simple and self-evident, isn't it, Randall?'

'I don't know,' I say, honestly. 'It's utterly beautiful, that's for sure.'

The adults laugh because I said 'utterly' which is not a word for children, even though they use it around us all the time.

'Thank you, sweetheart,' says Grandma Erra.

Then they all start talking grown-up talk about President Reagan (who Dad always calls 'that fourth-rate actor') sending troops to Beirut and I curl up on a big cushion on the floor and drift in and out of sleep a bit, thinking I'm the Dormouse like my mother and maybe they'll start pouring tea on me before long, at one point I doze off completely but then I wake up because everyone burst out laughing but I didn't hear what made them laugh, Grandma Erra raises her voice suddenly saying that the only instrument that ever accompanied her singing is a lute, Dad and Mercedes look at each other with little frowns on their faces like what is she talking about and Dad says 'Excuse me but I don't think I ever once saw a lutanist among your musicians' and Erra smiles and says 'He may be invisible but he's there, he's the only one who's really there.' I might have dreamed it though, I'm not sure she said that thing about the lute, people's phrases often get distorted when they slide into your sleep.

At the end of the afternoon we all try to stand on our heads. Dad keeps falling over, Mercedes can get her legs up in the air but not in a straight line with her body, I get better with every try but Grandma Erra does it best and I wonder if this is what her life is like all the time or if it's just part of the special occasion due to a Sunday picnic on the floor.

That night in bed I try to do Mercedes' magic with words, I close my eyes and murmur *dog…cat…plate…*and so on, but it doesn't work nearly as well as when there's someone else to say the words for you and you're not expecting them. It's hard to surprise yourself, just like it's hard to tickle yourself, as Dad pointed out to me long ago. 'I can't make myself laugh by tickling myself,' he added, 'but I can make myself laugh by thinking about people trying to tickle themselves and failing.'

Mom calls again long distance and at first, hearing her voice, Dad sounds happy and then he sounds less and less happy. 'What do you mean?' he says. He listens some more and nods even though she can't see him and says, 'Incredible. Ukrainian, huh?…Yeah, that's right, they may have thrown the occasional pogrom just for fun, but they're not a final solution sort of people…Listen, Sadie, of course this is all very fascinating, but I didn't marry your ancestors, I married *you* and I sure wish I could spend some time with you once in a while.'

Another couple of minutes go by while I know Mom is talking up a storm on the other end of the line. Then Dad breaks in again. 'You're *what?*' he says. 'Chicago? What's in Chicago?…What are you, a detective now?…It's not the number of days I'm upset about, it's how you're filling up your mind with all this…'

But she doesn't let him finish his sentence, and after a while he says goodbye.

'Your Mom's going to make a little detour by way of Chicago on her way home,' is all he tells me. 'She won't be back until next Wednesday.'

In the meantime before she gets back there's this playwright friend of Dad's named Jacob who drops by to chew the rag. I really like Jacob because he's got a long black beard and a big voice full of laughter. One of his plays is being performed in a summer theatre up in Vermont and he wants Dad to drive up with him to see it. Dad says 'Hey, I'd love to but I've got this dwarf here to take care of.' 'So bring the dwarf!' says Jacob. 'What the hell—the more the merrier!' So it ends up that without even telling Mom about our plans, we leave New York City on Saturday morning in Jacob's old minibus which would give her a conniption fit it's so dirty and full of junk, and jounce our way all the way up to Brattleboro which is a long trek. To pass the time Jacob and Dad sing songs from Broadway musicals from when they were young but since they can never remember all the lyrics they start fooling around with them, one of them starts a song and then the other one comes in with a verse from another song and so on and so forth in alternation and the only rule is that it has to more or less make sense and be in the same key.

> *If I were a rich man, Ya ha deedle deedle, bubba bubba deedle deedle dum. All day long I'd Follow the Yellow Brick Road. Follow the Yellow Brick Road Wa-doo—Zim bam boodle-oo Hoodle ah da wa sa Scatty wah. Yeah! It ain't necessarily so. To get into Hebben, Don't snap for a sebben Beneath the Broadway lights! Oh, moon of Alabama If I were a biddy biddy rich Yidle-diddle-diddle-diddle man New York, New York, a helluva town, The Bronx is up, but the Battery's down, The people ride in a hole in the groun' Li'l David was small, but oh my! L'il David was small, but oh my! You'll find he is a whiz of a Wiz! If ever a Wiz! there was. If ever oh ever a Wiz! there was, the Wizard of Oz is one becoz, Becoz becoz becoz becoz becoz Moses supposes his toeses are Roses, But Moses supposes erroneously. Hooptie doodie doodle Li'l Moses was*

found in a stream L'il Moses was found in a stream He floated on
water Till ol Pharaoh's daughter said show me the way to the next
whisky bar Oh, don't ask why, oh, don't ask why…

It goes on and on and they're singing at the top of their lungs with
the windows rolled down and I must say I haven't seen my dad so
boisterous in a long time.

When we finally get to the theatre Dad sits me on his lap and
I sleep through most of the play which anyway I can't understand.
Afterwards there's a dinner party in Jacob's honour and I wonder
if Dad is jealous but he doesn't seem to be, he's wisecracking with
everybody and asking who made all the delicious food. Then it
turns out there are no rooms left in the B&B because Jacob
brought us along with him on the spur of the moment and all the
other rooms in town are reserved for tourists. Jacob says to just
give us some sleeping-bags, we'll camp out. So although it's about
two in the morning we bundle back into his minibus and drive
for a while until we find a calm spot, Dad gets out and moves a
barrier aside and then we curl up in our sleeping-bags on the
ground and stare at the stars. It's really gorgeous and there aren't
too many mosquitoes. Before I fall asleep I hear Dad and Jacob
talking about how it reminds them of their young hippie days
when people used to want to go back to nature as much as possible
and everyone had long hair and naked breasts and it was a gas.

I'm the first to wake up in the morning, very early when
everything is peaceful. I see we're surrounded by meadows and it's
so early that the air is cool and there's still dew on the grass glittering in the clear light. Some cows are mooing from a nearby farm.
I get up and walk barefoot in the green wet grasses and then I slip
into a little thicket at the edge of the field. The sunrays are just
filtering through it and I sit on an old tree stump and think how

relieved I am that Mom isn't with us on this trip, she'd be fussing about our catching cold and not having brushed our teeth. I gently stroke my bat birthmark and it says I can do the magic now, so I try. I think of the word *dew*...I think of the word *dawn*...I think of the word *summer*...and it happens.

A few minutes later a car pulls up to where Jacob's minibus is parked and stops with screeching brakes, a man gets out and he's carrying a rifle. He strides over to Dad and Jacob who are still sound asleep on the ground and he doesn't see me because of the thicket but I can see him and he looks mad.

'What the fuck are you guys doing on my property?' he yells.

Dad and Jacob sort of sit up rubbing their eyes and vaguely straightening their clothes.

'Get the hell up!' the man yells, nudging them with his rifle to show that he means business. He can't seem to speak in anything besides a yell. 'See that sign over there?' he yells. 'It says PRIVATE PROPERTY. Can't you guys fucking well read?'

'Sure,' says Dad. 'We saw the sign...'

'Of course we saw the sign,' says Jacob. 'We moved it, so we must have seen it. But we didn't steal it.'

'What?'

'We didn't steal the sign,' says Dad. 'We figured since it said PRIVATE PROPERTY, it must belong to someone. So we didn't take it.'

'Though it certainly would have come in handy for making a bonfire,' says Jacob softly as he puts his sandals on. 'The evening was rather chilly.'

'You assholes make one more wisecrack and I'm calling the police,' yells the farmer.

'Where's your son, Aron?' says Jacob.

'You mean you've got *kids* with you? JESUS H. CHRIST!'

'I'm right here, Dad,' I say, emerging from the thicket. My voice is high and squeaky because of the gun though I wish it wasn't.

'Now get the fuck outta here—you hear me?'

'Take it easy, take it easy,' says Jacob, bending to pick our blankets up off the ground. 'We're on our way.'

'I'm waitin'!' the man yells. 'I'm watchin' you! I'm countin' to ten!'

As Jacob backs the minibus out of his field Dad waves at him just to prove that he's not humiliated. The man's face turns purple with rage; he raises his rifle again and I cringe, almost feeling the explosion of the windshield if he got mad enough to shoot. A few moments later Dad turns to me in the back seat.

'You okay, Ran?' he says softly.

'Yeah... You didn't have to wave.'

'You're right. That was a dumb-ass thing to do.'

It goes without saying that this whole outing will be part of our gentlemen's agreement.

The next Wednesday we go meet Mom at JFK which means John Fitzgerald Kennedy who was a President of the United States who got shot to death when Mom was just seven years old and saw it on TV. She can still remember Jackie Kennedy the President's wife in a pink suit clambering all over their brand new armoured Lincoln picking up pieces of his brain, and she says she can't understand what the point of having an armoured car is if you're going to roll the roof down and wave at everybody as you drive through the crowds (I'm sure glad that Vermont farmer didn't shoot at us because Jacob's minibus was *not* armoured)!

We wait a long time watching the passengers of the Chicago flight come through the swinging doors. It's weird to look at all these faces one after another and see instantly that they're not your mother and just sort of dismiss them as if they were nobody whereas to the people waiting for them *they're* the ones who are important and your mother is nobody. At last—click—'There she is!' says Dad.

There she is indeed, dragging her suitcase, and when she sees us her face doesn't light up the way Grandma Erra's would, it just sort of registers our presence like Oh good, there you are now let's go home. Still, she crouches down beside her suitcase so that I can rush into her arms and she can hug me, but the minute I'm in her arms she says 'Dammit!' and it's a bit disappointing to hear that word just as you're hugging your mother for the first time in more than a fortnight but it's because crouching down made a button pop off the waist of her pants and she thinks it means she's gained weight which isn't necessarily true, everyone's stomach gets fatter when they crouch down. She picks up the button and stands up fussing with her pants whereas Dad was intending to kiss her hello so he just takes her suitcase and then we head for the parking lot.

I'm holding her hand. Her hand is with me here in New York City but her head must still be travelling all over the place because without even asking us how we've been doing she launches into a spiel. Her tone of voice sounds like trouble and more trouble so I let the words happen up there at adult mouth level while I stay down close to the floor and study the thousands of feet rushing past in all directions. I think about what would happen if a bomb fell on JFK and all these people suddenly found themselves dead or dismembered and flailing in their blood. My bat birthmark tells me to turn up the sound of the bomber planes as loud as I can in my head and just revel in the screaming the shattering glass the groaning and droning, the high sigh whistle that bombs make as they fall in movies, and then the explosion again and again.

In the car Mom's voice is excited and it goes on and on about what she learned in Chicago from this old lady named Miss Mulyk, who used to work with an agency for displaced persons in Germany after the war and that's when she met Erra. Dad just nods and grunts every now and then because he can't get a word in edgewise. I think of the way Mercedes pronounces one word at a time, I think of her three examples and try as hard as I can to see the fairy's iridescent wings but my mother's words crowd and jumble the air in the car. Some words keep coming back over and over: *fountain of life...incredible...Nazis...archives destroyed...fountain of life...incredible...blood...my own mother...fountain of life...*

'What's a fountain of life, Mom?'

Silence in the front seat.

'Mom?'

'Sadie,' Dad says with a sigh, 'maybe this conversation can wait a bit, what do you think?'

'Yes of course it can,' says Mom abruptly, swivelling around in her seat and sticking out her hand towards me so that I can hold it again which I do, but I can feel my stomach all tense with her nervousness as if something awful were about to happen. She still doesn't say 'What have you guys been up to?' She just watches the Manhattan Bridge zoom by with all the traffic on it. Then after a while she goes back to telling Dad about what she learned from Erra's sister Greta and especially from this Miss Mulyk in Chicago. Apparently Erra's German parents didn't die when their village got bombed like Erra always told her, in fact they weren't even her parents, she was really Ukrainian to begin with but first she got stolen to Germany and the agency found her thanks to her birthmark so she got adopted to Canada, the dead parents were her real Ukrainian parents.

'I don't get it,' says Dad. 'If her real parents were dead, how did the agency hear about her in the first place? How did they find her? Who told them she had a birthmark?'

'I don't know everything yet,' says Mom. 'My research is just beginning. I went to Germany to find answers and what I've come back with is a whole new set of questions!'

It's too complicated for me, I mean how many parents can one little girl have, so I fall asleep in the car and I don't even know who carries me to bed.

The thing about grown-ups is that they make all the decisions and there's nothing you can do about it.

The next morning over breakfast Mom says 'Guess what, Randall?' and I don't even say 'What?' because I don't feel like it; I know I'm going to get the what whether I like it or not.

I get it. It falls on my head like a ceiling.

The what is that we're going to move, we're leaving New York City. I can't believe it. For my mother's research, we actually have to move. I look at Dad but he's not contradicting her, he's going along with it. No one asks my opinion. I try to block out the whole situation with a fabulous shimmering atomic aura like in the first episode of 'Spider-Man' but it doesn't work; this is really truly happening. We're going to live in a city named Haifa in Israel. Miss Mulyk who I wish Mom had never met in Chicago told her about a professor at the university in Haifa who is the world specialist on fountains of life. That's what Mom is suddenly interested in, even though I still don't know what it is, because it seems that Grandma Erra spent some time in one as a baby, in between her Ukrainian and German families. Maybe it's like a fountain of youth which is what's always kept her looking so young? Anyway, Mom is going to work with this man's archive in Haifa. Everything's going so fast I don't understand what the connections are, I don't know even what an archive is. For me in Haifa there'll be a school called Hebrew Reali and I have to take Hebrew lessons for the rest of the summer because if you don't speak Hebrew they won't let you into this school.

'What about my friends?' I want to shout, but my parents don't give a shit. You're not supposed to say shit but I don't give a shit that you're not supposed to say shit. 'It's only for a year' they say, but to me a year is forever. In a year I'll be *seven years old*. I can't believe it. When we get back to New York I'll be *seven years old* and left out, my friends won't want to play with me anymore. I don't want to leave New York and I know for sure Dad doesn't either. He tries to joke about it, saying that we're going from Reagan to Begin which is at least keeping it poetic. He says we don't have much choice in the matter so we should try to think of it as an adventure. He says he doesn't mind schlepping his writer's block across the Atlantic Ocean as long as Mom pays for the transport because it weighs a ton.

I'm furious with my mother. I could kill her.

I start drawing people without stomachs again on purpose.

I draw women getting their breasts cut off.

I draw big daggers plunging into women's backs but I make sure the women don't look like my mother just in case she finds my drawings.

Mom hires a Hebrew tutor for me and I expect the rest of my summer to be completely spoiled by the lessons. 'Don't worry, Randall,' says Mom when she sees me sitting there pouting with my arms firmly crossed on my chest, waiting for the tutor to arrive. She strokes my head to show me that she does care about how I feel. I don't answer because I'm enjoying my pouting stance and even more enjoying making her feel guilty about it. She runs off to the university to look for some more evil, so when the doorbell rings Dad's the one who opens the door for the tutor. His name is Daniel and he's quite frail and thin with a light brown beard and a soft voice and incredibly expressive hands that move all the time like birds.

We sit down together at the dining room table and he smiles and holds out his right hand to me and says 'Shalom' which Mom always told me meant Peace but now I gather it means Hello so I say 'Shalom' back and shake his long white hand which the skin is very soft on. He's brought a briefcase and I think oh no it's really going to be like school but the briefcase turns out to be full of games and pictures. So the first thing we do is play a game of checkers which I'm good at and I beat him within five minutes and this gives him the chance to teach me how to say you (atem), me (ani), here (kan), there (sham), yes (ken), no (lo), help (ezra), and thank you (toda). By the end of the game he looks so flabber-gasted by my talent that I'm laughing my head off and he teaches me the word for laughing which is tsahaq. After this come pictures and instead of stupid things like flowers and kittens he has pictures of cars and bicycles, blue jeans and boots, soldiers and marbles, all of which will definitely come in handy as vocabulary. Daniel's hands flutter and dart all over the place and I can hardly take my eyes off them they're so expressive. I ask him how to say bat and he tells me, so now I know the secret name for my birthmark in Hebrew: atalef.

The world isn't quite the same when everything in it has two different names; this is a weird idea to think about.

After a few days I start looking forward to our lessons because when I remember what he's taught me Daniel is full of praise and smiles, and eager to get me moving on to the next stage. By early August I'm making full sentences, saying stuff like The weather is rotten (Mezeg avir garoua), and I'm hungry (Ani raev), and Shall we take a little walk? (Netayel Ktzat?) I like the feel of this language in my throat, especially the *ayin* and the *h'et* sounds which are rough and scrapy.

I appreciate Daniel more and more and I ask him for words that are more difficult like death (mavet), and loneliness (bdidout); he knows these are important subjects and he asks me questions about them. I'm supposed to avoid using English, so when I don't know the words in Hebrew I act them out as if we were playing charades, he nods and gives me the missing words. I tell him about Grandpa's funeral, about playing hide-and-seek and being abandoned by my cousins, about Grandma Erra smoking cigars and standing on her head, even about her second husband Janek blowing his brains out. He corrects my mistakes gently, always nodding as if to say *Yes that's right*, then repeating my sentence with the correction in it so that I can say it again without the mistake. Now Hebrew lessons are my favourite part of the day and I don't want the summer to end because it will mean not seeing Daniel anymore.

One day I ask him 'How do you say fountain of life in Hebrew?' because I keep hearing about them all the time and hopefully he can explain to me what they are. His smile slowly evaporates and his delicate bird hands flutter soundlessly to the table. 'I'm sorry? Ani lo mevin,' he says, which means I don't understand. So I pronounce the words again and add, in English: 'Mom thinks Grandma Erra was once in a fountain of life in Germany, but I don't know what that is.'

Daniel remains silent for so long that it scares me. He's looking not at me but at his hands on the table, as motionless as if the birds were dead. Finally he gathers up all his papers and taps them on the dining-room table to make a neat sheaf and puts them away in his briefcase. Then he snaps the briefcase shut and goes down the hallway and knocks on the door to my father's study. When Dad opens the door Daniel says to him in a low voice: 'I came here under the impression that I was to teach a young Jewish boy, not the offspring of S.S.,' then turns on his heel and leaves the apartment. His step is as soft and springy as ever but I can tell it's for the last time because he doesn't say 'Lehitra ot.'

I feel terrible because I lost a friend and I don't even understand why but it must be my fault so I burst into tears. Dad picks me up and just clasps me in his arms with my legs around his waist and lets me sob into his shoulder without asking any questions.

We go out for a walk around the block and decide it'll be best not to tell Mom about Daniel's resignation because we're leaving next Sunday and classes were going to end in a few days anyway. In the meantime we can pretend he's still coming and I'll keep on practising with the Hebrew he's already taught me which is quite a lot.

Mom comes home in excellent spirits because she's been very efficient which always makes her happy. At supper, without even noticing how delicious Dad's lasagna is, she announces: 'Everything's set up. Haifa is supposed to be a very beautiful city. I've rented an apartment for us on Hatzvi Street, which is walking distance from Randall's school. I'll be able to take the bus up to the university and Dad will have all the peace and quiet he needs for his work.'

'Yeah, right,' says Dad. 'Israel is a really peaceful quiet country these days because they've sent most of their soldiers up to Lebanon.'

'Oh, and Randall—guess what!' says Mom. 'There's a *zoo* not far away! We'll go to the zoo together—that'll be fun, won't it?'

I don't answer because there's a zoo right here in Central Park and she hasn't taken me there once. To say nothing of the fact that according to Dad they don't play much baseball in Israel, and you can't go tobogganing there because they don't get any snow in the wintertime.

I hold Marvin really tight in bed that night. I'm going to take him with me to Israel and I hope he can protect me with the idea that he used to belong to Grandma Erra. I really wish Grandma Erra could come with us but of course she's on tour again and I don't even think she knows about the real reason for our year in Israel which is that Mom wants to check out her fountain of life connections.

That night I dream we're in a coffee shop and a woman has been murdered. She's lying on the floor in a pool of blood with her limbs all akimbo amidst the legs of tables and customers but no one seems to notice her. 'Dad!' I say. 'Dad, look! There's a dead woman on the floor!' But Dad's busy talking to Mom and they don't pay any attention to me so I start feeling really upset. Just then a waiter arrives in a white uniform, bends down and starts laying white teacloths flat in the scarlet puddle, they soak up the blood and he wrings them out into a basin. 'Oh,' I say to him 'so you knew about it!' 'Of course, young man,' he answers. 'We do everything in our power to guarantee irreproachable service.'

We're in the plane, it's my first plane flight ever, Mom and Dad are both reading books and I'm sitting in between them holding Marvin and feeling scared. Finally Dad picks up on my fear so he takes out his writing notebook and we play games in it like hangman and tic-tac-toe. There are almost no kids on the flight apart from a couple of babies who keep squalling all the time. Dad asks the stewardess if she couldn't perhaps slip some heroin into their baby bottles to make them stop wailing. This makes the stewardess laugh, but the word 'wailing' reminds Mom of a place she's reading about in her guide book called the Wailing Wall, where the Jews can go to lament about all the catastrophes that have befallen them over the centuries.

'Enough of this weeping and wailing,' says Dad. 'Two thousand years, enough already! I'm going to write a play called *The Giggling Wall,* about a holy site where people can go to tell each other jokes and crack up and feel better. One hour of compulsory laughter every day,' he says. 'A joke before every meal. The Church of Mirth and Merriment.'

'I used to have a dog named Mirth,' says Mom, but then the meal service begins and what with passing out our napkins and plastic cutlery and keeping an eye on me to make sure I won't spill anything and calculating how many calories are in the food she's eating, she forgets to tell me about her dog.

After the meal she makes me go brush my teeth in the bathroom using my finger.

Tel Aviv airport is a haze of heat and loud voices. Two women have come from Haifa University to meet us, they speak to me in Hebrew. 'Baroukh haba,' they say. 'Ma Schlomkha?' and when I answer them hesitantly 'Tov me'od,' their faces light up. If I listen hard I can pick up bits and snatches of what's being said around me thanks to Daniel. He squeezed quite an amazing number of Hebrew words into my head before that fateful day.

Haifa is a bright white city with blue water around it wherever you look. You think the sea is on one side but then it's on the other side too because it's a promontory and built on a steep hill so you can see in all directions. The sun is shining strong and Hatzvi Street where the two ladies take us way up on the hill is completely lined with trees. A quiet street with birds singing in it. I wasn't expecting this though I don't know what I was expecting. The light comes through the branches of the trees in the same way the meaning comes through the language: dappled. Hebrew is a dappled language to me like Hatzvi is a dappled street. It's actually very beautiful here. The women help us carry our luggage up the steps to our new house, it's all clean and calm and a far cry from East 54th Street, that's for sure. One downer: there's no TV.

Dad gets started right away with the most important thing for him which is the food shopping. He takes me with him to a supermarket where the aisles are very narrow. When we get to the cash register there are shopping carts standing there with no people attached to them because people put their shopping carts in line and then go do their shopping as fast as they can so as not to miss their turn at the cash register. This seems surprising to me but Dad says we probably have a number of surprises in store for us here.

Just about everybody in Haifa seems to be Jewish with the exception of some Arabs except that Dad says you shouldn't call them Arabs because Arabs can be anything, Christian or Jewish or Muslim, but Mom says that doesn't prevent them from being Arabs. There are no black people at all.

In just two days I have to take my test for entering Hebrew Reali which I'm nervous about. Dad spends mornings with me going over lists of words because as Mom says the best thing is to take the bull (shor) by the horns. Dad's pronunciation and memory aren't as good as mine are by a long shot, which he says is because as you get older your brain cells get used to doing the same thing all the time and you can't teach an old dog new tricks. Then we go for a walk in the neighbourhood before it gets too hot out and try to remember the words for everything we see, we keep score and I beat him hands down. Sitting in the park on Panorama Street we can see the whole city laid out beneath us with the Mediterranean Sea surrounding it. 'Look,' says Dad, 'There, straight ahead. See that white bit of land sticking out on the left? That's Lebanon. There's a war raging there this very minute. Reagan and Begin have both sent troops to take part in the fun. They're called *peace-keeping* forces, because they want to make sure that everything *keeps* falling to *pieces*.'

We sit there on the bench staring out at the sea and the boats in the harbour and the green rolling hills beyond it and everything looks so calm it's hard to believe about the war.

Today's the day. We haven't even talked about what will happen if I fail the test, but I guess I'll get sent to some sort of kindergarten or other with little kids and feel like a nincompoop for the rest of the year so it's important. Mom walks with me to the school which is just two blocks away on Ha'Yam Street except that it's not on the road itself but down at the bottom of a ravine, you get there by descending several flights of wooden stairs. When we reach the top of the staircase Mom is squeezing my hand so hard and her chin is jutting out with so much determination that it makes my stomach ache, so I decide to count the steps under my breath. About halfway down I hit the number forty-four and that reminds me of Grandma Erra because of her age and suddenly I remember how I promised her never to lose contact with my bat so I stroke my atalef birthmark and try to calm down. I look around me and see that the staircase is surrounded by tall green eucalyptus trees that smell sweet with thin dangling leaves. In my head I think of Mercedes and slowly say the words for all the trees I can recognise in English and in Hebrew: palm (tamar), orange (tapouz), olive (zayit), fig (teena), eucalyptus (ekaliptous), and it makes me feel better. Then we arrive in the schoolyard and there are streaks of colour everywhere, children running and playing, cats slinking in corners, flowerpots with tall pink flowers, plus I can hear a rooster crowing in the distance and Mom says it must be from the zoo which is just on the far side of the ravine.

I'm not afraid anymore. I know I'm going to pass the test, and I do.

Suddenly I feel like a different person. Sure and strong, as if the world belonged to me. Dad takes me to buy the school uniform which is spiffy with khaki pants and shirt and a blue woollen sweater, on the shirt and sweater is the school emblem namely a cotton dark blue triangle on the left chest with the motto

'Vehatznea Lechet' meaning be modest in your ways. Every day the Hebrew language opens up to me a little more and changes the world around me with its music. The teacher and the other kids are all interested in me because I'm from America, a country which is a special friend to Israel which I hadn't realised before. They go out of their way to be nice to me and explain things to me and play basketball with me and ask me questions about the United States of America. I've never had this sort of red carpet treatment before, anywhere.

I begin to love Hebrew Reali. After a few days Mom says that if I promise to wait for the green light before crossing Ha'Yam Road I can walk to school all by myself, so I promise and it makes me feel grown up. In the first week at school we all learn the alphabet together and at home I spend hours drawing the beautiful letters and whispering their names in a magic tone like Mercedes. (I teach them to Marvin, too.)

Mom goes up to the university every day and works on her important archive with her important professor and feels she's on the brink of an important discovery. Whenever she thinks I'm out of earshot she talks to Dad about her fountains of life but it's hard to be out of earshot with a voice like my mother's. 'These places were *unbelievable*, Aron,' she says. 'There's never been anything like them on the face of the earth. Palaces of fertility! The country was being bombed, people were hungry and sick and scared to death, they sat there day after day and watched as truckloads of treasures were brought to these whores. *They* got real coffee, fresh fruit and vegetables, oatmeal, meat, cod liver oil, candies, cookies, butter, eggs and chocolate, while everyone around them starved. The pregnant ladies lay around like princesses, sunning themselves and twiddling their thumbs while waiting for their babies to be born. No marriage, no baptism, nothing but a ceremony of welcome into the Great Reich. In 1940, concentration camp inmates carved *ten thousand wooden candelabras* for birthday celebrations in these centres, can you believe it?'

Mom is always happy when she can hold forth against evil.

Dad on the other hand doesn't seem to be adjusting well to life here in Haifa. As far as I can tell, he basically sits around smoking cigarettes and reading newspapers all day long, plus he seems to be losing his sense of humour; he doesn't tell jokes or play checkers with me anymore and his shoulders seem to be slumping as if he were discouraged. He says he doesn't like what's going on up there in Lebanon and he can't write funny plays in a country that's at war. Mom says the Arabs started it by making terrorist incursions into the north and what was Israel supposed to do, stand there with its arms crossed? Dad says if we start playing the who-started-it game we can go back to Hitler, or the Treaty of Versailles, or the guy who shot Archduke Francis Ferdinand—or the assassin's *mother*, hey, why not? It's all *her* fault if people are killing each other in Lebanon these days! Mom says he shouldn't worry so much about Lebanon, he should be thinking about Rosh Ha'shana which is coming up in just a few days and how are we going to celebrate. Dad says he doesn't give a flying fuck about Rosh Ha'shana and Mom says he should be ashamed of using such language in front of his son. I try to imagine what a flying fuck is but I can't.

I leave earlier every day to get away from the squabbling in the house, which is worse than usual because it's about politics. When Mom and Dad start fighting, I lapse into Hebrew in my head and it blots out their words. I'm thinking in whole sentences now.

The morning air is delicious. I'm running down the ninety-seven steps—early for school, so early that the staircase is empty—hopping, leaping, taking them two, then three at a time—but in the middle of the last flight I land on a dried-out olive or a pebble that rolls under my left foot, I get thrown off balance and go flying through the air and make a bad landing on the pavement of the courtyard. My elation jolts to a halt. Breath knocked out of me, ears ringing with the shock, I gulp for air. When I slowly roll over to sit up, I see that my right knee is bleeding and I've got pebbles embedded in the flaming red palms of my hands. Birds twitter in the trees and a donkey brays from the zoo down below as if nothing had happened. I feel woozy. My knee hurts so much I can't even get to my feet. Will I pass out from the pain here, all alone?

Suddenly someone is behind me, touching my shoulder.

'Were you trying to fly, Randall?' says a soft voice in English and I turn my head and see the most beautiful girl in the world kneeling next to me as if I were dreaming. She's about nine years old with shiny black hair twisted into braids and enormous eyes full of kindness and brownish-golden skin. On her the light blue shirt and skirt of the school uniform looks like something straight out of Saks Fifth Avenue. She's so beautiful that I completely forget about the pain in my knee.

'You know my name?' I say.

'Who doesn't?' she says. 'You're the bigshot American from New York.'

So saying, she draws a handkerchief from her shirt pocket, dips it into a watering can next to the flowerpots, and carefully wipes the dirt and pebbles and blood off my kneecap. As I watch the sure and gentle movements of her hands, I fall head over heels in love with her, even if she's much too old for me.

I ask her what her name is.

'Nouzha,' she says, taking my hand in hers and helping me to my feet.

'Lucky thing for me you got here so early.'

'Yes, I'm almost always the first one here because my father drops me off on his way to work, but this morning you beat me.'

'Why do you speak such good English?'

'We lived in Boston when I was little and my father was studying to be a doctor.'

'My Mom is studying to be a doctor, too,' I say, basically just to have something in common with her.

'Oh, that's good—she'll look after your knee then.'

'No, not that kind of doctor...A doctor of evil.'

'You mean to get rid of evil spirits?'

'Yeah, I guess so...Something like that.'

'Ah.'

Nouzha nods very seriously and I wish I could go on talking to her forever but meanwhile the schoolyard has been filling up and now the bell rings and we have to go to our respective classes. She's in Grade Four.

At lunchtime I see her from afar in the cafeteria and she smiles at me and her smile is like nothing I've ever received before, it makes my stomach melt. What can I do? I'd do anything to make myself interesting to this human being. I'd die for her. I'd eat my shoes for her. I want to marry her.

Nouzha. Nouzha. Nouzha. What a wonderful name.

When school gets out I catch up with her as she's heading for the staircase and think: Let my friends make fun of me for talking to an older girl, who cares?

'Er…could you give me a hand?' I say, which is the first thing that comes into my mind. 'My knee still hurts a lot.'

She takes my elbow politely and I start hopping up the steps as slowly and laboriously as I can, leaning on her and smiling up at her to show her how grateful I am.

'It's a relief to find someone who speaks good English,' I say. 'Hebrew is difficult when it's not your mother tongue.'

'It's not mine, either.'

'It isn't?'

'Nope. Mine's Arabic.'

'Well! So both of us are foreigners,' I say, rejoicing to have found some sort of resemblance between us.

'Not at all. You don't even know what country you're in, do you? The true name of this country is Palestine. I'm an Arab from Palestine. This is my country. The Jews are the foreigners here.'

'I thought…it belonged…'

'The Jews invaded it. You're Jewish, don't you even know the history of your own people?'

'Oh, I'm not really very Jewish,' I say, nervous to see that we've already started up the last flight of stairs.

Nouzha laughs. 'What does that mean, not really very Jewish?'

'Well, like, my mother wasn't born a Jew and we don't keep the holidays or anything. I'm basically an American, when you come right down to it.'

'America is on the Jews' side.'

'Well, I'm not on anybody's side except yours, which is lucky because otherwise I'd never be able to make it up these stairs.'

I'm pretty proud of that comeback, but now unfortunately we've reached the top. I'm sweating from the exertion of all that phoney hopping and Nouzha looks at me and smiles. She's not really *that* much taller than me. If I stood on tiptoe, I could kiss her with no problem whatsoever.

'I'll wait for your dad with you if you don't mind. You're my first Arab acquaintance so it's interesting talking to you.'

'You can't wait with me here. My father doesn't want me to be with Jews outside of school.'

'Then…excuse me, but why does he send you to Hebrew Reali?'

'Because it's the best school in the neighbourhood, that's all. He wants all his kids to get a good education and fight to get our country back. You Americans don't know anything.'

'Teach me. I'll learn. I promise, Nouzha. I really want to learn. Give me a history lesson.'

'We can meet up at recess tomorrow if you want…under the hibiscus bush at the bottom of the hill, you know where I mean? Now disappear—that's my father's car there, at the next light.'

Nouzha.
Nouzha's glances.
Nouzha's smile.
Nouzha's hand on my elbow.
I'm in love, I tell Marvin.

The leafy branches of the hibiscus bush curve gently down to the ground and there's an open space beneath them, it's a sweet-smelling hiding-place and no one can see us under there. Nouzha and I sit side by side with our knees drawn up to our chins, looking down towards the bottom of the valley.

'Now I'm going to tell you the true story of Haifa,' says Nouzha and I can tell she's about to give me a spiel that someone else has made her learn off by heart, but I don't mind because her voice is as warm and trickly as maple syrup.

'A long, long time ago, a hundred years ago, all sorts of people lived in this city together. First the Palestinians, like both my parents' families from way back—and then, because of the deep-water port, a whole slew of Druzes from Lebanon, plus Jews from Turkey and North Africa, plus some crazy Germans who founded a Knights Templar colony here and made it into the German quarter...not to mention the Bahais who built their temple and gardens right on the hill so they'd stick out like a sore thumb. Then came Zionism. That's when the Jews decided to return to Palestine where they used to live, ignoring the minor detail that two thousand years had gone by and there were now several million Palestinians living here with their own customs and traditions. The Jews were determined to take over the whole country. Sometimes they'd just go into Arab towns and murder everyone, like at Deir Yassine. My father was eight years old in April 1948, when Jewish cars started driving through Haifa with loudspeakers shouting 'Deir Yassine! Deir Yassine!' and in the background a recording of the people in Deir Yassine screaming and crying as they were murdered. It made the Haifa Palestinians panic and scramble for their lives. They fled the city by the thousands, and the Jews just took over. My father's family got completely broken up, some of his aunts and uncles and cousins ran all the way to Lebanon but his parents landed on the West Bank, in Nabulus. My grandmother still lives there.'

'*My* grandmother is a famous singer,' I say, trying to get Nouzha a little bit interested in me, too.

She gives me a blank stare.

'Her name is Erra,' I insist. 'You must have heard of her?'

She shakes her head. No. She actually, really and truly, has never even *heard* of Grandma Erra! This sort of stuns me because I was sure she was world famous.

'She does magic with her voice,' I add lamely, wondering where I can go from there. 'And…and she thinks *I* can do magic, too.'

'Why is that?'

'Well, it's really a secret,' I say with a mysterious look on my face. 'But I can share it with you, as long as you don't think I'm too Jewish to be your friend.'

She hesitates, then nods her assent.

'You see, my Grandma Erra and I…We have the same spot on our bodies. Look.'

I push my shirt collar slowly aside, revealing the perfect round birthmark on my shoulder.

Nouzha studies it carefully. 'Do you do ceremonies with it?' she asks.

'Er…No, not exactly. But to me it's almost alive,' I say, stroking it. 'It's like a tiny little bat who talks to me and tells me what to do.'

'It's like a mandal,' she whispers.

'What's that?'

'A circle drawn on the ground, where magic rituals are performed. I have a sign, too—a zahry.'

She holds out the palm of her right hand and shows me a small purplish spot at its centre, just above the life line.

'Last month,' she says, gripping her knees again, 'my parents took me to see my grandmother in this little village near Nabulus, it's just a few hours away from Haifa but it's a whole different world…When my grandmother saw my hand was zahry, she cried out for joy. I love my grandmother so much—just like you, yes?'

'Yes.'

'She told me I was a nazir, which means that I can see the malak, the angel who gives orders and answers questions. Only a young child can be a medium for the malak. My grandmother wants to know the fate of her brother, Salim. She's had no news of him in years. She doesn't know if he's in hiding or if the Jews have already murdered him. So she brought me to see the sheik. He looked closely at my hand and nodded very gravely; he said we'd perform a mandal on my next visit.'

I'm feeling a bit swamped by all her fancy words but as long as she thinks we've got something in common it's fine with me so I keep on asking questions.

'How will he put you in touch with this…angel?'

'First he has to prepare for it with lots of prayers and incantations. On the day when I come, he'll burn some incense, put a drop of ink in the palm of my hand and then, when the ink is dry, a drop of oil.'

Nouzha pauses. She rubs her nose. I love it when she rubs her nose.

'Yeah?' I say, a bit dubiously.

'Then my grandmother will ask the question about where her brother is, and if I stare hard at the drop of oil in the palm of my hand, I'll be able to see the malak there and he'll answer all her questions with my voice.'

'That's pretty incredible,' I say.

'Yes but it's true,' says Nouzha intensely. 'And *you* must be a chosen one, too, because of the mandal on your shoulder.'

Just then the end of recess bell rings and, separately and silently, we depart from our fragrant dappled hiding-place.

'Did the Jews invade Israel?' I ask that night in a really soft voice as we're having supper, and Mom laughs in a sort of bark.

'Who put *that* idea in your head?', she asks, which makes me squirm.

'I just overheard it somewhere, I can't remember where,' I say lamely.

'Well the answer is no. The Jews didn't *invade* Israel, they *fled* to Israel.'

'Palestine,' says Dad.

'Palestine, it was called then,' says Mom. 'They were fed up with being harassed and murdered all over Europe for centuries, so they decided they needed a country of their own.'

'Unfortunately, that country was already heavily populated,' says Dad.

'Aron, let's not get into that again,' says Mom with her voice rising like a siren in a way that scares me. 'After six million dead in six years, where were they supposed to go? What were they supposed to do? Sit back and say go ahead, please, enjoy yourselves, kill us all?'

She's screaming now and Dad gets up to clear the table without a single word so her last words *kill us all* keep ringing in our ears. Dad starts washing the dishes and Mom suddenly feels embarrassed about her outburst so she tells me to go to bed even though it's only seven o'clock which is way before my bedtime.

I wish and hope that Nouzha is right when she says I'm a chosen one but I don't know what I'm chosen for and now I feel even more torn apart than usual, not just between Mom and Dad and between Hebrew Reali and Nouzha but also between Mom and Nouzha whereas I love them all. It's upsetting to me and I don't see why people can't just relax and try to get along.

I sit on my bed and grab Marvin and shake him really hard.

'Are you Jewish, Marvin?' I ask him and he shakes his head no. 'Are you German?' No. 'Are you Arab, then?' Still no. 'Palestinian?' I shake him harder and harder. 'Come on, Marvin, it's too easy to just sit here on a bed staring up at the ceiling all day long. You've got to take sides, you've got to believe in something and fight for it,' I say, punching him in the stomach, 'or else you'll die.'

Just then Dad knocks on my door and I jump out of my skin and let go of Marvin.

'Ready for bed, big guy?'

'I'm getting into my pyjamas,' I call out, scrambling to rip off my shirt so it will be the truth.

Dad comes in and sits down with a sigh on the edge of my bed. 'You know what the big problem is, with human beings?' he says.

'What, Dad?'

'They've got guts where their brains should be. That's the problem. Wherever you look, that's the problem. Want a paddle-whacking?'

'No, thanks. I'm a bit too tired tonight.'

'Okay, Buster, get a good sleep. And don't pay too much attention to your crazy old parents, okay?'

'Okay, Dad.'

'Okay?'

'Yeah, okay.'

Nouzha has been very nice to me since I showed her my birth-mark, and even if I have the uneasy feeling that her niceness is slightly based on a misunderstanding, I make the most of it, namely the joy of being beside her. She lives down on Abbas Street in midtown which isn't really *that* far away but since for obvious reasons we can't invite each other over, we have to be content with our hibiscus talks during recess.

'Do you believe in these things?' she asks me.

'Sure, I guess so.'

'Do you know about the evil eye?'

'…'

'All you have to do is look at someone, wishing them ill, and bad luck will befall them. It's called daraba bil-'ayn, hitting them with your eye. Do you know how to do that?'

I consider telling her that in my country we give each other the finger, not the eye, but decide against it.

'No, I don't think so.'

'I'm sure you must have the same powers, Randall, because of your mandal. Randall, mandal—it even rhymes! You should try it, starting on small things; you'll be amazed how powerful it is.'

'But what if somebody gives me the eye right back?'

'Then you have to cancel it out as fast as you can by saying "Ma sh'a Allah kan," what happens is God's will. That will swerve the arrow of the evil eye off track so it can't hurt you. Ma sh'a Allah kan. Repeat?'

'Ma sh'a Allah kan,' I say, only to me it means: Nouzha you have the deepest softest eyes in the universe and I am madly in love with you. 'Ma sh'a Allah kan.'

'Good, she says. You learn fast.'

Mom looks triumphant when she gets home that night, her eyes are blazing.

'I've found her!' she says. 'I've found her, it boggles my mind! There's a record of a girl baby, "approximately one year of age," who spent two and a half months at the Steinhöring Centre in Bavaria in the winter of 1939–1940. She had a mole on her left arm, Aron!!'

Dad doesn't even bother to glance up from his newspaper. He says with a glum look on his face, 'The last of the French and Italian troops just pulled out of Beirut, following the example of the Americans.'

'She'd been brought in from a city called Uzhhorod in Ruthenia, the westernmost part of the Ukraine, which Germany had invaded some months earlier. Himmler in person measured her birthmark—exactly 18 mm in diameter at the time—and recorded its existence in her file. He decided to spare her in spite of this terrible defect. And why did he spare her?'

'Habib broke his promise. Weinberger broke his promise. They were supposed to hang around and protect the refugees after Arafat's departure.'

'Because of her blond hair and blue eyes. Because she was so cute, so irresistibly Aryan. Are you listening to me, Aron?'

'Reagan and Begin have got their Gemayel guy in place.'

'So he gave her to one of his pals, a big-shot S.S. whose daughter had been pestering him for a little sister. His wife couldn't have any more kids.'

'Tzahal has its tanks stationed around West Beirut.'

'Can you believe it, Aron? From Ruthenia to Bavaria, and then after the war she gets flipped across the ocean to Canada! Can you believe it?'

'Operation Peace in Galilee, they call it.'

'All the pieces of the puzzle are falling into place...'

'Now the shit's gonna hit the fan.'

'Randall, go to your room.'

I'm only too happy to go to my room and plunge into my homework for the day about body parts. Rosh is head, beten is stomach, gav is back, regel is foot, berekh is knee, kaf yad is hand, etsba is finger, peh is mouth, Nouzha is beautiful, I am nervous, my dad is furious, my mom is crazy, soon it will be Rosh Ha'shana and the shit's gonna hit the fan.

The next day Gemayel gets assassinated like JFK except that he just got elected three days ago which is a very short term in office. At school during recess the teachers talk about nothing else, but their Hebrew goes way too fast for me and I can't get the gist of what's going on. Nouzha tells me they're upset because Gemayel was their pawn, he was put there by the Israelis and the Americans, and I know what pawn means because Dad once tried to teach me chess. As we're going down the hall we pass a huddle of big kids wearing kippas, one of them raises his voice and I see Nouzha go pale.

'What did he say?' I ask her.

'He said "Those bloody Palestinians, we should bomb them off the face of the earth."'

I keep feeling more and more tense. Marvin is of no help to me whatsoever, my atalef-birthmark remains stubbornly silent and Grandma Erra is so far away she might as well be on another planet.

I have a nightmare and wake up yelling and Mom comes running into my room in her nightgown saying 'What is it, Randall? What is it?' but I can't catch the memory of the nightmare in words, it just sort of disintegrates into little pieces that quickly fade away and dissolve into nothingness. I start feeling guilty, like I dragged my mother out of bed in the middle of the night and now I can't even remember what scared me so much, I feel like I should come up with *something* to justify the disturbance but the more I cast about for a story to tell, the more my mind goes blank and I can't say anything except 'I'm sorry, Mom. I'm sorry, Mom. I'm sorry.'

When I get up the next morning Dad's got the radio on and he's already smoking a cigarette at seven o'clock in the morning with Mom still in the house which is a bad sign.

Mom comes into the kitchen with her hair in curlers and says, 'Aron?'

He's not listening to her, he's listening to the radio, so she raises her voice.

'Aron…I want you to know that I'm deeply grateful to you for coming with me to Haifa. I know it's not easy for you to be surrounded by a foreign language. I know your inspiration usually comes from the conversations you overhear in the streets and coffee shops and parks, I know you miss Manhattan. Believe me, I'm not at all indifferent to that fact. I realise you've made an enormous sacrifice for my sake and I want you to know how much I appreciate it.'

She looks a bit peculiar making this formal speech with curlers in her hair and no make-up on, I wonder if she rehearsed it in front of the mirror the way she rehearses her lectures. As for me, I've still got one more piece of toast to finish but I'm chewing as fast as I can because Dad is still listening to the radio and Mom is turning red with the effort of not losing patience with him.

'Aron,' she says. 'It's the eve of Rosh Ha'shana and I want for us to turn over a new leaf. Now listen to me, *please*. Rosh Ha'shana is just a way of saying Hey, let's stop for a moment and take stock, let's cast off our sins and make some new resolutions.'

But Dad is still ignoring her, he's still bent over the radio listening really closely so finally she stops being patient and strides across the kitchen in her housecoat and turns the radio off.

Dad turns it back on.

She turns it off again.

He turns it back on.

I'm not particularly eager to sit in on the rest of this quarrel so I scuttle off to my room to get ready for school. Just as I'm leaving the kitchen, I hear Mom saying 'Seriously, Aron, don't you think it would be healthy for the two of us to make some new resolutions?'

But Dad doesn't answer her, he doesn't make a wisecrack, he doesn't even wish me a good day at school, he walks out of the house slamming the door and I know he's gone down to HaNasi Street to buy all the English-language newspapers he can get his hands on.

I can't really explain it but the atmosphere is heavy at school that day, too—as if there was going to be a thunderstorm whereas the sky is blue as blue and the sun is pounding down. My atalef says 'Look out Randall, Look out Randall,' but I have no idea what to look out for. At lunchtime Nouzha whispers to me: 'Sharon just invaded West Beirut, do you realise that?' and I nod but I don't know who Sharon is and I wish I could just go play baseball in Central Park.

When I get home from school I go into my room it's really

really hot I can't stand it being so hot I want to explode I want everything to explode I go whirling around my bedroom with my arms out like a mad spinning aeroplane saying 'ROSH, ROSH, ROSH HA'SHANA' and in this activity Rosh means head and Ha'shana means explode because I feel like my head is going to explode, I can't figure things out and it's really disturbing me.

We have supper in silence.

I go back into my room and draw people without stomachs then without heads then without arms then without legs; I put their legs on their necks and their arms on their stomachs, I draw disembodied breasts flying through the air and my atalef-birthmark says 'Wow! Look out, Randall!' but he doesn't tell me what to look out for and I don't know where to turn.

I dream that Dad goes out and slams the door forever. The door keeps slamming and slamming in my dream and then I realise that nobody can slam a door that often so it must be gunshot. Tanks. Bombs.

I wake up the next morning and walk into the kitchen in my bare feet and see something I've never seen before, my father crying. He's slumped over the *Herald Tribune* on the kitchen table and sobbing loudly. I don't even dare to ask him what's the matter but when I go over to stand close to him he grabs me and hangs onto me as if he needed me to protect him whereas parents are usually supposed to protect their children so I don't know what to do. I can hardly recognise him his face is so congested and his eyes are so red he must have been sobbing for a long time already. I can't read the headlines of the newspaper that are bothering him so much but I start crying too and I say 'What's the matter, Dad?

What's the matter?' in a high little voice. He just squeezes me even tighter which is beginning to choke the air out of me so when Mom comes into the kitchen I'm actually relieved.

'Happy Rosh Ha'shana!' she says because that's what she's gotten herself all revved up to say in advance and she doesn't quite notice that something is wrong in time to stop the words from coming out.

'Sadie,' says Dad, 'we are getting the fuck out of this country.'

This sort of stuns my mother who stops dead in the middle of the kitchen with the Rosh Ha'shana smile still hovering on her lips.

'Look—look—look,' says Dad, pointing to the *Herald Tribune* and my heart starts whamming against my chest as Mom with a scared look on her face sits down and reads the headlines and some of the other stuff on the front page. Meanwhile Dad has slumped to the table and started sobbing again which is just unbearable, and within about thirty seconds Mom starts saying 'Oh my God oh my God oh my…' and then she adds: 'That's *terrible*.' And what I gather is that my drawings have come true, that up in Lebanon people's bodies are getting hacked to pieces with arms and legs and heads flying through the air hundreds of dead bodies thousands of dead bodies dead children dead horses dead old people families stacked up and stinking. 'It's still happening,' my father says. 'It's happening right this minute! They're killing all the refugees in Sabra and Shatila! Look what this fucking country is doing!'

'But Aron,' says Mom, still reading the newspaper and fortunately not talking about new years and new leaves anymore, 'it's not the Israelis, can't you read? It's the Phalangists, the Lebanese Christians, it's all part of the civil war in Lebanon.'

'Don't tell me it's not the Israelis!' shouts Dad and I think it's the first time in my life I've heard him raise his voice. 'They got Arafat and the PLO out of there. They convinced the peacekeeping armies to leave so they'd have their hands free. They helped prepare the whole thing. They encouraged it. Aided and abetted it. Protected it. Watched it. They're still watching it, calmly, with binoculars and telescopes, from the roof of the Kuwait Embassy. There's an *excellent* view of Shatila from up there.'

'Stop blaming Israel for everything!' screams Mom at this point, so loud I think she must have a sore throat immediately afterwards.

The whole weekend this fighting and screaming goes on, with periods of silence and more listening to the radio and reading newspapers and more disagreements about who's to blame for the bodies piling up in Lebanon and getting all puffed up and making a stench because of the terrible heat and being shovelled into pits by bulldozers. I feel in a state of miserable confusion because it's never been this bad in our household before and despite my love of Hebrew and Nouzha I almost wish we'd never come to Haifa.

On Sunday it's a relief to go back to school again. The heat is already intense at seven-thirty a.m. and just as I'm crossing Ha'Yam Road I see Nouzha's father dropping her off at the top of the stairs and my heart leaps. Nouzha is my only hope. She'll be able to explain things to me. I run after her and say 'Nouzha!' so she'll stop and wait for me but she doesn't stop so I run even faster and catch up with her on the third set of steps and say 'Hey, Nouzha, what's going on?' and she turns and looks at me with a poisoned arrow in her eyes and I can't remember the magic formula to deflect it, I know it's Allah something or other, but I'm too shocked by her expression to remember the rest of it.

Finally when we get to the third landing she stops and says, without looking at me, with her beautiful profile frozen into stone: 'I've come to get my things. My father is waiting for me. Hebrew Reali is finished. Jews are finished. Even you, you are finished. Yes, Randall. Your mother is finished, your father is finished, all of you are guilty and will be my enemies forever. I had dozens of relatives in Shatila.'

Then her face closes up and that's the last word she says to me: 'Shatila.' She speeds up going down the rest of the stairs so she won't have to be with me anymore and I grab onto the railing because I feel dizzy.

School takes place as if nothing had happened which is a good thing, but at recess and lunchtime my head starts ringing again with everything I don't understand, and I'm not exactly eager to go back to the house.

No one is home when I get there so I go into my room.

It's so hot. 'It's really hot, Marvin, isn't it?' Marvin nods his head. 'You must be even hotter than I am with that fur coat on, aren't you?' He nods. 'Are you really uncomfortable with the heat?' He nods. 'Here, let me see if I can make you feel more comfortable.' I go into my parents' bedroom and get the scissors out of the drawer in Mom's desk and come back and look at Marvin for a long time, holding the scissors in my hand. His bleary blind eye makes him look sad but sweet, he cocks his head to one side and I stick him in the stomach with the scissors, piercing him right through his fur coat. 'Here, we'll just try and get this thing off you, all right?' and he nods. So I cut into him. The scissors are good and sharp, and Marvin's guts start spilling out. They're made of stuff that's like cotton batting, all bunched up in little yellowish-white balls. I cut and slit. I slit his throat. 'Are you feeling better now, Marvin?' I ask, and he nods. I slit the stitching along his arms and then his legs. 'Is this helping you, Marvin?' and he says yes, it is. I cut off his little ears and his little tail and I open the back of his head to see what his brains look like but they look exactly the same as his guts. He's a really old bear. Older than I am, older than Mom and Dad. I gather up all the pieces and put them in a plastic bag and take it to the kitchen. Then I get some ice cubes out of the freezer and put them in the bag with him and say, 'Are you feeling cooler now, Marvin?' and he says yes. So I knot the bag shut and stuff it down to the very bottom of the garbage can, covering it over with the rest of the garbage and saying 'Happy heaven, Marvin,' and then I wash my hands and feel better.

Dad comes home a while later and the minute I see his face I can tell he's decided to behave like a father again which is a huge relief. He hugs me without crushing me and says, 'Hey, how about the two of us going to the zoo?' As we walk down HaTishbi Street he asks me to test his Hebrew again and I'm glad everything is getting back to normal. Hakol beseder, I say to myself, all is well.

I soon gather that this visit to the zoo is basically, for Dad, to help him say something difficult because it's easier to say difficult stuff when you're looking at monkeys and tigers instead of the person you're talking to. 'Listen, Ran...' he says. 'I want you to know that your mother and I patched things up this morning. What's going on in Lebanon is so horrendous that we don't want to be having wars on the home front too—right?'

'Right.'

'So we've decided to avoid the subject of politics completely and just try to make the most of our stay in Haifa and consider ourselves lucky that our own family is in one piece. We've got a good family, right?'

'Right.'

'And I don't want you to worry, that's the important thing. Mom and I get upset about this and that, but we're going to stick it out and stick together and *you* shouldn't worry. It's a crisis, yes, but crises are part of life. Okay?'

'Okay,' I say, thinking about Marvin in his melted ice cubes down at the bottom of the garbage can.

So we settle into sort of a new atmosphere with Mom and Dad making conscious efforts to be polite to each other and express interest in each other's activities and carefully avoid the subject of the war. Dad has made a New Year's resolution to keep to a strict regimen of writing every day from eight to twelve and one to five even though he rarely seems delighted with the results. Mom has gotten tired of the long bus ride up to the university so she's decided to rent a car. When she tells us this at supper one night it almost causes a fight because Dad says it seems like an unnecessary expense and Mom says 'It's definitely not your money I'm spending, Aron, I can hardly remember the last time you brought home a paycheck,' which is an unkind jab reminding Dad that he's not yet very successful as a playwright, but Dad swallows his pride and asks her what kind of car she's thinking of and the conversation goes on from there.

It turns out that the car is a bonus for everyone because on weekends we can drive up the mountain to the beautiful Carmel Natural Reserve and go for walks amongst the trees and birds and flowering bushes and it makes us feel like a truly happy united family like everybody else. The only problem is that Mom is a not-that-terrific driver and she says Israelis drive like madmen so she's always jittery wondering if she's got enough time to pass, or indignant because somebody didn't respect her right of way. Sometimes when she pulls out into the left lane and there's a big truck hurtling straight at us, Dad involuntarily clutches hold of the door so Mom gives up trying to pass and swerves back into the right lane, furious with Dad because he seems to be doubting her driving skills whereas he himself never even got his licence. All this makes for a slightly upsetting atmosphere in the car but it's worth it anyway for the Reserve.

At school I throw myself into basketball and other sports activities to get rid of the ache in my heart about Nouzha's absence. I stroke my atalef-birthmark every morning to feel a little bit in touch with her zahry, the purple spot in her hand. And who knows, maybe we'll see each other again some day and be friends again despite all the conflicts in the world, because I truly love her.

September draws to an end and October slides by and then it's Hallowe'en. I think about how the leaves must be changing colours in Central Park, and also about how I'll be a different person by the time we get back to New York City and will I still be friends with my old friends like Barry.

I'm mulling over all these thoughts in my mind walking back from school. When I get home I see Dad's office door wide open which is unusual at this time of day with his new regimen. I go looking for him in the living room and suddenly there's this big *bang* behind me and I jump out of my skin. It's Dad who's all made up as a clown with a big dumb grin on his face and he just busted a balloon. For Hallowe'en he bought a bunch of candy and balloons and a make-up kit which is really nice of him as a surprise. Just as he's starting to put green make-up on my nose, the phone rings and I wish it wouldn't because it might spoil our attempts at having fun.

Dad goes off to the kitchen to answer the phone and his 'Hello!' is the only thing he says in a voice loud enough for me to hear.

The phone call doesn't last long but then I hear him making another call so I get mad and come into the kitchen and say 'What's up?'

He's calling a taxi, of all things.

'What about our game?' I say in a whiny, obstreperous tone of voice, but the glance he gives me banishes my annoyance and pours a flush of pure fear through my body.

It's clear that he's forgotten about everything in the world except the words he just heard over the telephone, and now, as he picks me up in his arms and strides to the front door to wait for the taxi, those words come tumbling through his bright candy-pink lips. Every sentence he says is softer than the one before.

'Mom had an accident. She went through the railing down on Stella Maris Boulevard. She's in the hospital. Randall, it sounds bad.'

The taxi driver's eyebrows shoot up when he sees us and Dad remembers he's still got his clown face on, which is no longer appropriate to the situation. So in the taxi he takes a handkerchief out of his pocket and wipes at the make-up, which mucks the colours together but eventually he gets most of it off, there's just some purple left around his ears which I don't tell him about because I know he's got more important things on his mind.

Children aren't supposed to come into intensive care but Dad, who is a good actor, decides to play the brash brazen American who knows his rights and will thump his fist on the reception desk until he gets them, so in the end I'm allowed to stay with him. He squeezes my hand as we go into the room where they've put Mom. I feel real small and scared when I see her because she's hooked up to all these machines and I've never seen anything like it before except on TV, and I can hardly breathe for dreading that my own mother is going to die. She's asleep and I look at her face and murmur really softly 'I'm sorry Mom I'm sorry Mom I'm sorry, please stay alive.' Dad and the doctor go into a corner of the room and start talking together in low voices and all I can think about is how Dad still has purple make-up around his ears and is the doctor going to notice it. I remember a photo in one of the Arab newspapers he bought when Sabra and Shatila happened, there was a baby's head and one of his arms lying on the body of a little boy about my age, seven or eight, who must have been his brother. Behind them amidst the rubble of their house was their mother, but all you could see of her was her enormous rear end in a flowered dress. Even though she was dead, it looked like she still wanted to be a wall to protect her dead children.

When Dad comes back from his conversation with the doctor I can tell from the stunned look on his face that today is going to be a turning point in our lives. There will be, as they say, a before and an after October 31st, 1982. He sits down by Mom's bed and takes her hand without moving it because she's got tubes going into her arm. He bends down and kisses her fingers murmuring 'Sexy Sadie' over and over again, which I haven't heard him say in a long time. Just then her eyes flutter open and she whispers our names, so at least her brain isn't broken: 'Aron…Randall…Aron… Randall…oh my God…' I smile at her with my sincerest loving smile so she'll want to come back to life, and I think how good I'll be from now on if she doesn't die.

When we get home Dad makes supper very seriously. He makes a dish I love which is chicken soup with yoghurt in it. He asks me to help him peel the carrots and onions, he cuts up the chicken liver and gizzard into tiny pieces and shows me how, when you thicken soup with egg yolk, you have to add the soup to the yolk a few drops at a time while stirring it with a whisk and not just dump the yolk into the hot soup which would make it lumpy and spoil the smooth texture. He asks me to set the table, too, which I do very carefully because it feels important and solemn. We sit down together and raise our glasses to Mom's health and then we sip our soup in silence for a while. The idea with this soup is that first you drink the broth and then you eat the meat and vegetables.

'Some of Mom's vertebrae got broken in the accident,' says Dad just as I'm sinking my teeth into the chicken neck. This is usually my favourite part of the soup, but all of a sudden it looks like vertebrae so I put it back in my plate.

'It wasn't her fault. She was coming up the hill near the Carmelite Monastery and some asshole came careening around that bend on the left side of the road and sent her flying through the railing. We're lucky she's alive, Ran. We're goddamn lucky she's alive. This is the sort of moment when you wish you believed in God so you could thank somebody.'

'But will she get better?'

'Hm,' says Dad, peppering his carrots to stall for time. 'Better, yes. But not all better.'

Again I remember the dead mother's flowered rear end and her little baby's head lying on his big brother's stomach. I can hardly go on with my meal.

'She'll be needing a wheelchair from now on.'

'You mean she'll be handicapped?'

Dad puts down his soup spoon so he can reach out his right hand and pat my left one very gently.

'That's right, Ran. She won't be able to walk anymore. Unfortunately, those two vertebrae are the ones that control her legs. It's a hell of a blow, I'm still reeling from it myself. But we'll be strong about it, okay? You mom has always been more of a talker than a walker anyhow. She'll still be able to talk her head off…and do her research…and travel…Nowadays, they've got excellent…'

He doesn't finish this sentence because he's got salt tears running slowly down his face and dripping onto his plate, but at least he doesn't break down and sob the way he did for Sabra and Shatila…

Why do I keep thinking about Sabra and Shatila?

Then it comes to me. It hits me so hard that I almost fall off my chair.

Nouzha. Nouzha's evil eye. Nouzha threw her eye at me that day on the staircase—daraba bil-'ayn—and wished for some terrible misfortune to befall me. *She's to blame for Mom's accident*, I'm sure of it. Her own family got hacked to pieces in Shatila and she decided to take her revenge on the Jews and I was her closest Jewish friend and I was so upset that I forgot the formula to deflect the evil eye. 'Ma sh'a Allah kan'—now I remember it completely but it's too late—what happens is God's will.

III

Sadie, 1962

'Have you made your bed, Sadie?'

'Yes' I have made my bed Sadie (and thus deserve to have my breakfast).

Gran bends over and brushes the top of my head with her lips. She's still in her dressing-gown but she's already made up her face and doesn't want to smudge her lipstick by giving me a real kiss which I'm not sure if she knows what that is anyway. Her hair is brushed and combed and styled, dark brown these days although the truth about her hair is that it's completely grey and she dyes it brown so no one will know she's old. An interesting thing to think about is the question of which is the real Gran—when she puts on her glasses or when she takes them off, when she dyes her hair or when she lets it grow out grey, when she's all bare naked in the bathtub or when she's dressed to the hilt, I mean what does *real* mean is an interesting question, I think.

She scoops a perfect poached egg out of the egg poacher, sets it on my plate next to the perfect slice of toast and pours me a perfect glass of milk.

'Sadie how many times do I have to tell you not to come

downstairs in your bare feet. It's twenty degrees below zero outside.'

'But it's seventy above inside!'

'Don't talk back to me, young lady. I want you to make a New Year's resolution to put on your slippers without being told, all right? Now scoot, I'll cover your egg to keep it warm for you, quick quick!'

She wants to get it right, she and Grandad failed with my mother, think they must have been too lax and are determined not to make the same mistakes this time around so I get discipline. Hate these big furry slippers, Mommy's Christmas present, the word *present* as usual meaning *absent*—she had a gig on Christmas Day. (*She* didn't want to live with her parents so why does she leave *me* with them?) I look at myself in the wardrobe mirror and let my true feelings show, crossing my eyes and baring my teeth in a monstrous grimace of rage and insanity (Gran says I shouldn't cross my eyes because some day they'll get stuck that way), then on my way downstairs I put the good-little-girl mask back on because if I'm nice and obedient and do everything right Mommy will take me to live with her and say 'It was just a game, darling, I was just testing your strength of character, now you've passed the test with flying colours and we can live together at last!'

The egg is warm and waiting, a white film over the yolk as there should be, the white cooked solid and the yolk liquid gold spilling over onto the china plate when I pierce it with my fork so I can mop it up with the buttered toast careful careful not to drip any yolk onto the table, Gran is watching, my Fiend is also watching as always and the silver fork is heavy in my hand, if you cut off my hand and put it on the bathroom scale would it weigh more or less than the silver fork? Ants carry loads many times their own weight. Gran weighs herself every morning (*after* going to the toilet and *before* breakfast, she says that's the time of day when you weigh the least because it's been hours since you ate), she teaches me all about good health and a balanced diet and how to cook so I'll grow up to be an excellent homemaker like herself and unlike Mommy who lives in Yorkville in a cruddy little flat teeming with friends and cockroaches and cleans house only when the mess threatens to overwhelm her.

'Now go upstairs and get ready for school, quick quick!'

Hm, I wouldn't of thought of that if she hadn't of told me. I say *wouldn't of* and *hadn't of* on purpose because I know it's wrong but I only think it I don't say it out loud, deep down I say all sorts of forbidden stuff including swearwords like shit and hell and damn and cripes, Mommy's boyfriends often talk that way in my presence (which I like), they swear and criticise the government and smoke cigarettes and call Mommy Krissy instead of Kristina and don't seem to mind about her having a little six-year-old bastard by the name of Sadie.

'Don't I have time for another piece of toast?' I say in my sweetest most placating hopeful darling voice.

'Oh, I suppose so,' says Gran crossing the kitchen to the brilliant silver toaster which she wipes and polishes every morning the minute breakfast is over, 'but it's more polite to say slice than piece.'

Grandad emerges then from his office downstairs which has a separate entry that gives directly onto Markham Street with a plaque saying *Dr Kriswaty, Psychiatric Consultations* so that his patients can go in and out without having to pass through the house because they don't want to be seen because they're ashamed because they're crazy. I'd never have thought there could be so many crazies in the city of Toronto but there are, an unending stream of them entering and leaving Grandad's office from morning to night (I used to stand at the window and watch for them because I was curious to see what they looked like but after a while I stopped because they looked like everybody else), and not only his but the offices of hundreds, maybe thousands of other psychiatrists, I wonder how they know the exact number of psychiatrists they need to train for the exact number of crazies but I guess they do, though there might be a few psychiatrists who can't find any patients and sit around all day twiddling their thumbs and waiting for the phone to ring, or some crazies who desperately ring up all the psychiatrists in the phone book and keep getting the same answer—'Nope, sorry, I'm full up'—but it doesn't seem that way, it seems as if the balance between the two populations was perfect. I wonder if there's a war or something and a lot of people start going crazy at the same time, do they automatically start training more psychiatrists at the university?

I'm not supposed to say *crazies* I'm supposed to say *patients. Slice* not *piece. Shouldn't have* not *shouldn't of.*

Just as he does every morning Grandad says 'Well, how are we this morning?' and sits down at the kitchen table with an air of exaggerated weariness and Gran wordlessly hands him a cup of coffee from the percolator, this is their eight-thirty ritual, it's been going on since long before I was born and it never varies except that sometimes, instead of 'Well how are we this morning?' Grandad says 'Ah why would anyone choose this profession? It's enough to make you tear your hair out,' which is a joke because Grandad is bald, he's got nothing but a fringe of short hair that goes around the bottom of his skull from ear to ear. His first crazy arrives at six-thirty so by eight-thirty he's seen two of them already, then after his coffee break he works from nine to twelve and then again from two to five which makes eight crazies a day every day of the week including Saturday which makes forty-eight crazies a week except that some of them come in twice or even three times a week so it's hard to calculate accurately. I don't know how the treatment works; does he give them small doses of happiness every time they come in, just enough to keep them going until their next appointment? And do they gradually build up enough happiness to be able to do without their sessions? But the thing is, Grandad himself is not exactly a brimming-over-with-joy kind of person, he's very silent and almost every time he opens his mouth what comes out of it is a bad joke and even if I've lived with him all my life I hardly know him. Now for instance, instead of talking to me as he drinks his coffee and I eat my toast, he reads the newspaper Gran has brought in for him from the porch.

'Sadie, you'll be late.'

I drag my feet going upstairs, I hate getting dressed but you can't go to school in your nightgown. Getting dressed always makes me feel my badness, especially in the wintertime because there are so many layers of clothing to put on, the badness is all buried deep inside but there's an outward sign of it which is an ugly brown birthmark the size of a nickel on my left buttock, almost no one knows it's there but I can never forget it, it's like a stain and because it's on the left I'm not allowed to lie on my left side in bed or hold a glass of milk in my left hand or step on a crack in the sidewalk with my left foot and if I do so accidentally I have to whisper 'Excuse me' five times in a row as fast as I can, or else. Mommy has a birthmark on the inside of her left arm and she's not ashamed of it because that's not a shameful place to have it, but for me to have it on my buttock is the *proof* of my dirtiness, you'd think I made a mistake wiping myself when I went to the bathroom and left a dollop of poop there by accident, it's the mark of the Fiend who presided over my birth, like he dipped his thumb in poop and pressed it onto my bum—*This one is mine*, he said in his evil voice *and I'll never let her go, she'll always be dirty and different.* Maybe that's why my father left: he took one look at me and said, Yech, that's disgusting, that's no daughter of mine and he turned on his heel and walked out of Mom's life once and for all so I have no memory of him, all I know is that his name was Mort which is short for Mortimer, that he had a black beard and a guitar, and that Gran and Grandad strongly disapproved of him. Mommy was only seventeen when she got mixed up with Mort and his beatnik crowd who were much older than she was, in their twenties, all obsessed with playing music and drinking wine and smoking kerouac, she dropped out of high school when she met Mort and I think they did morphine together at a party and my mother got pregnant without meaning to. Gran told me one day that she and Grandad were *so* upset when they found out—Mort could never support a family they said, he was irresponsible and incapable of supporting himself, this was a tragedy. 'You mean I shouldn't be here?' I asked her. 'You mean they didn't want me?' but all my questions on the subject have met with walls of silence.

For a while Mommy had another boyfriend named Jack who was a schoolteacher without a beard, I'll be forever grateful to Jack because he taught me how to read when I was five, even before I started school, but then he and Mommy quarrelled because he wanted Mommy to stop singing in public and she finally put her foot down (as she told me later), saying 'Jack, there are some things

I can live without. Singing is not one of them. You are.' And that was the end of that.

You have to put the garter belt on under your panties because if you put it on over your panties you can't pull your panties down to pee, it's only logical, so the very first thing to put on is the garter belt which has little hooks and eyes you fasten in the front and then hitch around until they're in the back and then there are the garters hanging down so you put on your woollen stockings before your panties too, otherwise the garters would get all caught up in the panties. Unfortunately I put the second stocking on backwards and have to start all over again; when I stand on my left foot to put my right foot into the stocking leg I lose my balance and have to sit down on the bed but then the foot gets stuck halfway down because the stocking is twisted and I'm all sweaty and flustered now because the clock is ticking on the mantelpiece and my Fiend is breathing down my neck and tapping his foot and saying *You're late, hurry up, you're late,* I can never ever do what's right because if I did, if I were truly a good girl instead of just pretending to be one, I'd be living with my mother and father like everybody else.

My panties finally cover over the birthmark but I can't forget about it being there.

After the panties comes the white blouse, you have to make sure the right buttons are lined up with the right buttonholes but even if I concentrate I often get it wrong and by the time I get to the last button I can see there's a piece of material hanging out on one side and I have to undo the whole thing, Gran has told me to start with the bottom button but I keep forgetting. Then comes the kilt with buttons in the back but since I can't button them up without looking I have to put the kilt on backwards then twist it around but it's hard to twist because it's tight around my waist and it pulls the blouse askew and it makes me frantic. Gran keeps saying she'll buy me a new kilt in a larger size but she never gets around to it because she's busy with her gardening and bridge clubs and ladies' luncheons and since the kilts are made especially for my school only one store in the city sells them and it's far away from where we live.

After the kilt comes the blazer which is easy (there are only two buttons) but you have to remember to hang onto the cuffs of your blouse when you slide your arm into the blazer sleeves and I forget so the blouse bunches up inside the blazer and I have to take it off and start over again and I still haven't brushed my teeth or combed my hair and it's quarter to nine, we have to leave the house in five minutes and my shoes need polishing but I won't bother with that (in my dream last night all my shoes were filthy, not a single pair was clean, I was ashamed, I had nothing to put on my feet), just as I'm crossing the room to get my shoes a sliver from the hardwood floor plunges deep into my heel, I shouldn't have *glided* on the floor, I should have picked up my feet and set them down carefully.

The truth about the world is that pain lurks in it everywhere and if there's the least chance of getting hurt, says Gran, I seem to find it (or it seems to find me is what *I* say). Gran has no patience for my pain, if I cry she says I'm trying to attract attention, last summer she sent me out to the corner store for a quart of milk saying 'Quick, quick' as usual so I ran as fast as I could, leaping and galloping and just as I was about to reach the store I tripped on the kerb and bang, the sidewalk came up and slammed into my chest knocking the breath out of me. Two ladies who happened to be going past kneeled down and said 'Oh my goodness, did you hurt yourself, dear?' and I got up, stunned and breathless and on the verge of tears but, knowing Gran would want me to be brave in public, I brushed the dirt off my clothes and said 'I'm okay' with a little laugh to reassure them. My knee and elbow were scraped so badly you could see the blood through the skin but I went into the store anyhow, holding back my tears, and bravely asked for a quart of milk and paid for it and stumbled and limped all the way home, still holding back my tears and when I finally got in the door after limping up the steps the tears rushed out of me in one fell swoop, I cried and groaned and sobbed in pain and when Gran came into the hallway to see what was the matter I showed her the scrapes, sobbing, and said 'I held it back as long as I could, Gran, I didn't cry when I was in the store or on my way home,' and she said, taking the milk and heading back to the kitchen, 'If you could hold it back in the store, you can hold it back here, too,' and she went back to making the angel food cake for her ladies' luncheon and didn't comfort me at all. Mommy would have comforted me if she'd known how bad the pain was but by the time I saw her again the scrapes were all healed and I couldn't even show them to her.

Everywhere I go dangers lie in wait for me—a shard of glass a furious wasp a hot toaster—they pounce on me as I go past and my body responds all by itself, the skin turns blue or the flesh swells and fills with pus or the skin opens, releasing a stream of blood, right now the sliver is making a throbbing pain in my left heel but I don't have time to take my stocking off again to look for it.

I hobble downstairs loathing life. Gran has already taken the car out of the garage, she's warming it up in front of the house and when I hobble out onto the front porch trying to button up my coat and put on my scarf at the same time she waves at me frantically meaning 'Hurry *up!*' Her breath is visible in the freezing air and so is the exhaust from the tailpipe, she's wearing leather gloves and when she stops for red lights her fingers tap the steering wheel impatiently but nonetheless, as usual, we get to school on time.

We sing 'O Canada' at nine o'clock and 'God Save the Queen' at four and all day long in between the two songs I suffer from either acute embarrassment or mortal boredom.

At morning recess I decide I can't stand the splinter pain anymore so I lock myself in one of the toilet stalls but since the doors don't go all the way down the other girls in the bathroom see that I've removed a shoe and a stocking and it makes them titter, 'What's going on in there, is she a Russian spy or something? Has she got a telephone hidden in her shoe?'

The other girls never choose me to be their skipping partner because I get my feet caught in the rope and make them lose. When I do a drawing in art class they say 'What's *that* supposed to be?' as if they couldn't tell. When we play musical chairs I'm always the first one to be eliminated because I get too wrapped up in the music and then I can't get into the chair fast enough when it stops. When we have a nuclear bomb alert and have to hide under our desks I can't stay in a squatting position for more than a couple of minutes whereas if there were real atom bombs falling on us you'd have to stay there for hours if not days. All the other girls are smug and competent and quick. They calmly snip away at paper snowflakes while I sweat and fret because my scissors are too dull. In the locker room they change smoothly into and out of their gym clothes while I struggle and blush. Their clothes are coopera-tive and neat, mine are rebellious: buttons jump off, stains blossom and hems surreptitiously unstitch themselves.

Today being Friday I have my piano lesson but because of the splinter I forgot to bring my music with me and Gran fumes as she drives us back home at top speed at four o'clock, making the wheels spin and shriek on the ice. 'We'll be late,' she says, 'Oh Sadie can't you take responsibility for your own things?'

'Now show me what you've learned since last week,' says Miss Kelly, towering over me. She puts her hands on my shoulders and pulls them back to make me straighten up, then puts a thumb under my chin to force me to lift it, then corrects the angle between my wrists and hands on the keyboard and reminds me that my fingers should always be curved as if I were holding a mandarin. I can't even get started, she interrupts my piece after three bars and makes me do exercises instead. 'Hold your third finger down and play chords with the second and fourth, the first and fifth in alternation. Hold your second finger on G and swing the thumb from C to C beneath it—*without* raising your wrist, Sadie!' she says sharply, tapping my wrist with a ruler and hitting the bump of the bone at the side which *really hurts* so I say 'Ow!' and tears start to my eyes. 'Sadie, how old are you?' says Miss Kelly and I say 'Six' and she says 'Well then stop acting like a baby, now take it again,' and we spend almost the whole hour doing these stupid exercises and there are only five minutes left over for my pieces, I only get to play one of them which is 'Edelweiss' but I'm so nervous that my hands are shaking and she says I played it better the week before and even as I play she's scribbling in my notebook with her purple ballpoint pen, underlining her instructions such as 'Curved fingers!' and 'Supple wrists!' and 'Watch the fingering!' Between now and next Friday I have to draw fifty treble and fifty bass clefs and learn to play the scales of G major and G minor 'Without a single mistake!' she writes, underlining the words so hard that her pen goes through the paper.

'Well?' says Gran as she discreetly hands Miss Kelly an envelope with the money in it for my lesson (they've spent so much money on my education and food and clothing and I'm not even their daughter, do I realise? do I realise?) 'How is she doing?'

'She needs to practise more,' says Miss Kelly menacingly.

'But she hasn't missed a day,' says Gran. 'I see to it…'

'Sitting at the piano isn't enough,' Miss Kelly interrupts. 'She needs to *work*, she needs to *concentrate*. No one can acquire good working habits for her. Musical talent may run in the family but nothing can take the place of *work, work, work.*'

My wrists are still red from where she hit me with the ruler and you're not allowed to yell at grown-ups but I'm really seething and boiling inside with a sense of injustice so I decide to tell on Miss Kelly the next time I see Mommy. Telling Gran wouldn't do any good, she'd just say I must have done something to deserve it, but Mommy won't be able to *bear* the idea of a strange woman martyrising her little girl with a ruler, she'll tell Gran I have to change piano teachers at once and if Gran says 'Good piano teachers are hard to come by, Miss Kelly has an excellent reputation, she prepares children for the Conservatory entrance examinations,' Mommy will answer 'Conservatory, Conshmervatory!'—I love it when she talks like that—'I want my daughter to be happy and if the only teachers you can find are sadists she'll just have to live without the piano, that's all.' Those words will be music to my ears, I'll never have to practise the piano again and I'll be able to read as much as I like. Gran says I'm damaging my eyesight reading and before you know it I'll need glasses (by which she means she'll have to buy me glasses) but at least when you're reading no one comes along and hits you with a ruler, you just sink into the page and the world gradually disappears.

A sadist is someone who enjoys hurting other people, why Mommy chose to give me a name that sounds so much like sadist I don't know, I asked her once and she said she liked the sound of it that's all. Sadie also has the word *sad* in it and even if she didn't do it on purpose what she ended up with (or rather *without*, most of the time) is one sad little girl.

Each day has its particular flavour of sadness, I recognise it the minute I wake up in the morning, Monday because it's the first day of the week and there are five whole days of school ahead of me, Tuesday because of ballet class, Wednesday because of gym at school, Thursday because of Brownies, Friday because of my piano lesson, Saturday because I have to change my bed and Sunday because of church.

At Brownies you have to learn to tie all these stupid knots which serve no purpose whatsoever because none of us have any plans to become sailors when we grow up. You have to stare at a whole bunch of different objects for thirty seconds and then turn around and try to remember them all without looking; I get stuck after about four. You have to wear a brown uniform that's even uglier than the school uniform and you have to *Be Prepared* though they never tell you for what and the joke about the Girl Guide who forgot to be prepared and got pregnant isn't funny. You're supposed to be the best at this, that or the other and win little ribbons and badges to pin to your chest but I'm the best at nothing and my chest stays empty.

At ballet you're supposed to be thin and graceful but my stomach sticks out and the pointe shoes pinch my feet until I can hardly even stand up much less dance.

All these activities are for my own good, their purpose is to turn me into a brilliant gifted well-coordinated outstanding homemaker and citizen but it's no use, I'll always feel fat and stupid, clumsy and left out, backwards and lopsided, *inadequate* to put it bluntly. No one can change my innermost nature which is almost not human at all. My teachers and grandparents think it's just a temporary problem so they keep chipping away at my brain and body, trying to sculpt me into something presentable and I go through the motions to make them happy, smiling and nodding and standing on tiptoe, twirling in my tutu and sweating over the different sorts of knots, I can fool them most of the time but I can't fool my Fiend, my Fiend knows I'm bad deep down and when the pressure builds up, all I can do is hit my head against the wall over and over again in the dark.

'Sadie it's time to practise your piano,' says Gran every evening at quarter past five. At exactly the same moment, Grandad emerges from his office after his last crazy and fetches the dog's leash to take him out to poop.

Gran and Grandad got a short-haired dog on purpose so he wouldn't be shedding hair all over the place, in other words the important thing about the dog they bought was the length of his hair, they didn't bother checking into his character. His name is Mirth which according to the dictionary means 'gaiety, joy or merriment, especially when characterised by laughter', which is just the opposite of this dog's personality, he's tiny and wriggly and snappy and when I try to pet him he twists away from me with a yelp as if I were going to strangle him or something.

'Where's my hunting hound?' says Grandad this evening, as he does every evening, and when Mirth trots up to him yapping and wagging his whole rear end in excitement, he says, 'Hey there, calm down or I shall have no choice but to muzzle you' and the whole thing is completely stupid and meanwhile this is when I have to practise the piano.

The instrument is sitting black and still in a corner of the living room, it doesn't seem as if it wants to say anything to me, it just seems like one silent piece of furniture amongst the others. I turn on the lamps, only two of them because you shouldn't waste electricity, the piano lamp so as to be able to read my music and the standing lamp so as not to be working in a pool of light which is bad for your eyesight. The piano has doilies on top of it to keep the wood from getting scratched by the little cut-glass sculptures and the framed photographs of Mommy when she was a little girl and Gran and Grandad when they got married and Grandad when he got his university diploma to be a psychiatrist, dressed in a long black gown with a flat square hat as if a book fell on his head. The diploma is now framed and hanging on the wall amidst several reproductions of paintings of bouquets of flowers. Sometimes in the springtime Gran cuts a few real flowers from her garden and puts them in a vase on the coffee table but I'm not allowed to get near them because I might upset the vase and spill water all over the rug and *then* what would happen? (Gran is always worried about the vase being upset but she doesn't care if her grand-daughter is upset, which I so often am.) She dusts all these objects every day and when I open the piano lid I also have to remove the long embroidered runner whose purpose is to protect the keyboard from dust so I must never forget to put it back in place when I'm finished practising though how a single mote of dust could get in there when the lid is closed I have no idea.

I fold the runner carefully and set it next to the photo of Mommy when she was about my age, the smile on her face is a genuine smile and not a mask like mine, she's wearing a bright blue dress and her blue eyes are gleaming. The girl in the photo listens to me practise and I try to live up to her but the more I play the more disappointed she gets and after a while I can't even look at her anymore, I feel so crushed. I start out with the scales which is like reciting the alphabet because it doesn't mean anything, I just do them over and over and over again, trying to swing that thumb under without lifting my wrist and keep my fingers curved and the tone exactly even and then after ten minutes it's time for arpeggios which are really difficult because my hands are so small and when I finally open the book with my pieces in it I feel discouraged because the pages are all mucked up with Miss Kelly's purple ink. She's drawn in the phrasing and circled the fingering and underlined *pp* for pianissimo because I played it too loud last week so all I can see are my mistakes and my mediocrity, the things I keep flubbing up week after week.

When Gran first bought me the book and I turned its clean new pages and saw the illustration for the piece called 'Edelweiss'—a little girl bending over these flowers in the Alps—I had feelings of purity, enhanced by the whiteness of the snow on the mountains and the little star-shaped flowers sprouting from their nest of green leaves even despite the snow, and the girl in the picture was just like I'm supposed to be, lovely with her dirndl and white blouse and smooth hairdo and white knee socks and smart boots. The words to the song were lovely, too:

Edelweiss, Edelweiss,
Every morning you greet me,
Small and white, clean and bright,

And then gradually the piece was spoiled by my learning it—by the mistakes I made, causing Miss Kelly to scribble purple comments all over the page including the illustration—so now when I try to play the song it just falls apart in my hands. Every bar is a hurdle to be gotten over. I'm so scared of making a mistake that I stare at the bar as if my eyes would pop out of my head and when it's time to go on to the next bar my eyes jump to the right but it's too late, I've already made a mistake and Gran calls out to me from the kitchen '*F-sharp*, Sadie! It's in the key signature!' (Gran used to play the piano even if I've never heard her once in my life so she has the right to correct me) so I start over again but this time my left hand forgets that it's supposed to hold the G over into the second bar because there's a tie, I break off and my right hand swiftly strikes my left hand and my left hand apologises saying 'I'm sorry I'm sorry I'm sorry I won't do it anymore' but my right hand is furious it says 'I'm fed up to the teeth with your bad behaviour, I will not put up with it one minute longer, do you hear me?' and my left hand cringes and cowers and goes back to the keyboard muttering 'I'm doing my best.' 'What did you say?' asks my right hand in a sharp angry voice. 'I said I was doing my best' says my left hand in a somewhat louder voice because it's on the defensive and has not, after all, committed a murder, only released the G a moment sooner than it should have—'Well you'll have to do better than your best,' shouts the right hand, 'because your best simply isn't good enough!'—all of this happens in a fraction of a second, Gran doesn't even notice there's been a pause in my playing, I start over. When the right hand makes a mistake, the left hand doesn't get to yell at it; it just notices the mistake and thinks resentful thoughts about the right hand without attacking it outright; the whole left side of my body is inferior because of the birthmark being where it is.

(Mom has a piano at her place in Yorkville and not only does she never close the lid, she doesn't even use music; she just picks out the chords she needs to sing from, and when she isn't singing she's smoking, which Gran says is a repulsive habit she hopes I'll never pick up.)

At last it's six o'clock and I get to stop playing the piano and set the table in the dining room. First the three place mats which will deftly catch any stray crumbs that might drift down from our fumbling fingers and would otherwise get stuck in the lace table-cloth where it would be devilishly difficult to get them out again. Then the big white plates with a gold circle around the edge and the small matching bread plates which you put on the top left. Then the heavy silverware which is kept in a velvet-lined box in the top drawer of the buffet. The fork goes to the left of the plate, the knife to the right with the cutting edge turned inwards because otherwise you might cut yourself picking it up (although people aren't supposed to pick up knives by their blades anyway), the soup spoon to the right of the knife because the meal begins with soup (at formal dinners where there are lots of different pieces of cutlery next to your plate Gran says you should never wonder which one to use first, the rule of etiquette is always start on the outside and work your way inwards) the dessert spoon face down above the plate with its handle on the right so you can reach it more easily with your right hand (too bad for left-handed people!), the water glass just above the knife and a little bit to the right. Meanwhile Grandad has come home from walking the dog and scooped Mirth up into his arms to wipe his paws with a rag (so he won't track slush and mud into the house), and turned on the TV for the evening news. There we see that Diefenbaker and Pearson have found something new to disagree about and the Berlin Wall is completely finished and President Kennedy is punishing Cuba for capturing all the pigs he sent over there last year. Lots of other conflicts in the world keep breaking out that I can't understand but whenever Mom is here they become cause for an argument like why are the USA spending a fortune to send rockets into space when millions of their own citizens are still struggling with being poor and jobless and black, which I would tend to agree with but her parents don't; they ask her if she's turning into Communist rabble or something. Gran and Grandad never argue, they hardly even talk at all. I think Grandad doesn't have the right to tell other people what his crazies tell him lying on the couch in his office all day long, and the only other thing he's interested in as far as I can tell is hockey (where Gordie Howe is his hero), but hockey leaves Gran completely cold. As for Gran, it would be quite a challenge for her to make her own daily activities sound adventuresome and thrilling, so at supper we basically eat and say 'Could you pass the butter please?' and 'A little more soup?' and stuff like that.

Days are long, even in winter when they're supposed to be short; weeks are longer and months are endless. I count them as they pass but I don't know what I'm counting towards. Life is interminable.

One Sunday afternoon late in January I think I'll die of boredom so I ask Gran if I can go out and make a snowman in the garden. She says it's too cold out but I plead with her until she relents, sighing, and helps me into my snowsuit and snowboots and woollen hat and mittens with the string going from sleeve to sleeve in the back under my coat (so I won't lose them) and just as she's tying up my scarf I realise I need to pee. 'I'm sorry,' Gran, I say in a small voice, 'but I have to go to the bathroom' and she gets furious and takes my snow clothes off as roughly as she can, saying 'You do everything in your power to exasperate me don't you Sadie?' and I say 'No, Gran, I don't, honest, I swear I didn't have to go to the bathroom five minutes ago!' and she says, 'Well, let this be a lesson to you. Maybe next time you'll pay closer attention to the signals'—and no matter how hard I plead with her she refuses to let me go outside after peeing.

In February an unusual event occurs which is that Lisa one of the girls in my class invites me to her birthday party. I know she's not inviting *me* as an individual, she's inviting all the girls in the class—'probably to show off how wealthy her parents are,' says Gran, 'they can afford to have a party for thirty people'—and she can't leave *just* me out, that would be too conspicuous. There, too, at Lisa's party, something terrible happens because of my need to pee. We're eating sloppy joes made by Lisa's mother which are open hamburgers served on toast and drenched in thick luscious gravy, I've never tasted anything so delicious and I'm absolutely drowning in pleasure, everyone is talking at once and having fun the way children are supposed to do at parties and I'm pretending to be part of the general gaiety when all of a sudden the lemonade I've been guzzling makes itself urgently felt down there and I blush, thinking I'm going to pee my pants which would be the ultimate humiliation, so I get up and ask Lisa's mother in a whisper where the bathroom is. She takes me down the hallway as if it were the most natural thing in the world to have to pee in the middle of a meal, not reprimanding me as Gran would have done, for which I'm grateful. I lock the door and pee to my heart's content and then I can't get the lock back open. It's like a nightmare, it's really like a nightmare, I keep fighting with the lock and it keeps refusing to open and I start to panic, maybe I'll be locked in this bathroom for the rest of my life, so I bang on the door and call for help. A few of the girls yell down the hallway 'What's up, Sadie?' 'I can't get out!' I say in a high, squeaky voice I can't even recognise. Finally Lisa's father comes and kneels down on the other side of the door and tells me in a very kind voice to calm down and then gives me precise instructions as to how to open the lock, and it works. When I finally come back to the table Lisa says 'So how's life in the bathroom, Sadie?' and everyone hoots with laughter and I'm convulsed with shame and the party is completely wrecked.

Now spring is on its way. Mommy will be joining us as she does every year for Easter dinner which takes place at lunchtime, so I decide to count the days till Easter Sunday. They go by, laggards dragging their feet, from forty-two all the way down to one which means tomorrow, and then at long last it is today. Mommy won't be coming to Saint Josaphat's with us in the morning, Gran says she stopped attending church when she got mixed up with that beatnik crowd of hers. 'Yes,' says Grandad, 'Godless people destined for damnation,' but I think he's only joking. (I'm not sure whether the two of them actually believe in miracles and resurrection and heaven and damnation or whether it's just a manner of speaking, they certainly don't seem to be expecting any miracles to come along to transform *their* lives.)

We rush home to get dinner ready for Mommy's arrival at twelve-thirty. The ham has been roasting in the oven all this time so that even as we were singing songs about Jesus being risen from the dead, Gran was worrying about her ham getting burned but as it turned out it didn't. Now Jesus has risen from the dead until next Christmas when he gets to be born again and the ham is cooked and the table is set and the clock is ticking, it's one o'clock and Mommy is late as usual, 'She can't be bothered with silly little things like being on time,' says Grandad (sarcastically). The food is on a low flame on the stove but the bread is already getting a bit stale and so is the smile of welcome that Gran glued to her face at twelve-thirty on the dot. Mirth can tell that something is wrong, he goes back and forth between Gran and Grandad, whining and smacking the floor with his tail, Grandad scratches him behind the ears and says, 'You'd never keep your parents waiting like this, would you, Mirth?' and, hearing his name, Mirth thinks it must be time for his walk so he yelps and Grandad pretends to think he meant 'No,' so he answers 'Of course you wouldn't.'

Before leaving for church this morning I combed my hair and gathered up the top part into an elastic band and tied a yellow ribbon around it so I'd look pretty as a picture for Mommy's arrival but as time goes by I can feel the elastic pulling at my scalp and making it itch so I scratch it and some strands of hair come loose and still the elastic is pulling at my scalp so finally I just yank off the ribbon and the elastic at the same time which uproots a few hairs and brings tears to my eyes. Gran says 'Sadie what on *earth* are you doing? Do you want to get hair in everyone's food? Go get rid of that and wash your hands, quick quick!' and while I'm in the upstairs bathroom, realising in the mirror that I look as dumpy and ordinary as usual and that I went through all that hairdo suffering for nothing, Mommy finally arrives.

I fly down the staircase and literally throw myself into her wide-open arms, she catches me and drags me up onto her lap saying 'My big girl, my darling girl' and covers my face with kisses.

'Can we get started, Kristina?' says Gran, 'it's one thirty-five, if we wait much longer the ham will be dried out completely' and Mommy looks into my eyes and says 'How's my sweet Sadie?' and I say 'Fine' and Gran picks me up off Mommy's lap rather roughly and sets me on my chair and Grandad, turning on the electric carving knife, makes his usual wisecrack about Jack the Ripper.

The thing about Mommy is not that she's the most gorgeous woman in the world, it's that she *radiates charm*. I remember her boyfriend Jack saying that once and it stuck in my mind because it's true. Today she's dressed all in black which Gran probably thinks is an inappropriate choice for Easter Sunday, tight black jeans and a black sweater and a bright pink scarf and big hoop earrings, that's all, no make-up, no fussy hairdo or anything, but the point is that because of her smile, because of her blue eyes and her readiness and her eagerness, she's always completely where she is, which makes me realise that as a general rule people are *not* where they are because their minds are always busy with something else—*not* you, *not* the myriad possibilities of the moment.

(Of course the intensity of my mother's presence makes its rarity in my life all the more unbearable to me.)

'So, Kristina,' says Grandad once the ham has been cut and the bowls of pineapple slices and sweet potatoes and snap beans passed around, 'I see you've got some pretty stiff competition these days.'

Mommy gives him a look that means What are you talking about?

'Paul Anka has hit the top of the charts again, and they're making a film about him.'

Mommy laughs. 'Paul Anka and I aren't working in the same universe.'

'It's immoral to air songs like that over the radio,' says Gran. 'Kissing on the phone, indeed!'

'I like that song,' I whisper.

'Good for you, Sadie,' says Mommy.

'Well,' says Grandad, 'humanity doesn't always progress, it sometimes regresses, that's all I can say. When you think that in two hundred years we've managed to go from the sublime operas of Mozart to something called…Ahuh-Ahuh. Is that supposed to be human language? What do you think Mirth?'

He laughs at his own little joke and slips a piece of fat to Mirth under the table.

'Richard!' says Gran. 'You know that dog shouldn't eat fat! He's got cholesterol!'

'I used to love eating fat,' says Mommy dreamily. 'I wanted to be the fat lady in the circus when I grew up.'

'You did?' says Grandad. (How could he not know? Has he forgotten?) 'Ah, yet another childhood dream come to naught.'

'You've actually *lost* weight since we saw you last,' says Gran.

'I'm doing fine,' says Mommy.

I stop listening and go into a daze, I've been waiting for this day for so long and now that it's here I don't know what to do with it, all I can do is stare at Mommy from across the table, she's got a golden halo around her head from the sunlight pouring in behind her through the window, *she's here she's here she's really here right now,* I just sit there listening to the music of her voice and watching the graceful movements of her hands and suddenly I hear her say 'Sadie, how would you like to spend next weekend over at my place?' and I can't believe my ears. Next weekend? Only *six days* from now? Gran and Grandad exchange glances that mean Oh dear oh dear we're afraid this woman will be a bad influence on our little Sadie, but then of course they remember that this woman is none other than their little Sadie's mother and even if she gave me to them when I was born because she was only eighteen and couldn't look after me, she's twenty-four now and has every right in the world to take me back and who knows, maybe if I behave well over at her place she'll decide to keep me. My heart thumps.

'Peter will drive me over to pick her up after lunch on Saturday and I'll bring her back to you sometime late Sunday afternoon. How does that sound?'

Silence.

'How does that sound to *you*, Sadie?' asks Mommy but just as I'm getting ready to say it sounds heavenly Grandad breaks in.

'Who is Peter?'

'Peter Silbermann. He's my new impresario.'

Silence. Again Gran and Grandad exchange glances.

'Peter…Silbermann?' says Gran in a way that sounds as if there were something wrong with the name.

'What's an impresario?' I ask, imagining an Italian Prince Charming with long wavy hair, laying his red cape down on mud puddles so that Mommy won't get her feet wet.

'The guy who's in charge of making me famous! He looks after my career, sets up my concerts for me, stuff like that.'

'Any concerts in view that aren't in beer halls or blind pigs?' asks Grandad.

'Yes, as a matter of fact,' says Mommy smiling sweetly. 'Shall I send you some tickets?'

'You know I can't understand your music, Kristina,' says Gran, shaking her head. 'I don't want to sound disparaging, but no one has ever made a successful career out of songs without words.'

'I'm the first!' says Mommy. 'Wouldn't want to do anything that had been done before!'

Gran purses her lips and stabs a piece of ham with her fork as if to say, When will this daughter of mine learn to face reality?

'Sadie has quite an appetite,' she says instead. 'I could make a macaroni casserole for your evening meal…'

'Casserole, shmasserole!' laughs Mommy. 'Sadie can survive for one weekend on her mother's diet of dry breadcrusts and whisky… can't you, darling?'

'Sure!' I say, wishing I could think of something humoristic to add but I can't, I'm too keyed-up at the prospect of spending a night in my mother's apartment.

'Well, all right,' sighs Gran. 'I'll pack her a little suitcase…Do you have an extra bed?'

'We could strap the little cot from the guest room onto the roof of Peter's car,' suggests Grandad.

'Don't be silly!' says Mommy. 'She can sleep on the couch…can't you, sweetheart?'

'Sure!' I say again, wondering if Mommy thinks I'm dumb for saying the same thing twice in a row, but the glance she gives me is warm and full of love.

'Okay, that's settled, then,' she says. 'And now, thank you for the delicious meal but I must be off—I have a rehearsal.'

'A rehearsal? On Easter Sunday?' says Gran.

'Do you think Jesus will hold it against me? I'm sure he has more important things to worry about.'

'Kristina!' says Gran, torn between the wish to rebuke Mommy for her blasphemy and the wish to keep her in her clutches a little longer. 'Won't you have some dessert? I made a chocolate cake yesterday especially for you.'

'You always forget—I don't like chocolate.'

And in a flurry of hugs and kisses and barks she is off. I stand at the window and watch her recede down the tree-lined street—walking jauntily, rhythmically, almost dancing, her pink scarf floating behind her—until she turns the corner and Gran says 'Sadie, come and help me clear the table.'

I will be good I will be perfect I will not make one single mistake for the next six days I will step on all the cracks with my right foot only, it's a promise, oh, Mommy Mommy Mommy Mommy Mommy...My love for my mother swells and fills my whole chest to bursting and I wish I could just *merge* with her, be the same *person* as she is, or the incredible voice that pours out of her throat when she sings.

It's true. Mommy is actually opening the door to her apartment with a key, Peter her imprecation is carrying my suitcase, we cross the threshold, we're inside, I'm part of my mother's life at last. It's a basement apartment, not really an apartment because it's just one big room, thrillingly dark like a cave, with little windows giving onto street level so you can watch people's shoes and boots going past. An artistic odour of smoke and incense and coffee hangs in the air and there are lots of books and shadows.

'Make yourself comfortable, sweetheart. Peter and I are going to work for a little while—you don't mind, do you?'

'Oh, no!'

I feel incredibly shy, as if I'd just met this marvellous woman for the first time and had to make a good impression on her whereas she genuinely is my mother. I curl up in a little ball on the couch.

Peter (tall and lanky with long black hair and glasses) sits down at the piano and Mommy goes over and stands next to him and I can see that to them the instrument is not an enemy but a friend, a real pal. Peter runs his fingers over the keyboard and the notes go rilling into the air like a river when it thaws.

'Sadie, you'll be our test audience for this new piece we're working on—all right?'

'Great!'

Touching the birthmark on the inside of her left elbow, Mommy warms up her voice with scales and arpeggios but in her case the exercises don't sound like reciting the alphabet, they sound like joy, like running barefoot in the sand. Then she nods to Peter. After several short sharp staccato notes he lands on a chord, Mommy's voice slips into the middle of the chord and gets a grip on its notes, then bounces into the sky—they're off. She slides on a jerky rhythm from achingly sweet high notes three octaves above middle C all the way down into the deep dark waters of the bass, where she moans gently, longingly, as if her life were seeping away from her. Sometimes she pops her lips and other times she thuds her hand against her chest to punctuate the music flowing from her throat. She seems to be telling me a story—not only the story of her life but the story of all humanity with its wars and famines and struggles, its triumphs and defeats, now her voice fills up with thick ripples of menace as if it were the ocean swollen with storm and now it becomes a long cascade of notes rushing down a cliffside like a waterfall, jouncing off rocks, frothing and gurgling and trickling as it hurtles towards the lush dark valley far below. The voice spins golden circles around my head like the rings of Saturn, then flings itself up and down like a chorus line of women dancing the French cancan, the voice weeps and shudders, twists itself around a low F like climbing ivy around a treetrunk, then dives deep into the crystal blue waters of the G-major chord Peter is harping on…I'm swept away. She's right: no one has ever used their voice like this before. My mother is unique, an inventor, a genius, a goddess of pure song. If Miss Kelly were here now she'd have a conniption fit and die on the spot, having been forced to realise how useless her own music is.

When the song ends Mommy's face is streaming with sweat (you're not supposed to say *sweat*, it's almost a dirty word, Grandad always says 'Horses sweat, men perspire and women only glow,' he also has another favourite proverb about horses and women that says 'You can take a horse to water but you can't make it drink, you can take a woman to culture but you can't make her think') and her T-shirt is stuck to her skin all over her front and back. Peter leaps up from the piano bench and takes her in his arms and whirls her around saying 'That was fantastic, Krissy!' and Mommy lets her head fall back as if she were a doll, and just goes with the movement.

'What do you say, little one?' she asks me when he puts her down.

'Wow!' (I still can't come up with a single intelligent sentence.)

'You like that?'

'Yes!'

'Think I can go somewhere with that?'

'*Yes!*'

'Oh, baby'—Mommy blows me a kiss—'we're gonna hit the stars together, you know that?'

'My turn for a Krissy-kiss,' says Peter, turning her to him and kissing her full on the open mouth like in the movies except that

Gran always turns off the TV set the minute they get started whereas here I get to watch the whole thing from beginning to end. When it's over Peter doesn't look as if it's over, he looks as if it's still going on, his lips are all wet and soft, he fishes in his pocket and pulls out a handful of spare change and says 'Maybe Sadie would like to go buy herself some candy at the corner store' and Mommy turns to me and says 'Good idea, would you like that Sadie?' but even though I adore candy which I'm mostly forbidden to eat except a little bit at Hallowe'en and Christmas because it makes your teeth rot, I don't feel like going out alone into this strange neighbourhood and looking for a store I've never been to before. 'No, that's all right,' I say but Peter comes over and thrusts the money into my hand and says 'I'm sure deep down this little girl is really dying for some candy' and Mommy brings me my coat and says 'Look darling, it's only four blocks away, straight down the street, we'll finish rehearsing while you're gone, that way you won't get bored listening to us.' 'I'm not bored!' I protest, but she shoos me out the door saying 'Off with you, my love. We'll all have a game of rummy together when you get back.'

The blocks are long and I'm afraid of getting lost, I'm afraid of dogs, I'm afraid of being kidnapped by a bunch of hoods but I want to prove to Mommy that I'm a big girl and wouldn't be a burden on her if she let me come to live with her so I swallow the fear each time it rises in my throat and makes me want to cry, my legs feel strange and faraway as if they were detached from my body, they want to run but I force them to walk left right left right with my right foot on the cracks wherever possible. Mommy's neighbourhood is more run-down than ours, the cracks have weeds growing in them and the paint on the houses is flaking and people are sitting out on their stoops chatting and drinking beer because it's the first warm day of the year and it feels like hours and hours have gone by when I get to the store at last.

I push open the door which causes a bell to jangle right above my head which causes me to leap out of my skin and scatter Peter's spare change all over the floor. The lady at the cash register says 'Oops!' in a nice way. Luckily there's no one else in the store to laugh at my clumsiness so I squat down and pick up the nickels and pennies one by one, they've rolled far and wide, some of them under the shelves, this also takes forever and by the time I get to my feet again I'm shaking with nervousness because I think the woman will be fed up waiting for me but she's just sitting there lazily turning the pages of a magazine and yawning and not even paying any attention to me. She's quite fat and must be going out somewhere special tonight because her hair is in curlers and she's wearing a green lamé dress that looks weird with the curlers but of course once her hair is styled she wouldn't want to pull the dress on over her head, I can understand that.

'I'd like some candy please,' I say as politely as possible but my voice is a whisper and the lady doesn't hear me. I repeat the sentence louder and, heaving herself to her feet, she waddles over to the candy bins and flips open their plastic lids and plunges her pudgy hands in amongst the jawbreakers and jellybeans and red and black shoestring licorice and sugared strawberries, slipping them into a brown paper bag and telling me how much it comes to as we go along. I count the money out onto the counter, hoping she won't notice that my fingers are all grubby from scrabbling on the floor and then, just as I'm getting ready to say Thank you very much, she says 'Would you mind zipping me up, dearie?' and turns around. I see that the zipper of her dress is only half done up and her back is white and fleshy like whale blubber and the dress is tight on her, my fingers fumble with the zipper to inch it up to the top I have to squash the flesh in thick folds under the shiny green material, I almost don't think I'll make it, my face is burning with embarrassment and meanwhile the woman is wiggling her shoulders around trying to make it easier for me but you can't suck in your back the way you can suck in your tummy and when I finally get the zipper all the way up she says 'Oooh, I'd better not *breathe* tonight!' Then she says 'Thanks a million, dearie,' and hands me two nigger babies as payment and I'm so nervous that I almost drop them but not quite.

When I finally get back to Mommy's place not having been torn limb from limb by any German shepherds in the meantime, Mommy is straightening the bed and her hair is all over her face and her face has changed and Peter is nowhere to be seen.

'Where's Peter?'

'He had to leave.'

'You said we'd play rummy together!'

'I know, darling, but he got a phone call, something came up, he told me to kiss you goodbye for him.'

I say nothing but I feel forlorn and somewhat swindled.

'Do you like Peter?' Mommy asks, lighting up a cigarette and pouring the smoke out through her two nostrils (which I love).

'He's all right.'

'He really likes you.'

'He doesn't even know me.'

'You know what he said about you?'

'No.'

'He said, "There's a lot going on in that little noggin of hers."'

'What's a noggin?'

Mommy laughs. 'Your head, little one!'

'Are you going to marry him?' I ask, thinking I might as well get it over with.

'How did you guess?' (This lands in my head with a thud.)

'You're going to marry him?' I repeat in a tiny, breathy voice.

'Come and sit in my lap, darling,' says Mommy, holding out her arms to me from where she's sitting on the edge of the bed. 'Listen, it's really a secret, you mustn't tell Gran and Grandad about it for the time being, okay? Peter is a fine person and he's taking my career in hand, he's setting up concerts for me coast to coast, I'll be on tour throughout most of the spring. He's going to make me famous, Sadie!'

'But do you love him?'

'Oh…love…' She looks deep into my eyes and says, 'You know, little one, I'm not sure I understand a hell of a lot about love, but I know one thing for sure: *I…love…you!* Okay? As for all the rest…just leave it up to me and don't worry about it.'

'And then maybe if you're married I can come and live with you because it won't seem so shameful?'

'Shameful! Oh, my baby! It's never been about shame, what *does* go on in that noggin of yours? It's been about money. And the way things seem to be developing, the answer to your question is one big…yes! But keep that under your hat, too, for the time being, all right? Promise?'

She rises and moves around the room switching on lamps because the sun is going down and you can hardly see anything anymore it's so dark. I follow her into the kitchen part of the room and she grabs me under the arms and hoists me up onto a tall stool at the bar so I can watch her cook.

'I'm gonna make us some hamburgers! What do you think of *that?*'

I wonder if I should tell her how I loved the sloppy joes at Lisa's birthday party but I decide not to because she might think I was ungrateful or criticising her cooking so I just say, 'Terrific!' She takes some meat out of the fridge and cuts it into pieces and feeds it through the meat grinder and this reminds her of a song, everything reminds my mother of a song and as she grinds the meat she sings this song about a little Dutchman named Johnny Burbeck who invents a sausage machine and the people in the neighbourhood are afraid he'll grind all their dogs and cats to sausage meat which makes me laugh out loud. In the last verse the machine gets broken and Johnny Burbeck crawls inside to fix it but his wife goes walking in her sleep and accidentally grinds her husband to sausage meat which is hilarious the way Mommy says it:

She gave the crank one hang of a yank
And Johhny Burbeck was meat!

She's motioning to me to join her in the chorus so I chime in, laughing delightedly:

Oh, Mister, Mister Johnny Burbeck,
How could you be so mean?
I told you you'd be sorry for
Inventing that machine!

and so on and so forth and I try to make my voice as full and rich as hers but it still comes out thin-sounding in comparison, like whey as compared to cream.

'Do you know what a hamburger is?' she asks me as she shapes the meat deftly into little patties with her bare hands.

The obvious answer can't be the right one so I say, 'No, what?'

'It's a person from Hamburg! And do you know what a wiener is?'

'No, what?'

'It's a person from Vienna! And do you know what a frankfurter is?'

'No, what?'

'It's a person from Frankfurt! And do you know what a steak is?'

'A person from Stakesville?' I say, trying to get into the whirl of things.

'No, silly, it's a thick slice of beef!' she laughs, and I'm positive that none of the girls in my class have mothers who fool around with them like this.

While she's got her back turned to me frying up the hamburgers, I remember I wanted to tell her about Miss Kelly hitting me with the ruler so even if it seems a bit irrelevant in the midst of such a good mood, I tell her.

She doesn't say anything.

'Did you hear me, Mommy?'

'Hm?'

'Did you hear me say that Miss Kelly hits me on the wrists with a ruler, *really hard*, almost every time I have a lesson?'

'Yes, I heard you, dear... That can't be very pleasant,' she says non-committally and I can tell that she's gone somewhere else, far away, I don't know where, so I try to go back to the mood of a minute ago and I say 'So if you grind Johnny Burbeck to meat he can't become a Dutchman again, he can only become a Hamburger' and Mommy shrieks with laughter.

For dessert we spoon grape jelly directly out of the jar which we'd never be able to do at Gran's and I get it all over my lips which makes them purple and Mommy sticks out her tongue and it's purple too which makes us giggle and she says 'Can you stick out your tongue and touch your nose?' so I try to but I can't and then she says 'It's easy, look!' and, sticking out her tongue, she touches her nose with her finger and I wonder if I might be able to do that trick in school on Monday to make myself a little more popular or if the girls would just say 'What a dumb joke.' I show Mommy how I can cross my eyes by keeping them focussed on my fingertip as it approaches my nose and Mommy doesn't tell me that I shouldn't cross my eyes because they'll get stuck that way and I wish the evening would never end.

We sleep together in her bed. At first her body is warm and close against mine and I think I'm in heaven but after a while she gets up and goes over to the kitchen counter and pours herself a glass of whisky and lights up a cigarette, I watch her through my eyelashes pretending to be asleep because I don't want to lose a single second of being in my mother's presence and then I fall asleep in spite of myself. In my dream I see Mommy slipping a tiny little baby into a brown envelope, writing the baby's name on it with a red felt pen and dropping it into somebody else's mailbox, then she does the same thing with another baby and I start feeling really upset at the idea of all these packages containing naked little babies with nothing to eat.

When I wake up in the morning Mommy is sound asleep beside me. Her left arm curved up around her head reveals her birthmark which I study for a while, wondering why it had to go down such a shameful place on *my* body and the minute I think of that, all the bad thoughts about being sullied and worthless come stampeding into my brain and my right foot starts kicking my left without my even telling it to and I'm scared it will wake Mommy up so I gingerly get up out of bed and go to the bathroom. Then I don't know what to do because she's still sleeping so I eat some jawbreakers and licorice for breakfast and my Fiend starts nattering at me saying *Fat little girl, candy will make you fatter* and I can't stop thinking about that so I go over to the bookcase to see if there are any children's books but there aren't so I eat some more candy and then I feel sick because of the smell of the greasy frying pan from last night so I go back to the bathroom and throw up. I don't want the weekend at Mommy's to be spoiled but I have to admit that right now I'm not having the time of my life, it's raining cats and dogs outside and I really wish Mommy would wake up but I don't dare to wake her because she might have spent the whole night thinking and drinking, that's often the case with artists, I've got a burning acid taste in my throat from throwing up so I go to the fridge to see if there's any milk but the fridge is empty apart from half a grapefruit and a piece of mouldy blue cheese that makes my stomach turn again so I slam the fridge door as fast as I can.

Mommy sits up in bed and I'm afraid she'll be mad at me for making a noise but she isn't. 'Yikes,' she says, 'What time is it? Eleven o'clock…Been up long, darling?' She swivels out of bed and the world becomes liveable again because she's slipping into her black slacks and giving me a hug and turning on the radio and talking to me as she lights her first cigarette of the day and makes a pot of coffee. 'Miserable weather,' she says. 'What a pity—I wanted to take you to the zoo.'

Peter arrives with a bag of groceries and ruffles my hair which

I dislike because I just combed it, a couple of friends drop by and then the phone rings and more friends come over and before long there are six strangers sitting around in my mother's apartment smoking and talking and laughing, two of the guys have beards and I wonder if my father Mort still has a beard and if any of these people are still friends with him and if they'll tell him they met his daughter Sadie the next time they see him and if he'll ask them questions about me. They all say 'Nice to meet you' but I don't find it nice to meet them because they're hogging my mother's attention on the one weekend I'm spending at her place. I notice that when people talk to Mommy they have a special tone of voice as if they were in awe of her, and the minute she opens her mouth they fall totally silent to listen, and when she jokes they laugh louder than for anyone else's jokes. After a while Peter picks me up and starts bouncing me on his knees singing *Walk, my horsie, walk* which is unfortunately something grown-ups often think they have to do with little children. I squirm to get away and then a woman says 'Any chance you might want to sing something for us, Krissy?' and Mommy says all right. She doesn't get up from her chair but closes her eyes and sits with her arms crossed, her right thumb pressed into the crook of her left arm, and warms up her vocal chords, allowing the sound to pass over them like the bow of a violin, gently, gently up and down, Peter goes over to the piano and gets a drone going by playing low F and A-flat in alternation and at first Mommy's voice moves down that pathway but then it starts flying above it, filling the room, passing through the walls and ceiling and embracing the heavens until we have to close our eyes, too, because the objects in front of us have become totally irrelevant, there's only Mommy's voice, its pure vitality, as if it were air to breathe or water to drink, as if it were love. When she stops we don't know what has happened to us, where we have been, and the woman who asked her to sing is in tears. There's a long pause of silence before a burst of applause.

'You're a magician, Krissy,' someone murmurs. 'An absolute sorceress.'

'Did you know your mother was a sorceress, my dear?' says a man I've never met before and I wish they'd just all go away, they're spoiling the whole weekend as far as I'm concerned but Mommy doesn't seem to realise this, our precious hours keep sliding by and at about three p.m. Peter makes a batch of scrambled eggs in the frying pan which Mommy hadn't even washed yet from last night, he serves it up in cups and bowls because there aren't enough plates to go around and I'm just beginning to think that this is a tiny bit fun when someone (for the sake of conversation, not because they really care) asks me where I go to school and I answer them and everyone starts oohing and aahing and saying 'My my, aren't we *fashionable!*' and I blush though it's certainly not my fault what school I go to and the more I blush the more embarrassed I feel because people can *see* that I'm embarrassed which embarrasses me even more, so at this point Mommy says, 'Well, *someone* in the family needs to be respectable, don't they?' which sets off a chorus of laughter and allows them to change the subject.

More time goes by and all of a sudden Mommy gets up and says, 'Okay, like, vanish, you guys. It's five o'clock, I've got a concert at seven and I need time to warm up. Sadie darling, you don't mind going home alone with Peter, do you?'

In a jiffy she has packed my bag and is handing it to me, the friends start heading for the exit, I feel tiny and lost in all the shuffle and scuffle and smoke but Mommy crouches down and puts her hands around my face and gives me a soft short kiss on the lips and says 'Now don't forget *anything* we said last night, okay?' and I nod solemnly, fighting back my tears and wondering when I'll be seeing her again and not daring to ask her. Then she whispers into my ear so that no one else can hear, 'What's a frankfurter?' 'A person from Frankfurt,' I whisper into her ear, but she whispers back into mine, 'No, silly, it's a sausage used in making hot dogs!' And she hugs me hard to her chest where the music vibrates and scoots me out the door.

Peter lets me sit up in the front seat with him which Gran never does. As we drive across the city in the sleety rain with the radio on and the windshield wipers sloshing back and forth I remember the glance Gran and Grandad exchanged at the mention of his name so I ask him a question: 'What kind of a name is Silbermann?'

'A Jewish kind of a name,' he says. 'How come?'

'And what's Jewish?'

'Well, that all depends. It's a long, long story with lots of unhappy endings.'

'Does it mean you don't go to church?'

'No, lots of Jews go to churches called synagogues. It's the *atheist* part of me that doesn't go to church, not the Jewish part.'

'What's atheist?'

'It means you don't believe in hokey-pokey like god and the devil.'

'What *do* you believe in, then?'

'Well…I believe in your mom, that's for sure. I believe in money, though up until now I haven't seen much proof of its existence. Definitely I believe in those windshield wipers, look what a good job they're doing! Uh…I believe in scrambled eggs, preferably with bagels and lox.'

'What's that?'

'Hmm…You've got a lot to learn, kid. Here we are…See you soon, eh?'

It's tough going back to normal life with memories of that weekend churning in my brain. It's tough waking up on Monday morning and realising there are five whole days of school to get through before the weekend and not even looking forward to the weekend either. Every fraction of every second grates on my nerves, from Gran asking me if I've made my bed to Mirth thumping the hardwood floor with his tail; I wish I could kick them both but I can't.

My ballet classes are even more excruciating than usual because my pointe shoes are getting too small for me, but Gran says there's no point in buying me a new pair now because there are only two months to go until summer vacation and my feet will grow over the summer so by September the new ones would be too small, too, so I just have to be patient.

At school I toy with the idea of telling Mommy's jokes about Hamburgers and Wieners but I'm afraid the other girls would just look at each other and raise their eyebrows and their supercilious silence would spoil the jokes forever. In drawing class I go over to sharpen my blue pencil and sticking it into the pencil sharpener reminds me of Mommy feeding chunks of beef through the meat grinder, which reminds me of Johnny Burbeck—*she gave the crank one hang of a yank*—and suddenly I see myself sharpening my finger instead of my pencil—round and round, grind and grind, the right hand sharpening the left, ripping off bits of flesh, cracking and crushing bones, whittle flick whittle flick, the blood dripping down…'Sadie what *is* taking you so long?' says the Art teacher because I'm just standing there staring at the pencil sharpener and not doing anything.

May comes stumbling in. I'm watching myself very closely and giving myself a score out of ten every day. The minute I get home from school I stand in front of my bedroom mirror and if my hair is messy or my shoes are untied or the hem of my skirt is hanging down I lose points. Other points can be lost for burping and farting or if I make Gran raise her voice at me or if Miss Kelly hits me with her ruler. I can think whatever I like but if I say a dirty word out loud (even in a whisper) or make a grammar mistake or pick up a glass with my left hand or sniff back my snot and swallow it instead of blowing my nose, I lose points.

One of my eye teeth falls out and I spend hours sucking at the hole in my gums, worrying it with my tongue, drinking the tiny metallic flow of my own blood and not wanting it to stop, wishing I could somehow eat myself. What would it be like to disappear through my own throat into my own stomach? I'd start with the fingernails, then the fingers, hands, elbows, shoulders…No, maybe I should start with the feet…But how would I go about eating my own head? Open my mouth so wide that it could bend back around and swallow the whole head in one gulp. Then there'd be nothing left of me but this trembly little stomach on the floor. Full at last.

I'm always hungry. Gran tells me to chew my food slowly and thoroughly instead of bolting it but no matter how slowly I chew it I always wish there was more and it's not polite to ask for third helpings. The only meal Gran doesn't supervise is my afternoon snack because she's busy in the garden at that time of day so I make myself two whopping peanut-butter-and-jelly sandwiches while her back is turned, spreading the stuff on the bread as thickly as possible and gulping it down almost without chewing it.

One day just as I'm sinking my teeth into this guilty sweet-and-salt delight, a man walks into the kitchen, soft and soundless as a cat. His eyebrows are bushy and his gaze is bright blue and the minute I set eyes on him I know he must be one of Grandad's crazies. Either he got lost trying to find the exit to the street or else he decided to explore the house on purpose. After a minute I say 'Hi!' and he says 'Hi, that looks good' and I say 'Do you want some?' gesturing towards the untouched sandwich on the plate and he says 'Oh no, thanks just the same. I'm Jasper—what's your name?' 'Sadie,' I say. 'Mind if I sit down?' he says, 'Be my guest,' I say, trembling pleasantly inside because this is an Event in my otherwise Uneventful Life and he says, glancing at the jars on the table: 'I used to love peanut butter and jelly too, when I was a kid'—but just then Mirth having smelled a stranger comes skidding into the kitchen and starts yapping and snapping at Jasper's ankles so I give him the kick I've been saving up for months and he howls in pain like the dog in the 'Tom and Jerry' cartoons but the man stands up with a distressed look on his face and says 'Hey, no, you shouldn't punish the dog, Sadie. Dogs can only be as intelligent as their owners. Poor thing, poor thing,' he says, bending down to comfort Mirth who's still keening, but just then Gran comes rushing up the back steps from the garden with a pair of shears in her hands which she brandishes at him screaming 'Get out! Get out! You leave my house this instant or I'll call the police!' and straightening up, Jasper gives me the saddest little smile. 'Nice talkin' to you, Sadie,' he murmurs, and the Event comes to an end before it could even get started.

One day reading his newspaper at the breakfast table Grandad gives a little grunt of surprise because there's a picture of Mommy in it with an article about her concert tour.

'Look at this,' he says to Gran and she comes around behind him and bends down and gives a little grunt herself when she sees her own daughter grinning out at her from the newspaper.

'For heaven's sake,' she says, and Grandad says, 'I don't know that heaven's got much to do with it. And I'm not sure I enjoy seeing my family name in the *Globe and Mail* in association with those inhuman onomatopoeia. What do you think, Mirth?'

Mirth barks joyfully at the unexpected possibility of a walk.

'Excellent!' says Grandad, slipping him a crust of toast. 'Another week or two of practice and you'll be ready to go on stage with Kristina!'

Why can't they be proud of Mommy for having a successful concert tour, instead of making fun of her? I'm very proud of her! I'm almost famous because my mother is in the newspaper but at school no one seems aware of this fact although the words *Krissy Kriswaty* were printed in fairly large letters and my name is Sadie Kriswaty and as far as I know there aren't that many Kriswatys in the city of Toronto. I don't want to bring it up myself because either they wouldn't believe me (which would be embarrassing) or they'd think I was boasting (which would be worse).

I read the article myself when I get home from school and though there are quite a few words I don't understand it makes me flush and sweat to think that this is actually my mother they're talking about. I can just see the spectators sitting there in Regina or Vancouver or wherever with their eyes widening in disbelief as this thin blond woman dressed all in black comes out on stage, greets her musicians, goes over to the microphone and opens her mouth and then, instead of singing 'Edelweiss' or 'My Favourite Things' or some such drivel, takes them on a trip around the universe. The music is her floor and she dances on it, leaping octaves effortlessly; when she goes way up into the high notes she can split her voice in two and sing with herself in harmony.

'She is unbelievable,' the article says, 'and the news of her talent is spreading like wildfire.' In the interview the journalist asks Krissy Kriswaty what she's got against words and she says that 'the voice is a language unto itself.' The journalist asks her what her plans are for the future and she answers that she's 'planning to get married in the near future' (might her manager Peter Silbermann be the lucky man? wonders the journalist) 'and move to New York City and make her first record there.'

(it doesn't say anything about the fact that she has a daughter)

In the same issue of the newspaper there's an article about how Marilyn Monroe sang 'Happy Birthday' to President Kennedy last night in a tight sexy dress and when she went back to her dressing-room afterwards she felt faint all of a sudden because her dress was cutting off her circulation and I can certainly identify with that from the times when my kilt gets too tight around my waist and I can hardly breathe, so they had to swiftly slash the dress to pieces to save her life whereas it cost twelve thousand dollars.

I read faster and faster and better and better, I read until I'm blue in the face, it's the only thing I'm good at, if someone were to tell me I'm not allowed to read anymore I'd have a conniption fit.

Stories about dogs who find their way home to their masters, travelling for miles through mountains and forests and rivers and ending up right on their own doorstep.

Stories about people walking through the desert until they're crazed with thirst, their lips cracked, their mouths parched, and seeing an oasis up ahead of them but it's only a mirage, there's nothing there at all. When you start seeing mirages it means you're going to die.

Stories about people who get lost in the Great North: wandering aimlessly through the snow until, exhausted, they lie down in a snowbank thinking it's a warm bed, freezing to death in the delusion of having reached home at last. But also the *Legend of Sam McGee* which is just the opposite, about a man who was part of an expedition to the North Pole and froze to death, his buddies tossed his corpse into the furnace and the next time they opened it were astonished to see him sitting there smoking his pipe and toasting his toes:

> *And he wore a smile you could see a mile, and he said: "Please close that door.*
> *It's fine in here, but I greatly fear you'll let in the cold and storm—*
> *Since I left Plumtree, down in Tennessee, it's the first time I've been warm.*

...*that* made me laugh.

Little Black Sambo also makes me laugh, when he fools the tigers and they start chasing around the tree with their tails in each other's mouths, running faster and faster until you can't see their legs anymore, and finally just melting into a great pool of butter at the foot of the tree.

I love books where people die.

I dream that my mother dies and there are hundreds of people at her funeral and Gran and Grandad are standing at the edge of her grave looking very sad and I say to them, 'But why weren't you nice to her when she was alive?'

Over the month of May my average daily score is eight out of ten which is not bad at all but then I make an appalling mistake. We're in the locker room getting changed after gym, and as I'm pulling down my gym pants my panties come with them and my bum gets bared, it only lasts two seconds but that's long enough: 'What's that on your rear end, Sadie?' Heather asks, pointing at my birthmark. 'Look, you guys!' and before I can pull my pants up the other girls have caught a glimpse of my birthmark and they start giggling about it and I'm crushed. My Fiend is absolutely furious and I know he's going to punish me for betraying him and sure enough, the minute I get home from school—before I can even have my snack or check my appearance in the mirror—he tells me to lock my bedroom door and bang my head against the wall a hundred times. *You still think your mother's going to come and get you?* he sneers. *Ha! You don't deserve her, you don't even know how to get dressed and undressed properly, so you can just go on living in this house for the rest of your life.*

Have all my points been cancelled by this mistake?

That evening I feel woozy because of the hundred knocks on my head and my piano practice is even worse than usual and I hardly touch my meal so Gran asks if I'm sick but I'm not allowed to say yes, I'm not allowed to say *anything* about what's going on but just then the phone rings and I rush to the kitchen to answer it.

'Hello?'

'My darling Sadie! I'm *back!*'

'MOMMY!'

Gran comes in and wrenches the receiver away from me muttering 'Who told you to answer the telephone? Go finish your meal!' Then she says, speaking into the receiver, 'Kristina, don't you know we're at the dinner table at six-fifteen?' but apparently Mommy doesn't answer that question, she talks and talks and after a while Gran says '*What?*' and closes the kitchen door which is quite a dramatic thing to do. For ten long minutes Grandad goes on eating all by himself and I sit there waiting and we don't say one single word to each other.

When Gran sits back down at the table you can tell the upshot of the conversation has taken her unawares because she keeps her eyes on her plate. 'Not only are Kristina and Peter getting married,' she tells Grandad...'not only do they want all of us to attend their wedding...but they're taking Sadie with them to New York City.'

A velvet blanket of bliss falls over me, like a god heaving a sigh. Ah...

So all my efforts haven't been in vain. Despite the unfortunate incident in the locker room, my good marks have borne their fruit. I'm leaving this house.

My real life can begin at last.

Nothing can faze me now. Miss Kelly can bash me over the head with her *Complete Piano Works of Ludwig von Beethoven*, the girls at school can form a circle around me and snigger and point to their hearts' content, my ballet teacher can make me stand in the corner because I flubbed my tiptoe-twirl for the seventh time in a row—it doesn't matter—I'm not part of this world anymore—I'm going to New York!

Gran is more tight-lipped than ever as she goes about preparing for Mommy's wedding in early June. She buys me a new dress—a puffy yellow thing made of stiff lace and taffeta with a black plastic belt around the waist. On the morning of the wedding day she takes me to the hairdresser's, the lady washes my hair with scalding hot water and sets it in brush curlers, rolling them so tightly I could scream and sticking pink plastic pins through them at a sharp angle against my skull. Then she sits me under the drier and turns it on, the curlers tug and prickle as I sit there sweating under the burning panting electric helmet and when it's finally over and she takes the curlers out I think I'm going to be lovely with ringlets but instead of leaving them alone she backcombs them until I look like a wildwoman, then pins the whole thing up into a beehive and sprays it stiff and I can't even recognise myself, it's a vastly inappropriate hairdo for a little girl. When I've finished struggling into my dress and stockings and shoes, Gran stands back to study the effect and gives a nod: 'Yes,' she says, 'that will do.'

The church is packed with people who are strangers to me apart from Gran and Grandpa and a couple of the friends who came to Mommy's place that day when I was there. I get to sit up in the front row between Gran and Peter, and since Gran is staring straight ahead of her, tense and taciturn, I talk to Peter while we wait for the ceremony to start.

'If you don't believe in all this hokey-pokey, how come you're getting married in a church?' I whisper.

'Your mom told me it was theatre,' he whispers back. 'We're doing this play about a wedding, you see? Everyone's got a role to play. That's a pretty snazzy costume you've got there, kiddo.'

'Thanks,' I say, grateful for the fib. 'You look good yourself.'

'So like…when my turn comes, I have to get up and go put a ring on Krissy's finger and say *I do*. And you know what, Sadie?'

'No, what?'

He bends down even closer to whisper to me conspiratorially: 'It didn't take me long to memorise my lines.'

I give a little snort of laughter and Gran jabs me with her elbow. Then the organ starts wheezing through 'Here Comes the Bride' and everyone turns around and we see Grandad coming slowly up the aisle holding Mommy by the elbow, she's wearing a long simple sleeveless white dress, her blond hair is twisted into a hundred tiny braids with white flowers in some of them, no one has ever been so beautiful in the history of the world.

'Look,' whispers Peter. 'Your grandma's weeping—right on cue! And now I get to make my entry. I've got stage fright, what's my line again?'

'"I do."'

'That's right. "I do." "I do." "I do."'

He walks slowly up to the altar and, a moment later, the actor who is playing the minister pronounces my mother and Peter Silbermann man and wife.

At the reception I can't keep my eyes or my hands off the food, it's not a sitting-down meal but a milling-around one with enormous trays of yummies on every table—paid for, I think, by Peter's parents who are wealthy; anyway Gran and Grandad could never have come up with the idea for all these small stuffed rolls and balls and honey-soaked pastries. I know Gran won't dare to reprimand me in front of all these people so I just go around cramming my mouth full of one delectable morsel after another and practically swooning with the pleasure of it, trying to keep the voice of my Fiend at bay for the time being, yes I know I'm eating too much but how often does a girl get to attend her own mother's wedding?

There are a few babes in arms and a few teenagers but I'm the only kid my age and height which is pretty much exactly the height of adult waistlines which puts my nose at the level of adult crotches, I can smell them as I wend my way through the crowd.

Peter's father taps on a champagne glass with a knife to get people's attention to make a speech, then Grandad also makes a speech, then Peter. Watching them, I think about the theatre idea and wonder if that's basically what everybody does, not only at weddings but all the time: maybe when Grandad listens to his crazies he's playing the *role* of a psychiatrist and when Miss Kelly hits me with the ruler she's playing the *role* of a nasty piano teacher; maybe everybody is really somebody else deep down but they all learn their lines and get their diplomas and go through life playing these roles and they get so used to it they just can't stop.

Mommy's different, though. To play the role of a singer you have to be a singer; there's no way you can cheat. My mother is possibly the only really-what-she-is person in this whole room.

Just as I've gotten to this point in my thinking I decide to step out onto the terrace to see what kind of food is on the tables there and I ram wham into a glass sliding door which I thought was open but was actually closed. Not only does the collision take my breath away and hurt my nose but the door shatters, scattering glass everywhere. The wedding guests turn towards me in dismay and the waiters come trotting up with brooms and my Fiend says *This is your punishment for being so greedy.*

'Oh, Sadie!' says Gran in exasperation but then her tone changes and she says 'Quick quick, come here,' because my nose is pouring blood and she wants to staunch the flow with a Kleenex before it can stain my new yellow dress.

To take people's attention off the accident, Peter's father

mercifully motions for the orchestra to start playing. The newly-weds begin to waltz around the room, the very picture of amorous grace—and then Mommy does something unexpected, she waltzes with Peter right over to the corner where Gran is dabbing at my face and the two of them swoop me up (beehive-hairdo, taffeta flounces, plastic belt, bloody nose and all) and continue dancing with me in their arms. When the piece comes to an end they set me down on a table so that I'm actually standing with my shoes on the white tablecloth—they can do anything they like because it's Their Day—each of them takes one of my hands and they turn to face the crowd and Mommy announces publicly and proudly, 'This is the new family: Peter, Kristina and Sadie!' Everyone applauds, and I look at Gran and Grandpa to see the effect this has on them but their faces look exactly the same as usual—pained and patient, as if attending their own daughter's wedding reception were neither more nor less thrilling than going to the toilet.

The rest of June is a long list of last times.

I change my sheets in this house for the last time (the top one on the bottom and a clean one on the top is Gran's unshakeable rule about sheet-changing, though I don't see why you can't just change both sheets every two weeks which would be less work). Miss Kelly's purple ballpoint pen defiles my music book for the last time, I hang up my pointe shoes and school uniform and Brownie uniform, arrange the embroidered runner on the keyboard and close the piano lid once and for all, bidding farewell to the coffee table and the diplomas and the painted flowers.

Grandad sits down to his breakfast and says 'Ah why would anyone choose this profession? It's enough to make you tear your hair out'—not for the last time, certainly, but *I* won't be hearing it again which makes it almost endearing to me. Gran asks me to dry the dishes, and my hands in the dishtowel lingeringly caress every gold-circled cup and plate, in the full and pleasant knowledge that I shall never dry them again.

On July 2nd, Gran folds all my clothes and stacks them neatly into boxes and on July 3rd Peter's car pulls up in front of the house and Mommy jumps out of it. Two hours later we're on the far side of the American border, roaring past the city of Rochester, New York.

I was so excited I almost didn't sleep at all for the whole night between July 2nd and July 3rd so after a while I start feeling sluggish and groggy and I fall asleep with my head on the box of books beside me in the back seat. When I wake up the air is thick with heat, I'm drenched in sweat and my head is achy, Mommy and Peter are talking together in low voices.

'If you really want us to be a family,' Peter says, 'we should all have the same name. It would be by far the simplest. Mr and Mrs Peter Silbermann and their daughter Sadie Silbermann.'

This is a shock to me because Peter isn't my father by any stretch of the imagination. But the truth of the matter is I don't even know my real father's last name, I got the name Kriswaty from my mother who got it from the psychiatrist on Markham Street. Maybe if I change both my name and my country of residence, my Fiend won't be able to find me anymore.

'So I'll be Mrs Silbermann from now on—is that what you're thinking?' says Mommy.

'Well,' says Peter (and I can tell he's lighting up a cigarette because he's talking through his teeth), 'I mean you could keep Krissy Kriswaty as your stage name. Double letters are catchy—

Marilyn Monroe, Brigitte Bardot, Doris Day…But the Mrs Silbermann identity would protect you the rest of the time—at PTA meetings, for instance.'

Mommy laughs. 'Somehow I don't think I'll be attending a helluva lot of PTA meetings,' she says. 'But I've decided to start using a new stage name.'

'Oh yeah?'

'Yeah.'

'What's that?'

'Erra.'

'What?'

'Erra.'

'How do you spell it?'

'E–R–R–A—Erra.'

'That's not even a name.'

'It is now!'

Mommy starts singing the name in a soft, eerie voice and I know she's got her finger on her birthmark.

'You can't do that, babe,' says Peter. 'I've devoted two years of my life to making Krissy Kriswaty a big name.'

'Peter, just because you put a ring on my finger doesn't suddenly give you the right to tell me what I can and cannot do.'

'It's not your husband talking, sweetheart. It's your manager.'

'Manager, shmanager! I'm the artist and I call the shots because if it weren't for the artist, the manager would have nothing to manage—am I right?'

Peter doesn't answer.

'I think this is an *excellent* time to change names,' Mommy insists. 'Krissy Kriswaty was a Canadian singer; her fame will remain in Canada. Erra, on the other hand, will be a world celebrity.'

'Who ever heard of such a name?' says Peter, shaking his head.

'Erra,' repeats Mommy firmly. She swivels around and, seeing that I'm awake, asks me what I think.

'What do I think about what?' I grumble, rubbing my eyes and pretending to have woken up that very minute.

'We're talking about name-changing. How would you like to be Sadie Silbermann from now on?'

'Wouldn't Peter have to adopt me first?'

'I can't do that, kiddo,' Peter says. 'Your real dad's still alive.'

'You mean you want all of us to lie?'

'*Lie?* No, of course not.'

'More like theatre, then?'

'Yeah, that's it, exactly. You get to play the role of Sadie Silbermann—how does that sound?'

'Snazzy,' I say.

Peter laughs as he stubs out his cigarette in the ashtray.

'Sadie is a nice Jewish name anyway. In Hebrew it means "princess".'

'It does?' says Mommy. 'I never knew that.'

'You didn't?'

'No.'

'Why did you call her Sadie then?'

'I just liked the name, that's all.'

'Well, now there's a *reason* for her to be called Sadie. You goys really need to have everything spelled out for you.'

I don't know why he said *goys* instead of *guys* but all of a sudden I like the name Sadie for the first time in my life because it reminds me of something besides *sad* and *sadist. Princess!*

'And from now on,' Mommy adds, 'whenever I sing I'm going

to be Erra. How does *that* sound?'

'Fine,' I say, sitting up with a bad crick in my neck from the position I fell asleep in but a good feeling in my heart, 'That sounds fine but I have to pee.'

New York City doesn't make a terrific first impression on me, it's sprawling and infinite like Toronto only more so and the first thing that happens is that Peter misses the exit we were supposed to get off at and Mommy says 'Oh, brilliant!' and for a moment there's a bad silence in the car. Eventually we find our address which is on Norfolk Street in a little fourth floor walk-up apartment that Peter got cheap because it belonged to a friend of a friend of his who didn't need it anymore because he died recently of a drug overdose.

'Wow this is what I call a *pad*,' says Peter when we walk in because the walls are all painted black with yellow panels, there are yellow and black curtains on the windows, and the ceiling is dark red. It's got a piano which Mommy says was an absolute prerequisite and indeed the first thing she does when we get the door open is go over to make sure the piano is in tune, which it is.

We drag all our boxes and suitcases up the stairs and I notice that my life with Gran and Grandad and Mirth is already beginning to seem vague and long-ago to me. In this apartment there's only one bedroom and it's mine; Mommy and Daddy (I'm going to try and get used to calling Peter Daddy) will be sleeping on a fold-out couch in the living room. I stick my head out my bedroom window and look down into the street where there are lots of kids playing and quite a surprising amount of garbage and dog poop on the sidewalk. A smell of foreignness wafts up to me which I like.

We have supper in a Chinese restaurant nearby because it's too late to go out food shopping and Peter tries to teach me how to use chopsticks but I keep dropping them on the floor and the waiter gets tired of bringing me new ones so I give up and use my fork instead. At the end of the meal Peter's fortune cookie says *You will earn much money soon*, which makes us laugh and Mommy's says *Luck is in the store for you* and mine says *Take edvantage of your new life* which I think is amazing even despite the spelling mistake.

The plans that have been made for me for the summer are fairly non-existent which is fine with me. Mommy and Peter-I-mean-Daddy are busy most of the day setting things up at the recording studio which makes them really stimulated and in a good mood. There's a library not far away and Mommy brings home great stacks of children's books for me to read and the summer turns into a sort of endless paradise with as much reading and sleeping and eating as I like and no particular rules from the outside world. As for the rules from inside…my Fiend still critically observes my every gesture but he seems to be keeping a low profile, he hasn't screamed at me or forced me to hurt myself since we moved to New York. Even getting dressed is less of a torment than it used to be, though admittedly it's always easier in the summertime because there are fewer clothes to put on.

So these are the first days of my actually having the experience of what is called a family. I love it. The weather is hot, and when the sunlight pouring into my bedroom window wakes me up in the morning I go into the living room and tickle Peter and Mommy's bare feet which are sticking out from under the sheet and they kick and grumble at me to leave them alone. It's a funny feeling to see my mother lying in bed all naked with a naked man but that's family life I guess so I'm eager to get used to it.

I learn how to make their morning coffee and bring it to them with cream and sugar on a tray.

Peter is really nice to me and he invents a game called the flipshot where we grab hands, I take a few little jumps then leap up to put my legs around his waist, then hang down backwards till my hair sweeps the floor, then bring my legs around front into an open V against his chest, then he heaves me up into a sitting position where my legs are knotted around his neck and finally he lowers me down again and flips me over in a backwards somersault—I'm on my feet! That's the flipshot and it's fun to do, even though he teases me about being plump and making him pant with exhaustion after only two or three times.

It's not long before a whole new group of friends start dropping by at our place, carbon copies of the Toronto friends as far as I can tell, same beards and long hair, same awed reverence for my mother and her voice, same habits of staying up late drinking wine and smoking kerouac and listening to music; when I get tired all I have to do is go into my room and shut the door and if I get curious I can always watch what's going on through the keyhole.

Of course the housekeeping is less than impeccable—but 'you can't have everything,' as Mommy always says, and when there's really no clean silverware or underwear left and scarcely any floorspace to walk on, she throws herself into house cleaning with a vengeance, and as she wipes and washes and sweeps and irons and shakes the rugs out the window she sings wacko versions of Paul Anka songs—*Put your shed on my boulder*, stuff like that.

On July 29th I turn seven and they take me to the Bronx Zoo to celebrate and when my feet get tired Daddy picks me up and carries me on his shoulders. It's fantastic to see the world from that height and also to feel his head between my thighs and his hands on my ankles. On the way home Mom buys me a bakery cake on the Grand Concourse and to my surprise it tastes better than any of Gran's homemade cakes, I tell Mom this when I ask for my third helping and she says that's because the bakeries leave out Gran's favourite ingredient which is guilt.

A few days later there's a big uproar because Marilyn Monroe committed suicide, whereas just a few months ago she was dealing with the problem of her dress being too tight. I watch Mommy and Daddy's faces watching the news about it and the shock on their faces makes a deep impression on me, Gran and Grandad would never look shocked no matter what happened, they would merely look disapproving and shake their heads.

One Sunday morning Mommy sleeps in late and when she still isn't up at eleven o'clock Daddy says 'How about if we go out and hustle us up some breakfast?' So we go out hand in hand and I feel proud and wide-awake and unique. We walk down Delancey and Rivington, then get onto Orchard Street where all the stores are open and spilling their wares out onto the sidewalk which you'd never see on a Sunday morning in Toronto. There are signs everywhere, I read them proudly and loudly as Daddy points to them: *Fine & Klein Handbags, Altman Luggage, Beckenstein 'World's Largest Selection Woollens Silks Draperies', You are Missing Plenty if you Don't Buy Here, Leather Outlet, Garments, Fabrics, Trimmings, Knitwear,* you name it, Daddy's got this big grin on his face and every now and then he stops to examine the merchandise and exchange a few words with the salesmen, all of whom compliment him on his cute little daughter which I have no wish to disillusion them about. He takes me into this enormous restaurant called Katz's and inside he points to more signs, one that says *Established 1888* and another with a funny slogan: *Send a salami to your boy in the army*—'That doesn't rhyme!' I giggle, and Peter answers, 'It does if you're from Brooklyn.' The place is packed full of mostly men and Peter says it's not actually a restaurant but a deli, which means that instead of sitting down at a table and ordering your food from a waiter you stand in line at the counter and stare goggle-eyed at all the different rolls and cold cuts and cheeses on display and when your turn comes you tell them what you want and they put it on a plate right in front of your eyes.

So Daddy says, 'Okay, kiddo, now's your chance to make the acquaintance of bagels and lox.' He orders exactly that and the two of us sit down at a little table in a corner and I sink my teeth into this new form of happiness and then he says, 'You were asking me about Jewishness?' and I nod with my mouth crammed full of lox which means smoked salmon and bagels which means a not-sweet doughnut and also cream cheese, and he says 'This is one of the more pleasant sides of being Jewish.'

I swallow my food and glance around at the deli and say, 'You mean everyone in here is Jewish?'

'Pretty much,' he says. 'Apart from a few tourists like yourself. We make a point of being as noisy and active as possible on Sunday morning, when the rest of the city is closed down supposedly for church.'

'But how can you *tell* they're Jewish?'

'Open your ears, kiddo.'

I open my mouth and take another enormous bite of my bagel and lox and say 'Yeah, I heard they were speaking German,' and Daddy instead of telling me not to talk with my mouth full says

'That's not German, Sadie, that's Yiddish,' and I say 'What's Yiddish?' and he says 'It's the language all the Jews in Eastern Europe used to speak and you should drink it in now because this is the last generation of yiddishophones, by the time you start bringing your own kids to Katz's there won't be any left.'

'And what are the more unpleasant sides?' I ask.

'Oh…you've got plenty of time to learn about that,' he says. 'Plenty of time.'

It becomes a Sunday morning custom between the two of us, going down to Houston and Ludlow and having breakfast at Katz's. Daddy lets me taste anything I like and I like everything I taste: dill pickles or pickled green tomatoes, monumental corned beef or smoked tongue or hot pastrami sandwiches, bagels or bialies, salt herring or salami pizza, the whole thing topped off with an apple strudel.

'Ye gods, Peter, you'll spoil her silly!' Mommy says when I tell her what I had for breakfast but Daddy says 'She deserves to be spoiled a bit, after the Spartan upbringing she had back in the Cold Country,' and even though I'm not sure what Spartan means I totally agree.

At last the summer paradise draws to an end and the first day of school is going to be tomorrow. *Are you ready, Sadie?* mutters my Fiend in a threatening tone of voice. *Ready for Second Grade?* but I tell myself it can't possibly be as bad as First Grade was, because I'll be attending a P.S. (which means public school) along with all the children in the neighbourhood, instead of a snotty snobby private girls' school where everyone came by car and wore a uniform, including on their soul.

It goes all right. Under my new identity as Sadie Silbermann I actually talk to some of the kids at P.S. 140 Nathan Straus and realise they think I'm Jewish like most of them are. I tell them I'm from Canada and they hardly even know where that is which is incredible to me so I tell them that Canada is actually *bigger* than the United States which makes them tap their foreheads as if I was crazy so I don't make a big thing out of it, I just shrug and say matter-of-factly: 'In *surface area* it's a little bit bigger but in *population* you guys are ten times as big as we are,' which makes them gape at my knowledgeability but they don't seem to hold it against me. I've got to be careful and figure out how to impress them with my intelligence without getting ostracised for being a goody-goody like last year which was terrible.

I tell Mommy I feel as if I'm walking on eggs and she says 'Yes I know, I went through the same thing because I also learned to read at five' (I forget to ask her who taught her to read—it can't have been Gran or Grandad, that's for sure!). 'The other kids don't like it when someone stands out like that,' she goes on. 'But don't forget, *all of them* are feeling their way around and sounding each other out these days just like you are; none of them is a god, you know what I mean?'

'Yeah,' I say, really happy to finally have someone who will listen to me and take my problems seriously instead of just telling me to make my bed and clear the table all the time.

The other children are quite a long ways behind me in all the subjects so I don't learn much in class, but at recess I learn a lot about the facts of life because I've never been with boys before and now they're all around me and the girls talk about them and I assume they talk about us, too. Not that I was totally innocent up to now, because back in Toronto when I'd go out with Grandad to take Mirth for a walk if we went past a female dog I'd sometimes see his thing come out, red and stiff, and he'd scrabble up on her from behind panting excitedly even if she was thrice as big as he was which was hilarious, once he actually started humping this white toy poodle before Grandad could yank him away with the leash saying 'Come, come, young man, you're in no position to raise a family,' which gave me food for thought because it reminded me of what he'd said about my father Mort.

Plus also in Grandad's medical encyclopaedia I used to see drawings of naked men and women with their breasts and penises hanging down and strange-sounding labels on their private parts like 'urethra' and 'uterus', but now the girls tell jokes about these parts and it's incredible to think it goes on all the time, respectable gentlemen in suits and ties behaving exactly like Mirth, getting all excited and sticking their thing into respectable ladies, and that in fact this is what marriage is all about, married couples do it whether they want to make babies or not which means that Mommy and Peter must do it (at night I sometimes hear them making noises but when I look through the keyhole it's too dark to see what's going on), even Gran and Grandad must have done it at some point or Mommy wouldn't have been born, and every single person in New York City and on this earth is the result of this rubbing and pushing and spurting activity for which the word is *fuck;* it's perfectly incredible and yet true.

At school the boys tease and pester the girls. The first time I get my hair pulled it makes me mad but then I realise it's just a way of being included so I learn to say *'Stop that!'* like the other girls, in a way which actually means the opposite, and I also learn to giggle and sigh and flash my eyes at certain boys so they'll know

I like them. At recess sometimes the boys run after the girls with their arms stretched out saying 'Jew! Jew!' and the girls act as if they're scared, running away from the boys and saying 'Nazi! Nazi!' which is a new word to me. I look it up in the dictionary but I can't understand what it means about a German political party or what it could possibly have to do with P.S.140 so I ask Daddy about it one Sunday morning at Katz's.

'What's a Nazi, Daddy?' I say in a loud clear voice that makes Peter start and turn red as a beet.

'Shhhh,' he says, as a number of heads have turned. (At once my Fiend murmurs *Now you've put your foot in it, Sadie, now you've gone and messed up this friendship the way you always mess up everything.*) Meanwhile Daddy has gotten a hold of himself by drinking the last drops of coffee in his cup and now he says to me in a low voice, winking at the same time, 'The Nazis were the most unpleasant aspect of being Jewish. Let's wait until we get outside…'

Once we're back on Orchard Street amidst the bolts of cloth and the suitcases and leather goods, he asks me where that question came from and I tell him about the game at school and his eyebrows go up above his glasses and make ripples in his brow. Then in a few words he tells me.

'The Nazis were Germans who wanted to wipe the Jews off the face of the earth.'

'But why?'

'Because they were Jews.'

'But *why*, Daddy?'

'Because it's much easier to teach people to be stupid than it is to teach them to be intelligent. For instance, if you tell people that all their problems come from the Jews they feel relieved because that's an easy thing to understand. The truth is *much* too complicated for most people.'

'So you mean they killed them?'

'Yup,' says Peter, going over to the newspaper stand and buying the *Sunday Times* which means we'll soon be heading home, it's always the last thing he buys because it's so heavy.

'How did *you* get away, then?'

He laughs.

'Fortunately,' he says, 'they didn't get around to the Toronto Jews. They got my grandparents in Germany, though.'

'Your *grandparents*?'

He nods. His eyes are darting all over the place looking for an excuse to change the subject so I wham him with three more questions at top speed.

'How did they catch them? How did they kill them? How many in all?'

But Daddy just ruffles my hair and says, 'You shouldn't worry your little noggin about these things, kiddo. They've got nothing to do with you. But…do me a favour…don't play that game at school, all right? When the others start playing it, you find yourself something important to do on the far side of the courtyard. Okay?'

'Okay,' I nod soberly, sincerely, my brain staggering under the burden of what it has just learned.

Meanwhile, as that *Sunday Times* and every other newspaper is telling us this fall, the world is a dangerous place to live because there are now Russian missiles stationed in Cuba and the Cold War might actually get hot again but President Kennedy has decided to be firm about it and not put up with Russia's misbehaviour. At school the teachers keep running us through air raid drills and more and more people are building nuclear shelters in case the Third World War breaks out.

Peter and Mommy refuse to join in the panic; all they do is joke about it. One day they spend our whole dinnertime telling me about how Westinghouse Electrical have sunk a time capsule into the ground beneath solid granite out in Flushing Meadow Park so that it will be perfectly preserved, that way if humanity gets wiped out completely and some extraterrestrials come along a few thousand years down the line and want to learn about the lifestyle of the species that used to inhabit this planet, they can see a typical 1962 apartment with all its furnishings and clothes and household appliances, by the end of the story Peter and Mommy are wiping tears of laughter from their eyes at the idea of these Martians turning on an electric fan and sticking their long green fingers into it to see how it works.

Mommy's record comes out with her new name on it in enormous golden letters—ERRA—and a stunning photo of her with her eyes closed and her mouth open in a song of joy, her hands raised and extended as if she were begging us to share the joy with her. The record company sets up a concert for her and advertises it with posters all over the city.

When I wake up the morning after the concert, she and Peter are still in the kitchen drinking champagne; they've been up all night.

'She brought the house down!' Peter tells me. He picks me up and whirls me around in the air until I'm dizzy and even gives me a sip from his champagne glass because it's really a red-letter day in our lives. Mommy plants a big kiss on my forehead and says 'Hey, my love. This is only the beginning.'

While I'm having breakfast Peter starts teasing Mommy about the way she touches her birthmark every time she starts to sing (he must be tipsy, otherwise he wouldn't dare to tease her).

'What is it, a tuning fork or something?' he asks.

'No, it's a talisman. Sadie's got one, t—' But she stops herself in mid-sentence, having seen my eyes widening in panic.

'What? A birthmark?' says Daddy.

'No, a talisman,' says Mommy nonchalantly. 'A little heart-shaped pebble she's been carrying around with her for…how long now, sweetheart?'

'Uh…three years,' I say, floored by my mother's ability to lie and so blithely make me join her in her lie.

'Three years!' she says to Peter. 'Do you realise? That's almost half her life!'

After breakfast I look up the word talisman in the dictionary and see that it's like a charm, 'anything thought to have magic power,' and I sure wish I had one but I don't.

A few days later Daddy takes the plane to go all the way to California and set up some Erra concerts there, he'll be gone for a whole month. I miss not having him around, especially on Sunday mornings, but it's also nice to have Mommy to myself and sometimes at bedtime she cuddles up with me and we have long conversations in the dark. One night I finally ask her who taught her how to read when she was five and she says 'You know what? The Ice Capades are coming to town, shall we go see the Ice Capades?' and I can hardly believe my ears how blatantly she changed the subject without paying any attention to my question, but I don't have the nerve to repeat it.

It's a Sunday afternoon in December and it's snowing. The whole neighbourhood is like a hush of wonder because the thickly falling snow makes people stay inside and conceals all the garbage and dog poop beneath a soft white coverlet. The streetlamps come on early, at about four o'clock, and I'm standing at my window just looking down at the beauty and silence of Norfolk Street when the doorbell rings.

It rings again and I go into the living room and realise that Mommy is having a bath and can't hear it because of the water running full blast. So I go open the door and a strange man is standing there on the landing who doesn't look anything like Mommy and Daddy's usual friends. He's blond and thin and gaunt and somehow strained, with hollowed cheeks and clenched jaws you can see moving under the skin of his cheeks. He scares me a little. I'm about to tell him he must have gotten the wrong apartment when he says in a strong yet uncertain voice: 'Erra is here?' (He's a foreigner. He rolls his r's.) I don't answer because he might be just some guy who attended her concert the other night and fell in love with her or something, which would be scary to have him come into the apartment with Daddy away in California.

'Erra is here?' he repeats in a louder voice that makes it sound like an emergency. 'Say her…say her it is Lute.'

Now I'm terrified. What should I do? 'Wait,' I say—and I slam the door in his face, leaving him out on the landing. He pounds on the door. I go running into the bathroom where Mommy is now basking in a tub full of bubblebath.

'Mommy!' I say, in such a weird little voice that she turns towards me right away.

'Sadie! What's wrong?'

The steam in the bathroom fills my nose and mouth and for a

minute everything is blotted out, I have no words in my head at all. Then finally, stammeringly—

'There's a man at the door for you. He says his name is Lute.'

'Luke?' says Mommy, frowning. 'I don't know any—'

'No, not Luke. *Lute.*'

Mommy freezes, and even though she's staring straight at me I can feel her going far away from me like the day I told her about getting hit with the ruler. She drops her eyes and says *Lute…*in a low voice I can hardly hear, and I can see her right hand pressing her birthmark as if she were about to sing. 'Lute…I can't believe it…'

'*Who is he*, Mommy?' I whisper. 'Do you know him? He scared me, so I shut the door in his face.'

'Oh, you shouldn't have done that, Sadie,' she says. 'Go tell him to come in and sit down. Tell him I'll be right there.'

I let the man in and say 'Please have a seat' which he doesn't understand so I motion to an armchair and he just barely sits down on the very edge of it and stares at the bathroom door so I go over and stand in the doorway to my bedroom, as far away from him as possible. When Mommy comes out of the bathroom she looks like an apparition in her long black velvet robe, her damp blond hair sticking out in all directions like the Little Prince. The stranger rises to his feet and the two of them stand there motionless with their eyes absolutely glued together, saying nothing.

I've never felt Mommy so far away from me as at this minute, not even in all my years of living apart from her. It's as if she were hypnotised, as if she'd become a different person. Then she whispers a word that sounds like 'Yanek,' whereas the man said his name was Lute. I don't understand what's going on and I don't like it. I clear my throat to make my mother snap out of her trance, come back to her senses and behave normally again ('My, my, my...it's been ages. What a pleasant surprise! Can I get you some tea or something?') But this is not what happens. What happens is that Mommy turns to me in slow motion with her eyes glazed over as if the soul of a dead person had gotten into her body, and murmurs, looking straight through me: 'Sadie...Go into your room, close the door, and don't come out until I tell you to.'

The words are like a slap in the face and I recoil but obey at once, not only closing but even locking my bedroom door so she'll know I'm obeying with a vengeance. Then I get my pillow out of my bed and put it on the floor in front of the door and kneel down on it and take the key out of the lock and peer through the keyhole.

It's as if I were watching a play. Mommy and the stranger stay right where they were for another minute or so without talking, then Mommy takes a few slow steps toward him and he holds out his arms and she walks right into them like a sleepwalker, they close around her and the strange blond man is crushing my mother against his chest and sobbing. Mommy starts crying too and then she starts laughing at the same time but what's more upsetting than anything else is that every word she says is in a language I've never heard her speak before. It could be Yiddish or German, they speak by bits and snatches between crying and laughing and breathing hard and looking at each other.

This goes on for a while and the snow is still falling in the street behind me. Mommy's hand goes up and strokes the blond man's cheekbone and she says something that sounds like 'My Yanek, my Yanek' except that she says *mine* instead of *my* and he murmurs her name too—her real name, not Erra—except that it sounds different in this language they're speaking, it sounds like 'Kristinka.'

He pulls at the dangling end of her belt and the knot comes untied and he slowly opens the black robe revealing her breasts and he kisses her on the neck and her head goes back and his own head moves down to kiss the base of her neck and I can't stop watching, she's saying words to him in this language which they share and which excludes me, now she's unbuttoning his shirt and kissing him on the mouth, now he's gripping her Little Prince head in his hands and then her robe falls to the ground. Now my mother is stark naked with this stranger who still has all his clothes on. She moves to open out the couch into a bed (which is the very same bed she shares with Daddy every night) and meanwhile the man undresses, slowly, until he's all naked too and I see his thing standing up and bobbing around.

He kneels on the bed and to my horror my mother kneels in front of him and bends down and takes his thing into her mouth which makes me so sick that I move away from the keyhole for a while with my heart pounding and just try to calm down by watching the snowflakes floating down in the light of the streetlamp and when I finally go back and get on my knees again my mother has turned her back to him and he's holding her hands tightly behind her back as if to handcuff her and meanwhile going in and out of her from behind, the way Mirth did with the white poodle only slowly very slowly and instead of panting he's moaning foreign words to her in a low voice and she's arching her back and making a deep sound with her throat and the whole thing is just unbearable so I turn my light back on and get into bed, shaking. My Fiend rises up in me stronger than ever before, devastating, almost destroying me, and says *You will let this happen Sadie because you are evil and a liar and your mother is evil and a liar and you have inherited her flaw, I possess you totally and for the rest of your life you will go on sinning just as she does. Never shall I release you, Sadie!* and I begin to shiver and shake in bed. *Get up*, he tells me. *Don't make any noise, you mustn't disturb your whore of a mother, she too is obeying me and must betray her husband to the hilt—to the hilt, do you hear me?—Now pull yourself together, go into your clothes closet and shut the door behind you and bang your head against the wall a hundred times and don't forget to count.*

I obey, shuddering and nauseous at the image of what my mother was doing a moment ago and what she might be doing now, when I've finished banging my head against the wall and come staggering out of the closet I have to pee very badly but Mommy told me to stay in my room so I'm desperate, I look for some sort of container to pee in and all I can find is the mug I use for my coloured crayons so I shake out all the crayons and pull down my pants and underpants and squat over the cup on the floor and try to pee into it but it's hard to aim, the pee gets all over the floor and I sop it up with some Kleenexes but then I don't know what to do with the Kleenexes and this is by far the worst day of my life because I'll never be able to trust my mother again.

Somehow I fall asleep because the next thing I know Mommy is banging on the door saying 'Sadie...Sadie...Supper's ready!' and I quickly put the pillow back on my bed so she won't know I was spying on her. 'How come you locked the door?' she asks when I open it and then she sees the mess of pee-soaked Kleenex on the floor and realises what has happened and says 'Oh my darling I'm so sorry!' but I don't answer her, I just go wash my hands in the bathroom and leave the mess there for her to clean up because it's her fault and I hate her guts.

Over dinner (which is macaroni and cheese) I go on sulking and she doesn't ask me why because she knows. Finally she puts down her fork and says, 'Sadie, you understand a lot for your age but there are some things children can't be expected to understand and I do not owe you an explanation.'

I say nothing so she says, 'Darling please don't be angry.'

I go on eating my macaroni and cheese and let her squirm for the next five minutes but finally I ask her, 'What language were you speaking?'

And she laughs and says, 'We were *trying* to speak German…But it's been so long since either of us used it, we can hardly speak it anymore.'

'Where did you learn *German*?!' I say, dreading her answer without knowing why.

At this she hesitates for quite a while. Then sighs. Then says, 'Oh, Sadie…I used to *be* German…A long, long time ago.'

And, sitting there staring into my eyes but with her own eyes far away, she suddenly reels off a series of strange syllables and I say 'What was that?' and she says with a faint laugh, 'The German alphabet, backwards!'

I don't know what to do with this information, I don't want to ask any more questions, I just want the day to be over I wish it had never begun I wish I hadn't answered the doorbell, I wish Peter hadn't gone to California, I wish the whole thing were a bad dream. And when I go to bed my mind churns for hours, wailing and screaming like the firetruck and ambulance and police car sirens outside: but if Mommy is German that means the Kriswatys aren't her parents which means they're not my grandparents either but it nonetheless remains that she's my mother and if my mother is German that means I'm half German at least—*Now you know where the evil comes from*, says my Fiend, *you've been living a lie since the day you were born*—unless, that is, she's not my mother either…

The next day at recess a boy runs after me saying 'Jew! Jew!' but since I promised Peter not to play this game I run as fast as I can and trip and fall and skin my knee and have to go to the infirmary, and when the nurse rolls down my stocking there's blood on my knee and I can hear my Fiend cackling with glee and saying *German blood, Sadie! Nazi blood!*

IV

Kristina, 1944-45

A scattering of ecstasies.

Amaze me, I say to the world.

Whirl me, thrill me, stun me, never stop.

Grandma's jewellery box: the key is on the bottom, you have to be careful to keep the lid closed when you turn the box upside down and wind it up and then when you set it back down and open the lid, tinkling music starts to play and an exquisite gold and white ballerina twirls round and round in front of a tiny mirror, one arm raised in a curve and the other held out in a curve in front of her. The ballerina isn't alive but she moves. 'Real ballerinas can spin as much as fifty times on tiptoe,' says Grandma, 'they keep their balance by looking straight in front of them every time they spin back to face the audience, try it Kristina' so I try it, though not on tiptoe, whirling and whirling with my arms stretched out till I'm gorgeously dizzy and fall to the floor, loving it, and Grandma laughs and says 'I guess you need a few lessons, sweetheart.'

The ballerina watches over Grandma's jewellery, it's all perfectly arranged in drawers lined with red velvet, sparkling necklaces and bracelets in the bottom drawer, glittering rings and earrings in the top. Grandma teaches me how to tell the difference between diamonds and rhinestones, diamonds have more colours in them when you hold them up to the light. Sometimes she lets me put on her diamond tiara and look at myself in the mirror, I blur my vision by lowering my eyelashes and for a moment I look as beautiful as a princess.

Grandpa brings home two little windmills, one for Greta one for me, their vanes all different colours, when you run with them they spin and the faster you run the faster they spin and if you run into the wind they spin so fast the colours blur, sometimes I think so fast my brain blurs, too.

The merry-go-round in the schoolyard is covered with snow in the wintertime but in the summer I can sit on it and Greta will push me, running along with it at first until she can't keep up, then standing still and shoving the bars as they go by to give them extra impetus, I'm hanging on to the centre pole for dear life and to keep from getting dizzy I look at Greta every time I come around, just as ballerinas look at the audience. Greta pushes me on the swings, too—higher and higher until I'm kicking the clouds and the wind is whistling in my ears, I put my head way back and watch the world whoosh at me upside down and my nose almost grazes the ground. Then I learn to gain impetus all by myself, sitting down, standing up, but it's better when Greta does it because I don't have to make an effort, I can just sit back and let it happen.

The schoolyard is the same thing as the courtyard because the school is the same thing as the house because Papa is a teacher when he isn't a soldier which he's been for so long now I can hardly remember him, but we still get to live in the school which is a lucky thing for us says Mama because we can wake up later than the other pupils and not have to walk to school through driving wind and snow or pouring rain or scorching sunlight, just whisk across the courtyard at the last minute and walk into class and say 'Heil Hitler.'

I haven't started school yet.

The tramway tracks make patterns in my brain as they flick past, they're not moving I tell myself, you're the one who's moving, but they enter my eyes and move and flash there like an endless silver ladder.

There's a clock tower next to the town hall and sometimes if we're out shopping for vegetables and it gets to be twelve o'clock Mama takes me there especially, because when the clock strikes noon a set of doors opens in the tower and a dozen painted wooden figures come sliding out, bowing and nodding, raising and lowering their arms and legs, their movements are human movements only jerkier and the expression on their faces is unchanging. They're not alive.

Greta and I beg Mama to let us ride on the carousel in the park, pleading cajoling and insisting until she relents although we can't afford it she says. I'm on a black horse, Greta's on a white one in front of me, my thighs squeeze the horse's huge hard body and my hands squeeze the pommel, the horse isn't alive and I am but it is making me move, up and down slowly, round and round as the platform revolves, it's dark out, the carousel is lit up, the loud piping music fills me to overflowing, we're moving with no effort and I can feel myself beginning to mingle with the high notes and the blinking lights and I wish it would never stop.

Music is movement invisible.

Grandpa is teaching me to sing harmony so that the Christmas carols will be even more beautiful than usual this year, he says I have the best voice in the family and I think he likes me better than Greta because of it. He's taught me so much and his head is full of knowledge because he went to the university when he was young and so did Papa. When I was little he taught me the difference between left and right. He crouched down facing me and said 'Look, Kristina—this is your left hand and this is your right, this is *my* left hand and this is *my* right' and I said 'So it's different for boys and girls?' and he burst out laughing. Then he started his explanation all over again crouching next to me instead of across from me.

When I look in the mirror and touch my left eye the Kristina in the mirror touches her right eye but it's still me.

Grandpa and I take a nap together every afternoon but I don't sleep, I lie there in the darkened bedroom looking at the stabs of sunlight coming through tiny holes in the blinds and trying to make a pattern out of them. When Grandpa starts to snore I push him gently on the shoulder and say 'Kurt' and he stops, it feels weird to call my grandfather by his first name but Grandma says that's the only thing that works and she's right, if I say 'Grandpa' he goes right on snoring with his mouth open and hairs in his nose.

I lie there thinking and stroking my birthmark, a perfectly

round spot the size of a penny at the crook of my left elbow, golden brown and slightly raised, my skin there is fuzzy like the skin of a peach and I love to stroke it. When no one is looking I bend and unbend my arm, very slowly, to watch the spot disappear and reappear.

'Did I ever tell you the story of the juniper bush?' says Grandpa after dinner and we all gather together around the wood stove and I curl up on Mama's lap in the armchair, the story is about a wicked stepmother who tells her stepson to help himself to an apple and while he's bending over the box of apples she slams the lid so hard that his head falls off and rolls amongst the apples and later on she chops him up and makes him into a stew, which his father finds delicious without knowing what he's eating, he sucks on the bones and tosses them under the table as he goes along but his sister gathers them up and everything turns out fine in the end. My favourite place in the world to be is on Mama's lap with my left thumb in my mouth, my right thumb stroking my birthmark and Grandpa telling the whole family a fairy tale.

Grandma says I shouldn't suck my thumb, she reads me the poem in *Struwwelpeter* about Conrad who was such a suck-a-thumb that finally the Great Tall Long-Legged Scissor-Man came in and cut off both his thumbs. His mother had *warned* him they wouldn't grow back again. When she comes home, he stands there and holds up his hands and they've only got four fingers each.

Grandpa has two fingers missing on his left hand from when he was in a different war when he was young but that doesn't stop him from playing the piano.

Fingers don't grow back.

Hair grows back, fingernails and toenails grow back, even in dead men they keep on growing, Grandpa says that hair and nails are dead cells that get pushed out of your body by living cells, all the dead parts of your body grow back but not the living parts, which is strange when you think about it. Eyes don't grow back but if you lose one you can have it replaced by a glass eye or else you can wear a patch. Teeth grow back but *only once,* if you get them knocked out a second time you're left with a hole forever. My brother Lothar got into a fistfight after a youth group meeting once and somebody punched him in the mouth and knocked one of his front teeth loose, there was a lot of blood but *fortunately* the tooth didn't fall out and the dentist could make it stick.

I've lost seven baby teeth so far.

Salamanders' tails grow back. I'm not sure exactly how *much* of them you can cut off, how high you can go without hitting a vital organ, I should ask Grandpa about that. I love salamanders—they can live in fire! Grandpa showed me how when you light a candle it's hotter just *above* the flame than *in* it. You can pass your hand through the flame without feeling any pain whereas if you hold your hand over it even for an instant it burns you.

At the circus people on horseback go leaping through hoops of fire. I've never seen a circus but Mama has told me about the acrobats and trapeze artists performing feats that make the audience gasp. Grandpa says that when you gasp it's because you've seen something shocking or dangerous and your body thinks you might be needing some extra oxygen to face up to an emergency so it draws a lot of air into your lungs really fast.

My dream for the future is to be the Fat Lady in the circus but just now there's a food shortage because we're losing the war so I can't even get started putting fat on my bones.

Everything you eat gets turned into your own body except the waste which comes out the other end, I don't know why they can't take the waste out of the food before we eat it so we wouldn't have to go to the bathroom all the time. When you think about it, says Grandpa, it's pretty amazing that cows turn grass into beef and we turn beef and carrots and potatoes and candies and apples into human bodies. We haven't had any beef in ages. The more you eat the more you grow and when you stop growing upwards you start growing outwards, says Grandpa who has a big belly. In the *Struwwelpeter* book, Augustus gets thinner and thinner and then he dies because he doesn't eat his soup and they put a cross on his grave.

Lothar is wearing a uniform because his turn has come to go to war even despite the fact that we've already lost France and England, every single man between sixteen and sixty has to go, luckily Grandpa is sixty-two or we wouldn't have any men at all in the house. Lothar kisses me and tosses me in the air, for an instant nothing is holding me and my heart goes flipflop, then he catches me in his arms and hugs me so hard the metal buttons dig into my chest and I squirm to get away, the hug is squeezing the air out of me plus my dress flew up when he tossed me and I'm afraid people can see my underpants. Finally he releases me saying 'Good-bye sweet Kristina' and I glance at Greta to see if she's jealous because after hugging her he didn't say 'Good-bye sweet Greta,' he didn't toss her in the air either because she's getting too big to pick up—but she's just standing there saying 'Lothar, don't go! Don't go, Lothar!' with tears and snot running down her face. Then Lothar turns around and as he walks towards the door the back of his uniform is a perfect rectangle.

Greta is prettier than I am but she's not as interesting and I think Grandpa likes me better because Greta sings off-key. Her skin is all white all over, she doesn't have a birthmark on her left arm and she doesn't get freckles in the summertime the way I do. Freckles make my face more interesting and they protect it from the sunlight. There's something blank about Greta, her personality is blank and flat like a placid lake whereas I am a volcano, I burn and smoulder deep down and when I sing it's like the lava overflowing. The two of us share a room, our beds are end to end and in the dresser drawers her clothes are on the right side and mine are on the left, she spends a lot of time fussing with her hair which is light brown and wavy whereas mine is blond and straight and I just brush it and have done with it, there are more important things in life. At night I lie awake thinking about a million ideas whereas Greta goes right to sleep and sleeps all night like a placid blank lake.

Grandpa grew up in Dresden and all of our china comes from his father's factory there, he says Dresden is the most beautiful city in the world because of its statues, he's got a whole album full of postcards of the city and sometimes for a treat he takes the album down and we pore over them together. He shows me stone men riding stone horses, stone angels lighted on cathedral doors, stone dolphins and mermaids on park fountains, stone wise men meting out justice on courthouse pediments, stone masks on the façade of the theatre and opera house, stone Negro slaves holding up balconies, staircases, and windowframes at the Zwinger palace, their muscles straining and their faces clenched with the effort but he says they're not really suffering because they're not alive, there's also a Pan which means half man half goat, and a centaur which means half man half horse, and twelve beautiful young women in niches surrounding a bath, all of them smiling as they unwind their clothing and reveal their bodies. Grandpa says they're called nymphs and they're allowed to take their clothes off in public because they don't really exist, they're just things people make up in their dreams. Same goes for the dozens of baby heads on the columns in the Zwinger gardens—they're just imaginary, the babies didn't get their heads cut off, you can imagine anything you want. None of this is moving but the idea of movement has been caught in stone, the wind raises stone rills in the horses' manes and the mermaids seem to rise up, their naked breasts streaming with stone water.

The people walking around in our city are alive and ugly compared to the nymphs and angels of Dresden, they look hurried and worried and especially hungry and they're not allowed take their clothes off in public, there are lots of men with an arm or a leg missing, sometimes both arms or both legs, arms and legs don't grow back again of course.

Papa comes homes on leave and I feel shy because I can hardly recognise him it's been so long. After kissing Mama and hugging Greta he picks me up under the armpits and whirls me, moving just his feet and making me go around and around in circles with his body standing straight in the middle like a maypole. 'Stop it Dieter' says Mama 'you'll make her sick' but she says it laughingly, not scoldingly, not once have I gotten sick.

He goes away again. Like all German men these days he has to try to kill as many Russians as he can, even despite the fact that we're losing the war and that Jesus said *Thou shalt not kill,* or maybe it was Moses. Grandpa says that sometimes you have no choice, you just have to kill or be killed, that's all there is to it. It bothers me when during grace he asks God to protect Papa and Lothar from the enemy because there must be families in Russia asking God to protect *their* men from the enemy, too, only when they say the enemy they mean us, and in church when the priest tells us to pray for Hitler I think how people in Russian churches must be praying for *their* Guide, and I can just imagine poor God sitting up there in the clouds and seizing His head in both hands and trying to figure out how to make everyone happy and realising that *unfortunately* it's just not possible.

On Wednesdays and Saturdays Greta and I have a bath together, she washes my hair because she's the older sister, she's supposed to know how to do it without getting soap in my eyes but sometimes soap gets into my eyes anyway and it stings and I'm sure she did it on purpose but she says she's sorry so I can't tell on her. Our favourite game in the tub is one we invented called Heil Hitler where you stand up and say 'Heil Hitler' in a funny voice, like the voice of a ghost or a madman or a clown or a snobbish lady, or else you get mixed up in the salute and raise your elbow instead of your arm, or you put one thumb on your nose and the other thumb on your pinky and wiggle all your fingers and say 'Heil Hitler,' but once I went too far and instead of raising my arm I raised my leg and just as I was saying 'Heil Hitler' I slipped in the tub and fell and banged my head on the edge so hard that I had to scream I couldn't help it, Mama came rushing in and when she saw me crying and Greta looking scared she gave Greta a terrible whack across the head without even asking what had happened and it was a long time before Greta forgave me and agreed to play Heil Hitler again.

We know it's not really a laughing matter because last year Lothar ran into our neighbour Mrs Webern in the hallway, and when he raised his arm and said 'Heil Hitler' she didn't answer so Lothar denounced her to the police and they came and arrested her. Already her husband had been taken away at the beginning of the war and now their children had to fend for themselves with the older ones looking after the younger. Mrs Webern was gone for three whole weeks and when she came back she said 'Heil Hitler' again just like everybody else.

We go to church every Sunday morning, all clean from our Saturday night baths and dressed up in our best clothes because it's the house of God, women have to cover their heads and men have to uncover theirs, it's not like left and right it really is a difference between boys and girls. When you walk into church you have to dip your fingertips into the holy water and make the sign of the cross and say 'In the name of the Father, the Son and the Holy Ghost,' which is not a scary kind of ghost but a sort of invisible spirit. I'm not sure what all three of them are doing on the sign of the cross since only Jesus died there. In church the prayers and sermons bore me so I take my revenge with the hymns, my voice is crystal clear and unwavering, it stands out among all the voices of the congregation, soaring up and flying through the steeple all the way to God in the clouds.

'Where is God, Grandpa?'

'God is everywhere, little one.'

'But if He's everywhere, what does He need a house for?'

Grandpa laughs and laughs, he repeats my question to Grandma and then to Mama, but he doesn't answer it.

'Is Jesus a magician, Grandpa?'

'A magician? Why?'

'Because he turned water into wine at the wedding in Cana.'

'No, that wasn't a trick, that was a miracle.'

'What's the difference?'

'Magic is based on illusion, Kristina. A magician could have changed the water from clear to red but it would still have tasted like water. A miracle is the real thing. At the wedding in Cana, the water *really* turned into wine that tasted like wine.'

'But when you take Communion?'

'Yes…?'

'Communion is a miracle, right?'

'Yes…?'

'So does the wine *really* turn into blood that tastes like blood?'

'Did God make everything, Grandpa?'

'Yes, Kristina, He made everything in the world.'

'Did He make war, then?'

'No, He made men…and men make war…and He wishes they wouldn't. They disappoint him.'

'But if He can do anything he wants, why didn't He make men the way He wanted them?'

So many of my questions go unanswered. When I grow up, in addition to being the Fat Lady in the circus and a famous singer, I'll read all the books in the world and put their knowledge together in my head so that when my children and grandchildren ask me questions I can always answer them.

We're not allowed to use electric lights in the evening because they could make us a target for the enemy planes that are trying to bomb us, not the same enemies as Papa and Lothar are fighting, Grandpa told me—not the Russians but the British and the Americans. 'The whole world is ganging up on Germany,' he said, 'is that fair? Imagine, my little Kristina, if you went out to the playground and all the other children ganged up on you and beat you up, would that be fair?' Almost every night now, a siren goes off and everyone in the building has to rush down and wait in the potato cellar to see if the enemy planes are going to see us and drop a bomb on us. Luckily our town is quite small and not an important target for the bombs. Sometimes at night the sky is red with the other cities burning nearby.

I make up a song where I use my voice to imitate everything that rings.

> *On Sundays church bells—ding, dong—time to pray.*
> *On weekdays school bells—dring, dring—time to learn.*
> *At night the sirens—rrr, rrrrr—time to die.*

Helga the maid overhears me singing it and tells me it isn't funny.

The summer ends and I begin school at last. Mama gives me a shiny paper cone with apples and candies and a pencilbox in it to sweeten my first day of school, and I get my own notebooks and a black slate and chalk and rulers and a leather satchel. Since all the teachers are away killing Russians these days, they've been replaced by smart young unmarried women or widows or old men who still remember about school. Our teacher is a woman, she's strict and efficient and it doesn't take her long to see I'm bright; in the first month of school she gives me a gold star for spelling, another one for arithmetic and another one for needle-work. There are three levels in the classroom and when I finish the first grade work I listen in on what the second and third grades are doing and I learn that, too. I'll go zooming past Greta the way the hare zooms past the tortoise; she'll glance up with a startled look on her face and all she'll see is dust. I wish I could learn everything at once instead of little by little. Like gulping down everything on the table and becoming the Fat Lady in the circus.

Now that I can read for myself, I learn all the poems in *Struwwelpeter* off by heart. The little girl who plays with matches and sets fire to her house and gets burned to death. Augustus who refuses to eat his soup for no good reason and starves to death. Especially Conrad who gets his thumbs cut off. I recite the poems over and over again, I invent tunes for them and sing them to myself, it puts me in a trance.

At recess I play Halt with the other girls in my class, I toss the ball up in the air as high as I can and meanwhile they scatter in all directions but the minute I catch the ball I shout 'Halt' and they have to freeze on the spot, they're not allowed to take one more step. I look around to see which one is closest and throw the ball at her, if it hits her she's out which means it's her turn to toss up the ball but if it misses her I don't mind because what I like best is the moment when I say 'Halt!' and look up and see everyone motionless, frozen in mid-gesture like the statues in the Zwinger gardens *stay still sit still stand still I'll teach you to keep still!*

Waking up, the words come to me like a live voice: *Six Years Old.* I gasp for joy and run downstairs, everyone says 'Happy birthday,

Kristina! Happy birthday,' hugging and kissing me. Mama has bought a pork bone with lots of fat on it to celebrate and when Greta and I get home from school at noon I see the pork bone lying on a newspaper on the kitchen table so while Mama's back is turned cooking the lentils I sneak up and grab it and sink my teeth into the fat, it's excruciatingly delicious but Mama whirls around and says 'Hey what are you doing? That's for the whole family and it's not even cooked yet! You'll make yourself sick, eating raw fat!' and I just laugh and run around to the other side of the table with the big bone in my mouth like a dog and she runs after me in her apron and I duck under the table and she bends down and catches my foot and I'm giggling on the floor with the pork bone in my mouth when the doorbell rings and Mama goes to answer it and I chew on the pork bone, wishing I could eat the whole thing but knowing that would make Mama seriously angry and I hear a man's voice and Mama doesn't answer him and there's a crash.

Gingerly, I set the bone back on the table. Grandma and Grandpa are rushing into the hallway from the living room and at the same time Greta and Helga the maid are running downstairs, the crash was Mama fainting on the floor. A messenger in uniform is kneeling next to her and Grandpa bends down to take the telegram out of her hand and straightens up slowly, reading it, and says in a hoarse whisper, 'Lothar is dead.' Then he and the messenger carry Mama to the living room couch and Helga brings a bowl of water and dips a cloth into it and presses it to Mama's forehead. Mama starts to moan and Grandma is crying and Greta is silent and Helga the maid is wringing her hands and now I think everybody is going to forget about my birthday because it's Lothar's deathday and for the rest of my life my birthday will be a sad occasion for the whole family but then I think no, it's not his deathday, he must have died a few days ago, it takes time for news to travel.

My brother is dead. I didn't know him well, he was too old, seventeen, and even before he went off to war he was away at youth group meetings all the time. My brother is dead and do I feel sad? I don't know.

Everything gets cancelled.

Sadness in the house. Mama's red eyes and black dresses. Grandma's motionlessness. Grandpa locking himself in his bedroom and listening to the radio. At school the teacher tells Greta to stand up in front of the class and say how proud she is that her brother gave his life for the Guide, she does it but her voice is trembly and tears glitter in the corners of her eyes and it doesn't sound like she means it.

'Can I play with your jewellery box, Grandma?'

'Leave me, Kristina, leave me.'

Will we manage to celebrate Christmas this year? I want to watch very closely and see if I can figure out what happens, I'm not sure if it's a miracle or a trick.

All of us gather together in the living room on Christmas Eve as night begins to fall and Mama doesn't light the fire in the big tiled stove, she only lights the snow-white candles on the Christmas tree. Grandpa sits down at the piano and now is the time to show the others how I've learned to sing harmony. We stand in a semi-circle around the tree and sing one carol after another, my voice is stronger and sweeter than anyone else's, I can feel it swelling in my chest and pouring out of my mouth exactly right, *Jingle bells, jingle bells, jingle all the way*, Greta sings off-key and sometimes I wish she'd just be content with mouthing the words, she spoils the beauty hitting wrong notes all the time and besides she gets the verses mixed up, launching into the third verse whereas we haven't sung the second one yet, she doesn't care about getting it right, I do, I know every word of every carol including the one Hitler likes about mothers—*Deep within your hearts beats the heart of a new world*—and as I sing these words I look up at Mama and shine my eyes at her so she won't be sad about Lothar being dead and Papa not being with us, she pats me on the head and I can tell she's proud of me, I want her to be proud to bursting.

Night seeps and creeps into the room as we sing, the candles on the Christmas tree seem to burn more brightly, the silver tinsel and coloured balls catch their light and glimmer in a heavenly way, Helga's white apron gleams and so does Grandpa's white hair. Grandpa knows the pieces off by heart so his fingers go on playing in the shadows without making a single mistake even if two of them are missing.

When we get to 'Silent Night' which is always the last carol, we sing it more and more softly with every verse, more and more softly so that the last words *heavenly peace* are like a whisper in the air, and then Grandma says 'Sssshhhhh' and everyone falls silent. I can hear the big clock ticking in the room and feel my heart thumping in my chest. When my heart stops beating I'll be dead. The pendulum isn't alive but it moves, swinging calmly back and forth, sometimes it stops but that doesn't mean it's dead it just means Grandpa forgot to wind it. Even if the clock gets broken some day and we can't fix it we won't say it's dead, we won't put it in a coffin and bury it, we'll just say it's useless and throw it away and get another one.

If your heart gets broken, that's just a manner of speaking.

At last Grandpa says a prayer to God in a low voice, thanking Him for the greatest Christmas gift of all, the gift of his son Jesus Christ—*Christ* and *Kristina* are the same word, it means anointed, they put anointment on you and you're blessed for your entire life long—'and now,' Grandpa says, 'You have called our Lothar to be at Your side just as You called Your own son Jesus,' but then his voice cracks and he can't go on, Mama stifles a sob, finally Grandpa's voice says 'Amen' which means So be it and everyone repeats 'Amen' in a soft echo and the silence returns and then the clock begins to chime. I count the seven chimes, wondering if it was seven o'clock at the beginning of the first one or at the end of the last one or exactly in the middle, halfway between the third and the fourth.

Nodding at Helga the maid, Grandma says, *'Now!'*

In a swift rustle, Helga crosses through the darkness to the double doors and slides them open—lo, lo, lo and behold! Yes, it has happened again! *How can it be?* We were all here, all of us, gathered together, no one was missing except for Papa who is off killing Russians *miles* away, and even as we were singing Christmas carols in the living room, the dining room table *set itself*. Oh, oh, oh, oh, white linen cloth fluttered across the room and spread itself gently over the table, Mama's best silverware and the plates from Dresden danced out of the cupboards and lined up along both sides, crystal glasses flew down from the buffet to stand at attention at the tip of each knife, and the Advent wreath with its four red candles burning floated over to serve as a centrepiece. Oh, oh—I cannot stop saying it—how did this happen? I look at Mama.

'Did you tell a neighbour to come and do this?' I ask her.

'Me?' she says, flushing. 'A neighbour? No, of course not.'

She's not allowed to lie so how did it happen? Every year the same mystery and I can't get to the bottom of it. Is it a miracle or a trick?

The meal is over, the spice cookies and Christmas bread weren't very good because the eggs were missing, Greta and I are sitting on the living room rug with our gifts in our laps and Mama is in the armchair, watching us and trying to smile.

'Hopefully more than one next year,' she says.

'That's what you said last year,' says Greta.

A W of pain appears between Mama's eyebrows but she erases it at once. She doesn't scold Greta for being selfish, doesn't say Greta do you realise your brother is dead and your country is at war.

'Go ahead and open your gifts, my darlings,' is all she says, but her voice is husky and I can tell she's worrying about Papa, she's already lost her son is she going to lose her husband too, lots of neighbours have lost both sons and husbands, *where is my beloved Dieter this Christmas morning*?

'Maybe Papa will be here next year too,' I say to comfort her, and she pats my hand.

'Go ahead, my darlings,' she repeats.

We seize the gifts and rip and tear—there is no tape, the wrapping paper is plain newspaper, in a matter of seconds my nimble fingers have the string off, the paper off, the box open, I look down and catch a glimpse of yellow fur and glinting metal, but before I even understand what it is Greta lets out a squeal of joy and my gaze snaps up and over to where she is sitting, holding up—a doll.

I freeze.

What can I say? There's been a mistake. Mama got the presents mixed up, the doll was meant for me and the—the, whatever it is—stuffed animal for Greta, why doesn't she say so right this minute, why doesn't she say Oh my goodness how silly of me, Greta! That's Kristina's doll and the teddy bear is for you, my darling.

The doll is mine and I know it. She's wearing a red velvet dress with white lace collar and cuffs, she has long brown hair, pink cheeks, pursed ruby lips and dark blue eyes that can actually (as Greta shows me from a distance) open and shut. When you hold her up straight she looks at you with her eyes wide open but when you lay her down the lids gently close and the lashes brush her cheeks and she seems to have drifted off to the sweetest of dreams. I love her. I even know her name, which is Annabella. She's *mine*. I have to turn my muscles to steel to keep from leaping across the room and wrenching my doll out of Greta's hands. Now Mama is saying 'What about you, Kristina? What did Father Christmas bring you?' and still I sit there stunned, not knowing how ever to be happy again. I don't care what's in my box, I only urgently burningly want to hold and hug and cherish and love forever beautiful Annabella in her red velvet dress. Greta is rocking her and singing to her now, off-key as usual, I see my white numb fingers slip beneath the furry thing and pull it out. A bear with a pair of cymbals in its paws. 'Oh, Kristina,' says Greta hypocritically, 'isn't that cute!' and I want to push her to the floor and capture Annabella and go flying out the window with her like Peter Pan with Wendy.

'Did you see, darling?' says Mama. 'There's a little key in its back, you can wind it up…Here, let me help you!'

Crouching down next to me she grasps the bear in her left hand

and twists the key with her right, once, twice, thrice, then sets the bear on the rug. It clashes its cymbals together, takes two steps forward and falls flat on its face.

'Hm,' says Mama, laughing. 'It doesn't seem to like the rug, let's try the table. Come, Kristina, look!'

And I force myself to look at the stupid bear clashing its stupid cymbals and jerking its legs forward. Left, right, left, right. The bear moves like a soldier but it's not alive. Soldiers move like robots and robots aren't alive but soldiers are—at least until, like Lothar, they get shot or stabbed through the heart or the brain or else blown up by a bomb or a hand grenade, then they stop moving forever and you put them in a coffin in a hole in the ground and no one ever sees them again because they've gone to heaven. I look at Mama, she's watching the bear and saying 'Left, right' and clapping in time with its movements, when it gets to the edge of the table she says 'About—face!' and turns it around and starts it marching in the other direction. Then its paces slow down and so do her words…'Left…right…' Halfway across the table the bear stops. It has wound down, ground to a halt, just like the clock when Grandpa forgets to wind it. Mama looks at me, her face bright with pride at having found such a wonderful gift for me. 'Now you wind it up, Kristina,' she says, and I want to die.

Greta has given Annabella another name, a name so ridiculous that I refuse to pronounce it. Every morning she leaves the doll sitting up straight on her bedcushion with its hands clasped demurely on its skirt. She's told me not to touch it, but every time she goes out to play with her friends I touch it and more than touch it, I talk and sing to it, pouring my heart into its heart.

I'm careful to put Annabella back on Greta's bedcushion exactly as I found her, sitting upright with her velvet dress spread out around her and her hands in her lap.

Grandma gives a shriek that makes my blood run cold, I know that's not really true, human beings are warm-blooded which means that their blood stays the same temperature no matter what, even in a horrendously cold winter like this one, the blood of the German soldiers is warm, at least until somebody shoots them and it starts spurting out of their chests, then it probably makes red icicles in the snow, so when Grandma shrieks my blood doesn't run cold but it does something very peculiar, I can feel it in my neck and wrists, and Mama calls—'*Kristina! Come quickly!*'—and I run downstairs so fast that I can't feel the separate steps under my feet.

They were doing the laundry and the vat tipped over, splashing boiling water and lye onto both of Grandma's hands. She's not shrieking anymore but she's whimpering like a puppy, rocking back and forth on a straight-backed chair and trying to cradle her scalded hands with her scalded hands. Mama is standing next to her looking overwhelmed, she's brought out ointments and bandages but doesn't dare to use them. 'Go get the doctor, Kristina,' she says without looking at me. 'Run, darling! Run as fast as you can!'

When you get a burn like that your skin puffs up into blisters that fill with pus, if you pop them the pus pours out and it hurts horribly but after a while a fresh new layer of skin comes to replace the old damaged one and the incredible thing is, Grandpa told me, that your lines and spots come back in all the same places, so criminals can't get ever rid of their fingerprints, not even by burning their fingertips on purpose.

The doctor is still bandaging Grandma's hands when another shrieking begins, upstairs.

Greta. Oh, no.

I left Annabella where I was playing with her—on my bed—and Greta has found her there. She doesn't even bother looking at me as she bursts into the kitchen, she just goes straight up to Mama and tells on me. And Mama, now grating potatoes for lunch with her mind still on Grandma's burned hands, says 'But Greta, you can share the doll with Kristina, can't you?' And Greta says 'No I can't, I don't want her grubby little fingers on that doll, she's *my private property!*' So Mama says 'Well if that's how you feel…Kristina darling, you have toys of your own and you mustn't touch Greta's things without asking.'

I feel desperate. I betrayed Annabella by leaving her on my bed; she must have tried with all her might to climb up over my bedstead and slide down Greta's but she just couldn't make it. And now the secret has been revealed. Now Greta knows I love her doll and that knowledge gives her power over me and I feel desperate.

After bedtime prayers, I lie on my stomach and start sobbing into my pillow, very softly so that Greta won't hear me. Suddenly Greta gets to her knees, sticks her head up over the bedstead and hisses something at me. I stop sobbing and prick up my ears which is a manner of speaking, only dogs and foxes really prick up their ears, she hisses again. It's a sister's hissing, a hissing about sisters, the sound it makes is like the iron when Mama presses it onto a damp cloth—here are the sizzling hot words that sink slowly into my brain and leave their burning imprint there: 'Anyway, you're not my sister.'

I hold my breath and say nothing.

'Did you hear me, Kristina? You're not my sister.'

What does she mean? That she disowns me? That she doesn't want to think of me as her sister anymore, doesn't want to be part of the same family as me?

The hissing goes on, each word singeing more deeply than the last.

'Mama and Papa aren't your parents. Grandma and Grandpa aren't your grandparents. None of us are any relation to you. You didn't come out of Mama's tummy the way Lothar and I did, you've got another mother somewhere but she didn't want you. You're *adopted*. I remember when they first brought you here. I was four years old and you were one and a half. It's a secret, I wasn't ever supposed to tell you, but you've been so hateful to me that I've got no choice. I'm not your sister. I have nothing to do with you. I wish you'd go back where you came from and I'd never have to see you again.'

She whams her body back down onto her bed, making the mattress springs squeak, and then a large new silence settles over the room. I'm lying on my back now, looking up at the high dark rectangles of the window curtains, my thoughts darting around in all directions to get away from what Greta just said. I push up my pyjama sleeve and stroke my birthmark gently in the dark, over and over again, until I fall asleep.

The next morning Greta wakes me with a kiss on the forehead.

'Breakfast is ready, Kristina,' she says lightly—and when I scramble out of bed she adds, 'Forget about what I said last night. I just made the whole thing up because I was mad at you for playing with my doll. I'm sorry if I hurt your feelings. Let's be friends again, all right? Listen…' I can tell that the effort she's making to be nice is almost killing her… 'I just don't want you to play with…' and she pronounces the ridiculous name she's given the doll…'because you're too little and you might get her collar dirty or break her eyes. But if you promise not to tell Mama what I said last night, I'll teach you everything I learn in school. Okay? Have we got an agreement?'

My head is a heavy boulder, I let it move up and down *once,* and stop; its balance is so precarious I fear it will roll off my shoulders and fall to the floor.

I spend the day in a daze. Mama asks me to help her fold the sheets, a chore I usually enjoy, each of us pinches two corners, my arms stretched out as far as they can go, we back away from each other until the sheet is taut, shake the sheet once, then bring the corners together, pick up the half sheet at the fold…But I feel like one of the automatons in the clock tower, as if I were made of wood and hooked up to some mechanism of whirring chains and springs, I keep the same expression on my face and just go through the motions, I can't talk.

'My, my little Kristina is quiet today,' says Mama when we've finished with the sheets. 'Are you still sad about the doll, dear?'

I nod and she sits down on a chair, lifts me onto her lap and folds me to her, I can feel the soft skin of her arms and the round-ness of her bosom beneath her housedress, and as she cuddles me I slip one thumb into my mouth and stroke my birthmark with the other, now I should feel happy except that Greta says this person isn't my mother and if she isn't my mother who is she and what am I doing here.

I go outside and stand by a snowbank, stiff as a soldier, and let myself fall face forward as if I'd been shot in the back, then lie there without moving until the snow begins to burn, the very-cold turns very-hot, and when by mistake you put your foot in the tub with all hot water it's the other way around, the shock feels icy cold at first. I turn and sit up in the snowbank, scoop up a handful of snow in my bare hands and rub it into my eyes until they sting.

Greta keeps her promise. As soon as the twelve days of Christmas are over and school starts up again she shares her homework with me, guides my hand to help it form cursive letters, instructs me in the heroic deeds of our Teutonic past, drills me in fractions and percentages. I gobble up her knowledge, digest it, shoot the answers back at her. The knowledge takes up room in my brain but still I can't forget what she said that night. And I promised. Even if I gave only the slightest of nods, it made the promise as solemn as a treaty—not the one with Russia, the one with Italy and Japan—a nod means yes and yes is a word and my word is my promise and I'm not allowed to say anything to Mama.

Grandpa? Grandma? I look at them, hesitate, reject the idea. Both of them are still grief-stricken at the loss of their grandson and I don't want to cause them further pain.

Looking at them, however, I gradually begin to *look* at them. And at Mama. And at Greta. I scrutinise their features one by one. After dinner I lock myself in the bathroom and confront the mirror. *Kristina*...how can I tell? My hair is blond, Mama's is light brown and so is Greta's but that proves nothing, Lothar's was blond. Papa's is dark blond, his eyes are green and mine are blue but so are Grandma's. Forget about eyes and hair. Why am I the only one in the family with a snub nose? Why is Greta's forehead higher than mine?

I go on like this for hours.

I start having bad dreams at night. In one of my dreams I'm sitting on the potty and a woman in white shoes and a white skirt walks past me and hits me so hard that I fall off, the potty gets knocked over, I fall into the pee, a boy points at me and screams with laughter as I sit there in the middle of the yellow puddle, other children mill about with no clothes on, whining and bawling, their noses running, dragging their blankets through the pee on the floor.

In another dream I climb up on a chair and look outside and see a trembling whimpering blue-skinned baby lying naked in the snow, left there to die.

Whom to ask? Not Mama. Not Grandma or Grandpa. Finally I know: Helga the maid. Hefty Helga of the starched white apron and the auburn hair, who's been with the family half her lifetime (as she likes to say). Mama hasn't been able to pay her wages these past two years but she's stayed with us anyway, doing the men's chores now that the men are gone, splitting wood and shovelling snow and carrying heavy loads, while Mama and Grandma do what *she* used to do, the cooking and the cleaning. She's an old maid. Once she and Mama were having tea in the kitchen and I heard her saying that soon she would be thirty and no one would ever marry her because all the young men were dead. Half of thirty is fifteen so she was fifteen when she moved in with the family so she would remember Greta's birth and mine.

A simple, innocent question: *Do you remember the day I was born?*

It takes me three days to work up my courage. Grandpa says that when you're afraid your heart beats faster because it wants to help you, it thinks your body might need a big burst of energy all at once if it has to put up a fight or run away, so it prepares you for the emergency by pumping lots of blood through your veins, but the result of the whole thing is that the pounding of your heart makes you *feel* afraid! Every time I find Helga alone and start working up my courage and tell myself: *Now! Ask her!* my heart starts pounding all by itself and my hands and feet go cold and I feel paralysed with fear, so I hum a little song and act as if I just happened to be passing through the room.

Then the day comes when I can't put it off anymore, I have to do it. Helga is knitting in the rocking chair next to the wood stove, Greta is upstairs, Mama and Grandma are in the kitchen and Grandpa is listening to the radio in his bedroom. In the hallway I make the sign of the cross as if I were about to enter church—and then, crossing my arms and pressing my thumb into my birthmark as hard as I can, I sit down on the footstool at Helga's feet.

Do it! I tell myself. *And be sure to watch her reaction!*

'Helga?' I say in an offhanded tone of voice.

'Hmmm…?'

'Do you remember the day I was born?'

My eyes leap at her.

She doesn't start or blush or stammer, her eyes are lowered towards her knitting but for the space of a second her needles stop moving and I have my answer.

Immobility is the truth.

Then the knitting resumes—one over, one under, one over, one under, Helga is making a pair of woollen socks and I am a stranger to this household.

'Of course I do,' she says, and I can tell she's disturbed so I press my advantage.

'Are you sure I'm not adopted?'

'*Adopted?*' she repeats, to gain time. 'A little foundling, you mean? Ha ha ha! You've been listening to too many of your grandpa's fairy tales, my little one!' She sets her rocking chair rocking and adds, 'Now run along and give your Mama a hand with dinner.'

I run along, not to the kitchen but to the toilet, I have my answer, I have my answer, I bring up everything my stomach contains and when there's nothing left to bring up I pull the chain and sit down on the toilet seat and let everything come out the other end and as I sit there sweating and letting the liquid waste flow out of me I see little babies lying on their backs and screaming as their diapers overflow with shit, bigger babies crawling on the floor their hands and faces smeared with shit, toddlers carrying rim-full potties out of doors and spilling the contents as they go, white-skirted females stomping around and yelling, delivering smacks left and right, I see white shoes striding, I see graceful bare feet with painted toenails, pink silk negligées and long blond braids and cascading tresses, I see breasts as large and lovely as those of the nymphs in the Zwinger niches—only moving, swinging, milking—and dozens of teeny babies like the angel heads on top of the columns fastening their lips to the nipples of these breasts and sucking at them fiercely, I see white uniforms stretched to bursting point by the stomachs swelling beneath them, I hear women's voices crying out, babies mewling and whimpering, every now and then the roar of a man. Then I get off the toilet, pull the chain and kneel down on the floor again, heaving and retching into the dark stench. Drops of sweat form on my forehead.

When I emerge at last Mama is coming down the hallway carrying a pile of plates for the dining room. Though the light is dim she sees how pale I am and instantly kneels to set the plates on the floor. 'My Kristina,' she says, 'whatever is the matter? Are you ill?'

I crumple against her so she picks me up and carries me all the way upstairs to my bedroom, leaving the plates right where they are. Gently she removes my clothes and helps me into my pyjamas, murmuring all the while in a soothing voice about how I have a fever, how I must rest, how she'll be back in a minute with camomile tea.

Some days pass. I'm floating on air. Usually when people say they're floating on air they mean they're light with happiness but I mean exactly the opposite. I'm light with unhappiness, as if I were a last wisp of fog about to be burned off by the sun. When no one is looking I stroke my birthmark, but it doesn't take away the ache at the pit of my stomach.

Who gave me my birthmark?

At night I'm afraid of having bad dreams about babies so I hum to myself to keep from falling asleep. Greta grumbles and tells me to shut up. Annabella smiles down at me from her high shelf and tells me not to worry, everything will be all right, but I feel extremely worried, I can't help it.

Grandpa teaches me a beautiful new song about edelweiss. When I've learned all the words to it, he plants a kiss on my forehead and says, 'You're the only one in the family with perfect pitch.'

Who gave me my voice?

It's Saturday lunchtime and after grace, just as we're raising the first spoonful of broth to our lips, Mama clears her throat and says, 'My darlings, I have an important announcement to make, listen to me carefully.'

We look up, hesitate, set down our spoons.

A silence. My stomach growls because it's hungry and Greta jabs at me with her elbow.

'Yes, go on,' says Grandpa, putting a hand on Mama's shoulder. 'You must tell them.'

'Well…Greta…Kristina…This afternoon, some men will…This afternoon, our family will…have a new member. A young boy named Johann. Papa knows all about it. He'll meet Johann the next time he comes home on leave. Johann's parents have both been killed in the war and he's all alone in the world, an orphan. So…I've offered to take him into our home and bring him up like my own son. Of course no one can ever replace Lothar in our hearts, yet you must treat him just as if he were your brother.'

As I sit there staring at Mama I feel the pressure of a gaze on my own face so I turn my head to the left and Greta drives her eyes into mine. It lasts only a second but the message comes through clear as a bell: *You see? It's happening for the second time. You were the first.* Then she bends over her soup and slurps it. As a rule you shouldn't slurp your food but with soup you're allowed to because otherwise you might burn your tongue and palate.

'How old is he?' I ask.

'Ten,' says Mama. 'Just a year older than Greta.'

I listen to the spoons tinking on the plates.

'When is he coming?'

'I told you—this afternoon.'

Afternoon begins at twelve noon and it's already twelve-thirty so it could be this very minute or in an hour or two or three or four, it's unbearable not to know. The afternoon is endless. Greta goes out sledding with friends and I take my nap with Grandpa and it's still only two o'clock, the clock is ticking, forcing time to go by, kicking it in the rear end: *Go on! Get on with you!* I could die of curiosity.

When the high G of the doorbell rings out at last, I harmonise around it with Ds and B-flats, softly singing Johann's name.

Two men have brought him and are hiding him from my view in the entryway as they stomp on the mat to shake the snow off their boots, I can't make anything out. Now they move into the dining room, still flanking him, Mama bends over the table to sign some papers, strange deep voices are saying things I can't understand, there's a clicking of heels, 'Heil Hitler,' 'Heil Hitler,' 'Heil Hitler,' the door closes behind the men and the event has taken place.

'Kristina, come and meet your brother!'

So saying, Mama moves to help the boy take off his coat but he shrugs her away and the shrug is violent. He takes off his own coat. As he's hanging it up on the coat-rack I come up to him and say 'Hello Johann' in my most beautiful voice, wishing I could sing it—'*Hello, Johann*'—but he doesn't answer. His eyes are open but they are closed: a wall more opaque than his forehead or his back. He's tall for ten and his face looks old for ten and his blue eyes are wide open but tightly closed and his jaw is clenched, I can see its bones working beneath the soft skin of his cheeks and I think: he's very handsome, my new brother.

Greta comes home from sledding, her cheeks bright red and her eyes aglow, Grandma has made hot chocolate in the kitchen and the whole family converges there, raising our cups and clinking them together in celebration of Johann's arrival but he stands there rigid as a stick, unspeaking and unsmiling. Mama and Grandma glance at each other, the hot chocolate slithers in silence down our throats into our stomachs, Helga carries Johann's suitcase up to his room which used to be Lothar's room and Johann follows her because she told him to but he does so with reluctance and resentment.

Sitting down at the piano Grandpa nods for me to come and sing with him and I fill my voice with warmth, hoping that Johann will hear it from upstairs and that its strains will soothe him, untense his body, he's in a state of shock because his parents are dead and we are strangers to him—but when he comes down for supper nothing has changed, his jaws are still working his eyes are still walls and his silence is intractable.

After grace (he bows his head but does not murmur 'Amen'), Mama questions him gently and when no answers are forthcoming she blushes. She turns to speak to Greta but stumbles in her words. Johann has brought silence into our household, his silence radiates outward, penetrating each of us by turn and striking us dumb. We're ill at ease, our conversation is stilted, what do we usually talk about? We can't remember.

After dinner we gather around the wood stove but I don't climb up onto Mama's lap and am careful not to suck my thumb because I don't want Johann to think of me as a baby. Grandpa tells us the story of the musicians of Bremen and all of us giggle when the cat, the dog, the rooster and the donkey scare the brigand half out of his wits, but Johann just sits there staring into the void, the shadows play on his cheekbones, our giggling falters and fades.

At school in the morning it's the same thing: the teacher introduces the new pupil to the class, she makes a speech of welcome for him and he stands there like a lead soldier, implacable, impervious and indifferent. He does everything he's told, with a slight delay to make it seem as if he's acting out of choice and not obedience—but he refuses to answer questions, read out loud, or utter so much as a single word.

No one scolds or punishes him.

It is thrilling. We are the orphans. I am song and he is silence. Can you hear me singing, you of the working jaws? From now on all my songs are for you.

We've run out of wood for the stove and Helga the maid is sick in bed.

'Johann,' says Mama, 'I need you to do me a favour, you're the strongest one in the family today, you must go out and fetch us a load of wood. Take the sled along, Kristina will show you the way. Bundle up now, both of you, it's snowing out there.' Handing him a bank note, she adds, smiling, 'Don't forget to bring me the change.'

As we go down the hall together, Mrs Webern who didn't used to say 'Heil Hitler' enthusiastically enough is letting herself into her apartment with her key; without turning around to greet us she mutters, 'How the family keeps growing!' in a sarcastic tone of voice but luckily Johann doesn't hear her.

We're walking side by side and for once, this winter, the cold is not unbearable. The large soft flakes come down, sticking to our hats and scarves, melting on our cheeks, catching in our eyelashes—this is my chance, I think. The wood seller is several blocks away, on the far side of the town square, the expedition will take us nearly an hour. And so I talk.

'Every single snowflake is different from every other snowflake,' I say. 'They look like stars but in fact stars aren't tiny and cold they're huge and hot, they're burning faraway suns, isn't that incredible?'

No answer.

'Johann,' I say, 'I know you think I'm not worth talking to because I'm just a little kid but Greta has been teaching me everything your class is learning and my memory is excellent and in addition to that I've got perfect pitch.'

No answer.

'Johann, I understand about your not feeling very comfortable yet with our family but I just wanted you to know that you can trust me, and in a way I really am your sister because I was adopted, too.'

Ah. He looks at me—really looks at me—for the first time. My heart quickens, my pace quickens, my tongue quickens.

'I don't belong to this family either,' I add, for good measure.

Johann is looking straight ahead but I can see his jaws beginning to relax a bit, and then—oh, victory—his mouth opens and his voice comes out, shaped into words:

'Is it true?' he says.

These are the words he utters but the shape of them in the air is strange—he has an accent.

I nod, and the relief of having someone to confess to wells up as tears though I'm not sad at all, I'm happy.

'At least we got adopted by a nice family,' I say.

'I'm not adopted,' he says, which is ridiculous because I saw Mama signing the adoption papers with my own eyes but I say nothing because I want him to continue.

'What is your name?' he asks then. I'm taken aback.

'My name? Kristina!'

'No, your true name—from before.'

I don't understand what he means but now we've reached the wood seller's and I can feel him withdrawing into silence again for protection the way a turtle withdraws its head and legs into its shell, he glances at me as I knock on the door and his glance means You do the talking so I do it. In a bright chirpy sparrow voice I say the words that have to be said, he hands the man the banknote and pockets the change, we're back outside.

The cold is sharper now and the daylight is waning, the sled was light when it was empty but now it's heavy, Johann's face strains pulling it, like the faces of the Negro slaves holding up the stone balconies at the Zwinger only Johann is alive so he really feels the weight and has no strength left over for conversation. By the time we reach the little park at the town centre he's panting hard and has to stop to rest.

Barely audible, the carousel's piping music wafts over to us from the far side of the park.

Johann turns to me and says, in his strange halting German-with-an-accent: 'Want to ride the carousel, phoney-Kristina?'

'We can't,' I say, laughing. 'It costs money.'

'We're rich!' he says, drawing Mama's change from his pocket and showing it to me, a treasure glinting from the dark cave of his glove.

'Johann, you're joking!'

'Johann you're joking,' he repeats, mocking me. 'No I'm not joking, and I'm not Johann either. Come along, little whatever-your-name-is!' And he takes me by the hand, hauling along the heavy sled with his other hand.

The carousel is at a halt when we reach it, the music has stopped too and you can tell that it's the end, night is beginning to fall and the last children and their mothers are moving away—'We can't go, Johann,' I say, 'it's not our money and they're closing anyway,' but Johann pulls me up to the ticket wicket and whispers fiercely into my ear '*Ask him,*' so I do, not in a chirping-bird voice this time but in a scared-little-mouse voice: 'Is it too late for the carousel, Sir?'

The man—a tired-looking man with grey hair and many lines in his face—was just locking up his cashbox. He looks down and sees us standing there in the falling snow, in the falling dusk, in a country that's losing the war. 'Oh,' he says, 'one more round won't make any difference—get on now, make it snappy.' Johann holds out Mama's coins to him but he waves them away—'Can't be bothered with that, the cashbox is locked. On you get—twice around and that's *all.*'

The music starts up again, loud, thrilling through me from head to foot as the man picks me up bodily and sets me on the back of the white horse, to my surprise Johann climbs up behind me and puts his arms around me to grip the reins, the carousel picks up speed and we rise and descend with the music, turn and turn with the music, the air is colder and darker by the second but my body is a fireball of joy. I'm laughing but the laughter is whipped out of me by the icy wind, the horses go up and down, the lights flash and the music pipes and when our two rounds are over I wave to the man and say 'Thank you!' he waves back at me and nods, he looks exhausted, he looks as if making two children happy is the only thing he can do in the world, the carousel goes round again, I say 'Thank you!' and he nods and sends us around again, then again, and every time I say 'Thank you!' he sends us around again, I wonder if it can last forever, what could ever make it stop?

How often can things be repeated can you die repeating the same word over and over forever and ever *dumbhead dumbhead dumbhead dumbhead dumbhead* until it loses its meaning how many times.

Just as we're reaching the house—before Mama screams at us for being late and scaring her half to death, before she punishes Johann by sending him up to bed without his supper, before the air raid siren wails in the middle of the night, toppling the whole family down into the basement in their pyjamas and bare feet—before all these things come to taint the wonder that kept my heart spinning and flashing and piping music throughout the long walk in the black night dark at Johann's side—yes, just as we're reaching the house, Johann drops the rope of the sled and takes me by the shoulders and turns me to him.

Putting a finger to his lips, he says to me in his slow strange German: 'Not Johann: Janek. Not German: Polish. Not adopted: stolen. My parents are always alive, they live in Szczecin. I am *stolen*. And so, little phoney-Kristina, are you.'

270

From that night onward I have a new life, a life of shadows and secrets and conspiracy with Janek-Johann. The finger on his lips was forever: no one must learn of what we share.

Almost every day we find a few minutes to continue our exploration of who we really are. Our conversations are whispered. The whispering makes everything we say important. He says my real name is spelled with y's instead of i's, Krystyna or maybe Krystka, when he pronounces it he rolls the *r* and it tickles me inside my stomach. He says I must never ever say 'Heil Hitler' again, only mouth the words so people will think I'm saying it. He says the Germans are our enemies, this whole family is our enemy even if they're nice to us, and when the war is over I'll go back to my real family and if I've forgotten my mother tongue I won't be able to speak to them and that would be terrible so he teaches me some words in Polish. Mother is matka, father is ojciec, brother is brat, sister is siostra, I love you is kocham was, dream is sen and song is s'piew.

'Don't you remember any of it?' he asks me.

'No.'

'Not even matka, what you used to call your mother?'

'No, but it's…coming back to me.'

'They must have stolen you when you were a baby, before you learned to talk. They must have ripped you from your mother's arms. I saw it happen, Krystka, more than once…'

I remember every word he teaches me and in return I gently but firmly correct his German, he makes progress but still refuses to open his mouth at the dinner table or at school.

We're sitting on the floor in the big clothes closet at the end of the hall, it's really a room unto itself, it's got a light in it.

'Everything in our papers is false,' he tells me. 'Our names, our ages, our places of birth.'

'Our *ages?*'

'Mine, anyway. They made me younger by two years.'

'You mean you're *twelve?*'

'Yes.'

'So twice as old as me!'

'And twice as angry. But you should be angry, too—just think, your real parents have probably been searching for you for years, weeping and wondering where you are. They must be in despair by now.'

'You think so?'

'Of course.'

'Who stole you?'

'The Brown Sisters.'

'What's that?'

And he describes the flock of evil crows that materialised one day in the streets of Szczecin. Dressed in straight brown dresses with stiff white collars and white cuffs—nightmare Annabellas—they stood outside his school and watched the children pouring out at noon. Studied them. Approached the chosen ones with sweets in their hands and smiles on their faces.

'How did they choose you?'

Johann turns away and I see his jaws working.

'*Us*, Krystka. They chose us because we looked like Germans. Because our hair was blond, our eyes blue, our skin perfectly white.'

'That can't be true.'

'What do you mean?'

'My skin isn't…'

Moving close to him I push up my sleeve, revealing my birth-mark. My heart is beating hard.

'It's a spot that makes me different from everyone else,' I tell him, 'and it's what makes me sing. When I touch it I can go inside my soul and gather up all the beauty there and fly out through my own mouth like a bird. You can touch it if you want to.'

Johann covers my birthmark gently with two fingers and frowns. I recoil. Does he think it's ugly?

'What's wrong?'

'No, nothing…I'm surprised, that's all. I saw children sent away for less than that.'

'Sent away…?'

'Tell me more about you, Krystynka. What else do you love besides singing?'

'Eating. Especially fat. When I grow up I want to be the Fat Lady in the circus.'

A shout of laughter escapes him. 'You've got a long way to go, little one,' he says, looking down at my stick legs.

The closet door flies open. Greta is standing there in the hallway, looking wounded and triumphant at the same time. She's heard us talking. Never, never has Johann said a word to her. He's closer in age to her than to me, and how can he be interested in an ugly bug like me when there's a charming young girl like her sitting next to him at the table? It's incomprehensible. She's burning with jealousy. Seizing my arm, she drags me to our bedroom and locks the door.

'What were you two doing in there?' she hisses at me. 'I'll tell on you!'

'Greta,' I say—strengthened by my new language, my new

brother, my new nationality—'there's nothing to tell.'

'You were whispering, I heard you!'

'It's not a crime to whisper…'

'But that means Johann knows how to talk! Why doesn't he talk to *us?*'

'Ask him.'

'He won't answer me.'

'That's *your* problem.'

'Do you know what, Kristina?'

'What?' I say, turning towards her.

She spits in my face. 'That's what!' she says.

Nothing could make me renounce my secret conversations with Johann, now peppered with words in Polish. All right is dobrze, yes is tak et no is z'aden, I am your daughter is Jestem waszym còrka. I want to know everything.

'The Brown Sisters took the chosen children by train to a place called Kalisz, where they handed us over to men in white coats, maybe doctors maybe not. Boys and girls were separated…'

'And then what?'

'Then we were measured.'

'To see how tall you were?'

'No. Yes. Everything. They made us take our clothes off and they measured every part of our body. Our heads, our ears, our noses. Our legs, our arms, our shoulders. Our fingers. Our toes. Our foreheads. Our penises, our testicles. The angle between our noses and our foreheads. The angle between our chins and our jaws. The distance between our eyebrows. Those whose eyebrows grew too close together were sent away. So were those who had birthmarks…big noses…little testicles…those whose feet turned in or out…Then they measured our health, our endurance, our coordination, our intelligence. Test after test after test. Those who got low marks were sent away.'

'Sent away…?'

'Sshh Krystka, let me tell you…They gave us new names and told us we were Germans from way back, we had German blood in our veins, our Polish identity was a mistake but it wasn't too late to correct it. Our fathers were traitors and had been shot. Our mothers were whores who didn't deserve to raise us. We would be given a German upbringing from now on. If we spoke together in Polish we would be punished. We spoke together in Polish. We were punished.'

'Oh, poor—'

'No. Don't ever say poor, if you say poor I'll stop talking.'

'I'm sorry,' I say quickly, in Polish. 'Ja jestem z'a uja ce.'

'They hit us on the head in the middle of the night'—closing his eyes Johann strikes the air violently with his hand—'*bang… bang…bang…bang…*We counted the blows and compared notes in the morning. Often more than a hundred blows, *bang…bang… bang…bang…*It hurts at first but after a while it stops hurting, you use the rhythm to turn it into something else, you think it's an axe chopping down a tree in the forest, or a hammer driving in a nail, *bang…bang…bang…bang…*You register the impact but not the pain, even the dizziness becomes a dullness. But still I wouldn't stop talking Polish. So a Brown Sister took me to the chapel and made me kneel down on the flagstones, it was the wintertime Krystka, she made me kneel for hours with my arms stretched out like this, she watched over me and every time I'd lower my arms she'd whip me. Lashing me on the back, on the neck, over the head, panting like a madwoman, grunting with satisfaction every time the whip landed. At last I couldn't take it anymore, I spun around and tore the whip from her hands, in one second the expression on her face went from evil pleasure to animal fear, now I was in power because I had the whip and I started whipping *her*, screaming at her in Polish, insulting her, calling her names as she huddled on the floor in a quaking shaking brown mound—I could have killed her, Krystka, I swear.'

He pauses. I say nothing. My eyes are open wide.

'When they found out what I'd done they locked me up in the broom closet for two days, in the dark, with nothing to eat or drink. I refused to call out for help, I had to prove my will was as strong as theirs, I simply sank into myself and waited. Then the head doctor summoned me into his office and told me: "Young man, you are excellent German material but there will be no more chances: the next time you break a rule you will be sent away."'

He pauses.

'So after that I stopped talking Polish. They tore my tongue out by the roots.'

'And mine, too.'

'And yours, too.'

In my dream a heavyset peasant woman with a kerchief on her head is bending over a garden plot, she looks like Grandma and she's pulling at something with all her might, grunting and red-faced with the effort, uprooting it and tossing it into a basket—what is she pulling up? 'Tough work,' she says, panting and straightening, wiping her brow with the back of her hand. Drawing closer, I see that her basket is filled with human tongues, still moving, their roots waving helplessly in the air, like tiny lobsters. 'Oh!' I say. 'If you tear them out by the roots they won't be able to talk anymore!'

'That's just the idea!' the woman says, and, bending down again, she returns to her labour.

'We were rounded up at Christmas of 1943,' says Johann, 'and for a whole year we had German drummed into us from morning to night. *Bang…bang…bang…bang…*like the blows to the head. German words, German history, German poems and fairy tales— and then, when winter rolled around again, German Christmas carols. 'Silent night, holy night'…'Oh come all ye faithful'…'Jingle bells, jingle bells'…*Bang, bang, bang, bang.* Oh, how I hate those stupid carols, phoney-Kristina, how I hate them! Don't you?'

'Ye-e-e-s, I guess so.'

I know I used to love them, but that was when I thought I belonged to this family and this language and this home. For the moment I haven't got much to put in their place, just a few words in Polish and my love for Johann, but it will come. I push the carols to the back of my head. At school when I learn to spell new words I think how they were banged into Johann's head, slapped and whipped into his memory, driven into his body against his will, the words sound evil to me now and learning them hurts but I tell myself they'll soon be replaced with words from my mother tongue and I'll be able to flush them out of my brain like when you flush the toilet and all your waste goes far away into the ocean. Grandpa says that people who go to hell are the waste of humanity but I don't want to quote Grandpa anymore, even if he's nice to me he's not my grandfather and I don't know what his wisdom is worth.

When he offers to teach me a new song I tell him I'm busy with my schoolwork and don't have time to sing. He looks sad so I give him a kiss on the forehead and tell him 'Maybe later, Grandpa.'

The real problem this creates is that if I don't sing in German what can I sing? All the church hymns and Christmas carols, all the beautiful songs that Grandpa taught me are off limits to me now. I ask Johann about this and he says 'I could teach you some songs in Polish but that would give us away. So for the time being, I'm afraid, you'll just have to sing without words.'

I learn to sing without words. I make sounds in the back of my throat, pushing my voice up higher and higher until it stabs the sky. I go down with it into my deepest self where the lava bubbles and boils.

'What do you and Johann talk about?' Greta asks me. She's combing Annabella's hair which doesn't grow and doesn't need to be washed twice a week the way ours does because there are no living cells pushing it out of her head.

'Ohhh...life.'

'What do you mean, life?'

'Look it up in the dictionary,' I say, surprised at my own nerve.

'You've had your last lesson with me, Kristina.'

'Yes? Then I'll tell Mama what you told me that night.'

'Go ahead and tell her. I dare you!'

At the end of January school closes down because of the cold. The air-raid alerts come day and night now, one after the other, it seems as if we're spending more than half our time in the potato cellar which is more boring than church, you have to sit still hour after hour with nothing to do but listen to people's snores and sighs and whimpers, and the smell is terrible. Something is happening, you can feel it, every day now we are silent as we sit around the table and it's not because of Johann's silence, it's something new and opaque and heavy, like an iron lid weighing down on us, crushing us, as if the whole world were grinding to a halt. We try to go about our usual activities, getting dressed in the morning, making our beds, setting the table, splitting wood, polishing silverware, folding sheets—but it's as if all this order and cleanliness and neatness were make-believe, as if the adults were just pretending for the children's sake and when I look into their eyes I see fear and chaos, if I look for too long I could fall into them and just keep on falling, through the eyes into the head and down into the guts and bowels the hellish darkness, it's because we're really losing the war now—or rather, since I'm Polish, because Germany is losing the war, I wish they'd just lose it and get it over with, how much losing does it take?

'Would you really have spent Mama's money on the carousel?' I say to Johann.

'Yes. The Germans stole my country, they stole me, what's a little spare change in comparison with that? You have to take sides, phoney-Kristina.'

'I'm on your side.'

'Prove it.'

'How?'

'The next time you play with phoney-Grandma's stupid jewellery box, steal one of her jewels.'

'I can't do that!'

'Then you're not on my side.'

'But what do you want her jewellery for?'

'Just do it and I'll tell you.'

The following day, I draw a pair of sparkling earrings from my pocket and dangle them in front of Janek's eyes. I hope he doesn't know the difference between diamonds and rhinestones.

He doesn't. His eyes widen and he makes a thumbs-up gesture, I tingle with pride.

'Now tell me what you want to do with them,' I say.

'It's just a start, phoney-Kristina, but it's a good start. You'll become a master thief. From now on, you'll take a small amount of money every day out of phoney-Grandpa's wallet, all right?'

'But what for?'

He takes my two little hands in his big ones and squeezes them.

'Are you with me, Krystynka?'

'Yes.'

'Do you love me?'

'More than anything in the world.'

'Then listen to me carefully...You and I are going to run away together. We'll sell the jewellery and get good money for it and find our way back to Poland. When we run out of money, you will sing. People will crowd around to hear you, I'll pass the hat and they'll pour all their treasures into it and we'll go on travelling.'

My heart thuds in my temples.

'But Janek,' I say, 'people will call the police if they see us on the road. Two runaway children—we'll stick out like a sore thumb.'

Johann laughs. 'There are refugees everywhere these days, haven't you noticed? Thousands of people are on the road. Children, old folks, you name it. Two more or two less...And the police have better things to do. No one will bother with us.'

'But Janek...I know we're living with the enemy but...If I...I mean, they love me, they've always been so kind to me, I can't…'

'Krystka. You have to make up your mind if you're a baby or a big girl, a German or a Pole. Think it over carefully, take your time, it's your decision. I'm leaving in the summertime, whether you come with me or not.'

This house without Johann again—unthinkable.

When Grandpa starts to snore, instead of pushing his shoulder and saying 'Kurt,' I get up out of bed and tiptoe over to the chair where he's left his jacket and go through the pockets. His wallet is in an inside pocket, I'm sweating and my hands are shaking, I wonder what purpose that serves, it seems to me it should be just the opposite—when you're nervous you need your hands to be steady and calm and do exactly as you tell them. There are only three banknotes in the billfold, I don't dare to take one, I'll tell Johann the wallet was empty, if Grandpa had had ten banknotes I would have taken one because it would have been only ten percent, but one out of three is more than thirty percent, it's thirty-three point three and an endless number of threes after the decimal, I learned percentages from Greta before she stopped teaching me, infinities are hiding everywhere.

The change purse is full of change, however. I extract half a dozen small coins, careful not to let them chink against each other in my hand, slip them into my shoe and go upstairs to join Johann.

'Terrific, little Krystka. Look, I've found a cache for us…I took some food.'

We crawl on our hands and knees through the hanging coats and dresses that smell of mothballs to the very back of the closet, where Johann moves aside a pair of old boots, maybe Grandpa's army boots from the other war. Behind them, stacked against the closet wall, I can make out packets of biscuits and sugar and dates…

'But Janek! The family doesn't have enough to eat as it is…'

'They're not my family, I want to go back to my family. Here—'

He holds out a little tin box and I drop the coins into it.

At night I lie awake wondering about my Polish family. Questions jump in my brain like fleas in a flea circus, Grandpa told me he saw a flea circus once in Berlin when he was a young man. How many brothers and sisters do I have? Have they forgotten me? Will they be nicer to me than Greta? Is my real Ojciec still alive? Does Matka have as warm a heart as Mama? Will I recognise her? She'll recognise me from my birthmark. She'll take one look at the inside of my left arm and cry out, rolling her *r*s the way Janek does: 'Krystyna! Krystyna! At last! My darling Krystyna!' and crush me to her chest and weep for joy.

What bothers me most is how Mama will feel when we run away, it will break her heart. But Janek tells me it's her own fault, she should have known better than to take stolen children into her home. She brought about her own unhappiness and there's nothing we can do about it.

'Now you must learn to lie to them.'

'No, Janek. What good would that do? We're already hiding from them, stealing from them, that's enough.'

'You've got to toughen up, phoney-Kristina. You need thicker skin or you'll never survive the long march home.'

'I can't do it, Janek.'

The next day when Greta goes up to our room after school she finds the contents of our dresser drawers on the floor. Panties, socks and leggings, undershirts and sweaters—dumped and scattered. At once she runs to the top of the staircase. 'Mama!' she cries. 'Come and see what Kristina did!'

I come upstairs on Mama's heels and stare at the havoc, thunderstruck.

'Did you do this?' Mama asks me in a tone of controlled anger.

It's out of the question for me to denounce Johann so I say 'Yes.' My stomach is trembling.

'*Why?*' Her voice is sharp.

'I…I was looking for something and just I forgot to…put everything back in place.'

'What were you looking for?'

'…'

'What were you looking for, Kristina?'

'…My little marching bear.'

'She's lying!' squeals Greta. 'Her bear is right there on the shelf as usual, she *never* keeps it in the dresser.'

Mama has told Grandpa. He summons me and stares at me with sad eyes.

'What's happening to you, little one?' he sighs. 'You have changed. Your mother tells me you're turning into a bad girl. Why did you make such a mess in your bedroom?'

'Because I felt like it.'

The corners of his mouth turn down, his sadness turns to

grimness, he puts one big hand around my two wrists, yanks me towards him and forces me down onto his lap. I squirm to get away but he presses me down with one big hand and starts spanking me with the other, *whack whack whack* on my buttocks which he's never done before, the pain outrages me, I scream and struggle and my struggling fuels his anger, the blows rain down thick and fast, I can feel my bum turning red which is because all the blood is rushing to the skin's surface to find out what on earth is going on, I wail and kick and at last, his anger spent, Grandpa pushes me away from him and I fall to the floor, crying and shaking uncontrollably, and he tells me to get out of his sight.

On my way out I go past Greta who was standing in the doorway watching the scene with Annabella in her arms. She smirks at me.

'Congratulations, Krystynka. You passed the test. Tell me…how was the pain?'

'Fine.'

'Can you stand more than that?'

'Tak.'

'Good. And you see how the Germans are?'

'Tak.'

It's Valentine's Day.

We're at the breakfast table dipping dry bread into bowls of steaming chicory—there's no chocolate left, no butter, no cheese, no ham, no jam—when it happens: the orderly surface splits apart and the chaos erupts right in the middle of our house. What it is is Grandpa sobbing in his bedroom. The minute the sobbing begins we all freeze like in the game Halt, Mama's eyes meet Grandma's across the table, I catch the flash of panic in their glance and understand: the worst has come to pass. But which worst? Papa is dead or Hitler is dead or what? *What is it?* The sobs grow louder and louder, Grandpa bursts out of his room and we hear the radio in the background, he's in his long underwear with his belly hanging down like a big white ball, his face is wet with tears and he's grabbing at his white hair making it stand up in tufts like a clown, doesn't he know he looks ridiculous? Doesn't he know better than to come out in his underwear in front of everyone?

'Kurt,' says Grandma, rising to go to him but he turns away and starts to bang his head against the wall, again and again, is he counting the blows like Johann at the home in Kalisz?

Then his sobs become a word: 'Dresden,' he is saying. 'Dresden, Dresden, Dresden, Dresden, Dresden,' if you say the same word a million times will it lose its meaning?

Mother sends us upstairs to our rooms, when we come down at noon the place is a shambles and no lunch is waiting for us. Helga is sweeping the dining room floor which is strewn with broken china made by Grandpa's father in Dresden and the beautiful clock has been smashed to bits and so has the jewellery box, the tiny ballerina has rolled into the hallway, looking straight ahead always straight ahead as she rolled so as not to lose her balance, strange men have come to take Grandpa away but he has locked himself in his room, one of the men accidentally steps on the ballerina and her head snaps off without his even noticing, Mama and Grandma side by side on the sofa have turned into statues, Helga tells us all to go back to our rooms.

Johann and I stand at the window looking down at the empty

courtyard. No one is playing there. Utter stillness. Stone cold. No birds. Bare trees.

'They deserved it,' says Johann.

'Who?'

'Everybody. All the Germans, it doesn't matter, they all deserve to die.'

'Don't say that, Janek,' I say to him in Polish. 'Don't say that, please.'

'It doesn't matter. All of them are monsters, Krystka. The year I was born the Germans chose a monster for their leader, all my life long they've been killing the Poles, killing our people, invading our land, destroying our cities, do you know that? Warsaw our capital was burned to the ground last year, do you know that?'

His voice is so low I can hardly hear it.

'But the children, Janek...the babies...'

'Do you think they spared the Polish babies? Krystyna, the children of monsters are monsters.'

'What about the animals? Did *they* deserve to die?'

There is a silence. I can feel him withdrawing from me again.

'Maybe it's too late for you,' he says at last. 'Maybe you were too young when you got stolen and they did succeed in making a German out of you. Maybe you and I are enemies, not friends.'

His words make the hairs prickle at the nape of my neck. I press my thumb into my birthmark.

'Please,' I whisper in desperation. 'Please, Janek. I'm Polish just like you are. We have to stick together.'

'Stick together...*against the enemy*.'

'Tak, tak.'

He puts an arm around me. 'All right,' he says in Polish. 'Dobrze.'

'Janek…if some people in Dresden had pet salamanders…they're still alive, aren't they? They can live in fire.'

'No, that's a legend…There were lots of salamanders in the forest near our home in Szczecin. Did you ever seen one up close?'

'No.'

'Your head is so full of ideas, Krystka, but you haven't lived. I'll bet you never took a walk in a forest?'

'No.'

'Salamanders are magical animals. They're black with orange spots, they have large mouths, black eyes and a warm presence. My brother and I used to watch for them in the forest. Always they would come out after it rained. You could see them lurking under tree roots, in dark, humid places. Once my brother captured one and we brought it home. We made a terrarium for it and tried to feed it, but it refused to eat. No matter what we brought—seeds, plants, earthworms, insects—it just left it there. Weeks passed, it ate nothing but didn't die, it only moved more slowly…After six months it was nothing but a skeleton covered with skin, you could see right through it, but still it was moving. Finally it secreted a white substance that covered its whole body…it dried out and began to rot…One day we came in to check on it and all we found was a little mound of gelatin.'

We have our lunch at teatime.

Grandpa has been taken away, Helga serves the meal which is nothing but boiled potatoes, Mama and Grandma don't even join us at the table so Greta says grace and when she gets to the end Johann says 'Amen' for the first time. So be it.

In my dream that night thousands of Dresden statues are lying on the ground a broken crucified Jesus a broken bearded philosopher a broken lovely goddess a headless man a manless head a sad broken saint a child musician with both hands missing a broken Virgin Mary staring in wonder at a reclining male nude, I see stone heads rolling, stone eyes flashing, stone horses with gaping wounds in their flanks, the Negro slaves have been mutilated, the nymphs and centaurs dismembered, the little angel heads have been stacked in a pyramid like cannonballs. 'Look, Kristina!' says Grandpa, pointing. I follow his finger and see that the Zwinger columns are now topped with the heads of real babies, screaming and wailing, I want to go to comfort them but Grandpa keeps pulling me along. 'Look *up*, Kristina!' he says—and, looking up, I see that naked human beings have been nailed to the pediments of the theatre, opera and courthouse, their blood pours down the walls. Real hands and faces decorate the façades, waving and winking and blinking at us as we go by. In the parks and gardens, real women's breasts spout milk—these are the city's new fountains. 'Look, Kristina,' says Grandpa, opening his arms wide to embrace the vast spectacle of the city—'we have won the war.'

The dreams overflow into the daytime days and nights are reversed people and statues are reversed chaos is everywhere it is the month of March cold clenches the world sirens wail nonstop the sky is bloody it is the month of April school starts up again the trees in the courtyard burst into blossom birds are singing the town is bombed the bomb falls right on the square and when we go out the next day the town hall and our church are smoking ruins, the carousel poles stick out in all directions and the horses lie on their sides or on their backs with their feet in the air, still curved in their galloping position, tall trees split down the middle bend over dangerously as if to listen to some truth or other coming from the ground, school stops again, Hitler is dead the radio says, it is the month of May flowers run rampant in the parks and school stops and the courtyard fills up to overflowing with refugees from the east, they swarm through the town, they've walked for endless miles carrying bags and bundles and babies, their skin is grey, they're stunned and starving and we huddle in our homes and wait, one day we hear screaming in the street and go to the open window to see what is happening, a woman's baby is dead but she refuses to let go of it, she screams and screams as people try to take it away from her, she seizes a suitcase from a pile of suitcases, dumps its contents on the ground, stuffs her baby into it and disappears into the crowd carrying the suitcase, it is the month of June and now, says Johann, Germany has been divided like a cake into four and each of the victors have been given a piece and our piece belongs to America.

Now there is a time of hunger and waiting, waiting, waiting for Papa to come home, is he a prisoner of the Russians or did he die in a battle or is he on his way home, no one knows, the hot days of the summer are here and the town is a seething mass of suffering with people snatching bread from each other's mouths but generously sharing their diseases, we've got nothing left to eat so Johann makes a list of all that's valuable in the house, Grandma's jewels and the unbroken cups and saucers from Dresden and the piano, he goes out into the crowd and meets people and makes deals with them, somehow he finds a man to buy the piano, a truck comes to take it away and in exchange we receive a big bag of potatoes, it is a miracle not a trick, the piano has turned into potatoes like water into wine and Johann is the hero of the day. He listens to the low sick conversations in the streets, learns what these people are running from, what they have seen and lost and endured, what they have left behind, and tells me.

'Give Johann the doll, Greta,' says Mama. 'He might be able to sell it, get us some bacon for it or a loaf of bread,' but Greta stubbornly shakes her head, clings to Annabella and refuses to part with her. 'Steal, then, Johann,' says Mama in a low voice. 'Steal whatever you can or we will starve.' Johann steals, but when Mama weeps in shame and gratitude at the food he brings, he will not even look at her.

It's a dusty dusk, Johann and I are perched on a bit of broken bench in a corner of the park, refugees in rags are sleeping in a jumble on the ground using their bundles of belongings as pillows, I close my eyes and listen to the strange orchestra of babies mewling, old men sighing, old women praying and our own stomachs growling, and then Johann says in a soft voice,

'The time has come, phoney-Kristina.'

'What time?'

'I told you I'd be leaving in the summer. Are you coming with me?'

'Janek! We can't leave *now*…and abandon the family…to…'

'It's August already. Soon the nights will be too cold for us to sleep outside. Are you coming with me?' he repeats in Polish, and I start to cry.

Crying is a mysterious thing. Grandpa used to tell me we have tear ducts to keep our eyeballs moist and protect our eyes which are fragile delicate incredible machines, but no one can explain how it is that when we're sad the tear ducts start working all by themselves, it's hard to see what the logical connection might be between grief and salt water but there it is, suddenly I miss Grandpa terribly and the more I cry the more I miss him, when you cry one thing leads to the other and everything you think about becomes an extra reason for crying, I miss Grandpa I miss Papa I miss Lothar I want the family to be reunited I want Mama to be happy again—

'Is it yes or no, my Krystynka?'

I throw myself against Johann who has suddenly become all the men in the world to me and sob against his chest and he puts an arm around me and pats me awkwardly on the head, people who are walking by glance at us and go on, they've seen too much, their cities have been burned they've seen charred people reduced to a third their natural size with flames of phosphorus still dancing on their backs, they've seen red purple and brown mummies frozen for eternity, they've seen streetcars packed with roasted passengers, they've seen women's hands lying on the ground, charred human heads the size of tennis balls, people reduced to little piles of ashes, other people boiled to the bone by exploded water heaters, they can no longer be bothered with trifles like the sobbing of little girls.

'You can tell me tomorrow. Tomorrow is my birthday, little Krystynka. I'll be thirteen and I'll leave at midnight.'

Grandpa used to say that tomorrow never comes and he told me the joke about the barbershop that attracted customers with its sign saying 'Free Shave Tomorrow,' people would come back the next day and expect to get a free shave but the barber would laugh at them in front of everyone and say, pointing at the sign, 'No, it's tomorrow, can't you read?' so they'd get a shave anyway and pay for it since they'd made the trip and eventually, Grandpa said, that man got to be the richest barber in Dresden.

Tomorrow never comes but the next day comes

The next day we're sitting around the kitchen table drinking tea and nibbling on potato peels when the doorbell rings and Mama starts violently, thinking it might be Papa until she realises that Papa has the key and wouldn't ring the doorbell to his own home but then he might have lost the key in the thick of the battle so there's at least a chance but no, it isn't Papa, Helga goes to answer the door and comes back with a lady.

The lady is so elegant that she seems like a creature from another planet, it's been ages since we saw anyone so well dressed well fed well groomed, her dark brown hair is sleekly styled in a chignon, she's wearing a uniform and leather shoes and carrying a briefcase. She introduces herself as Miss Mulyk and apologises for barging in on our meal like this and the minute she opens her mouth we know she's a foreigner and Mama sends all the children out of the room.

We sit waiting in the living room. There's nothing to do so we do nothing. The clock is no longer there to tick and tock and tell us that time is passing but the sky slowly changes colour so it's passing anyway. It comes to me that today is Janek's birthday but this feels like the wrong time to remind him of that. Now the four women in the kitchen are raising their voices, Grandma's voice has grown shrill but we can't make out the words, only the melody, a melody of pain. At last Helga comes to the living room door and summons Johann and me—'Not you, Greta,' she adds when Greta gets up to join us, 'only Johann and Kristina.'

I look at Greta and she looks at me and in that instant we know we have reached the end of our thorny sisterhood.

The kitchen table is covered with papers and photographs, Helga and Grandma are sitting on either side of Mama, I can see their six feet lined up under the table but I can't look up at their faces because I know Mama's eyes are red from weeping and I don't want to see them.

Haltingly, the strange lady says a few words in Polish to Johann.

'Tak,' he says and Mama moans.

Then the lady turns to me. I expect her to address me in Polish too and I'm getting ready to explain that my mother tongue is rusty from disuse but instead she holds out her hand to me and says, in German, 'Would you mind coming over here, my dear?'

'*No!*' wails Mama in a voice I've never heard before, a gut voice rich with pain as dark as loam. *'Not Kristina!'*

The lady tells Mama to please, please calm down. 'I know how hard this must be for you,' she says. She asks Helga to bring her a glass of water but Helga doesn't move. The lady holds out her hand to me again and Mama collapses weeping on the table.

I walk slowly across the kitchen and take Miss Mulyk's hand and say solemnly, in Polish: 'I am Polish, too.'

The lady raises her eyebrows. 'No my dear, I don't think so,' she says—and, so saying, she releases my right hand and takes my left hand and gently turns it over and before I know it she's studying the inside of my left arm. It's a hot day, I'm wearing a sleeveless top so it's easy for her to see my birthmark and, having seen it, she adds, 'In fact I'm quite certain that you're Ukrainian…and that your real name is Klarysa.'

I look at Johann in a state of shock as if the floor had fallen out from under my feet. He meets my gaze and his eyes are filled with confusion. *Who are you?* they are asking and I don't know the answer. All these months I've been getting ready for the reunion with Matka and Ojciec in Poland; if *they're* not expecting me, then who is? Where and what is Ukrainia? My stomach clenches and I'm afraid I'll throw up like on the day I first learned I was adopted. But I was alone then, it was before Janek came into my life, I get a grip on his eyes and they're saying *No matter what happens, you and I will stay together.*

When Miss Mulyk has left, I go into the bathroom which is the only place I can sing to myself in private and turn the taps on full blast so that no one will hear me. Can I sing in German again if it turns out that I'm Ukrainian whereas I thought I was Polish? Very softly, with my thumb caressing my birthmark, I sing the song about the edelweiss, to thank Grandpa for everything he taught me in this house.

That night Greta comes and stands by my bed in the dark, she has Annabella in her arms and she says 'Kristina, the American lady is going to take you away, isn't that right?'

'I think so,' I whisper.

'She's going to send you back to your real parents in the Ukraine, isn't she?'

'I guess so.'

'Well then listen to me. We haven't been good friends over the past year but I'm going to miss you, the house will feel empty without you—and what's worse, I won't have a little sister to pick on anymore.' She hesitates then adds, 'I'm going to sleep with the doll tonight and then…when you go away…you can take her with you. She'll be something for you to…remember this family by.'

I throw my arms around her neck and the two of us hug and it feels strange because we've never hugged before and we'll never hug again and I say 'Thank you very, very much, Greta. I'll never forget this.'

Helga spends the morning packing our things, towards noon I see my suitcase open on the bed with everything I own in the world in it, from my toothbrush to the wind-up bear but best of all beautiful Annabella lying on top with her red velvet dress spread out around her. In the early afternoon Janek and I stand at the window and watch Miss Mulyk's car drive up and park in the street in front of our house. Two men are with her, one of whom has black skin and Janek says that means they must all be Americans. Mama has been locked up in her room all day, she didn't join us for lunch but when the doorbell rings she comes out with her hair freshly combed and lipstick on her lips, I can tell she's doing her best to seem composed, but when she sees Helga and Johann carrying the suitcases down the stairs she collapses all over again and I hear the same rich loam sound as the day before, a scary sound as if her voice were heaving upwards from the bowels of the earth. She rushes at me, sweeps me up and clutches me to her, moaning 'Kristina, Kristina' and the men take our suitcases and Johann follows them out to the car without a single word, without a thank you or a farewell to either Mama or Greta or Helga or Grandma, then Miss Mulyk comes over and gently but firmly convinces Mama to release me, which I must say is a relief because she was choking me.

After we've closed the door Mama gives a long piercing scream that echoes down the hallway. Curious neighbours open their doors a crack to peer at us and Mrs Webern instead of hiding behind her door is standing right in front of it, she watches us go by with her arms crossed and her eyes like burning torches but Miss Mulyk looks straight ahead like a ballerina and tells me in a low voice 'Be brave, Klarysa.'

The two men are up front and I'm squashed in between Janek and the lady in the back, the drive seems endless, it's a hot August day and I'm pouring with sweat. Grandpa used to say that sweating is the body's automatic cooling system, sweat is secreted by ducts in your forehead and your underarms and I don't know where else, and when it evaporates it cools you off but today my sweat doesn't evaporate it just keeps pouring out. No one says anything but I can see that Janek's jaw muscles have started working again. I close my eyes and pretend to be asleep. After a while I look at Miss Mulyk through my eyelashes and to my surprise she's brushing away a tear and I wonder what *she's* crying about but maybe everyone has good reason to cry these days, even Americans. I finally do fall asleep with my head on Johann's shoulder.

The car drops me off in front of a house and I go up to the door and try the doorknob, it's not locked, full of anticipation I let myself in, walk down a long hallway and enter a large room blazing with artificial light, a woman is standing on the far side of the room with her back to me and I say to myself At last! At last! I've found my real mother at last...'Mama?' I say and she doesn't answer me or turn around so I go up to her and touch her on the hand and say 'Mama?' but she's made of stone.

When I wake up we have arrived, my head is heavy and I need to pee, it's almost dark out.

As we're getting out of the car Janek whispers 'I saw some nuns as we drove up, it brings back bad memories, I won't be staying long.'

'Were they brown sisters?' I whisper back.

'No, black and white,' he says, 'but still German.'

The men take our suitcases somewhere.

'You'll be spending a while in this centre,' Miss Mulyk explains to us as we go up the stairs to the entry. 'It takes time for all the paperwork to be ironed out. The girls' wing is on the left and the boys' on the right, but you'll be seeing each other daily at mealtimes, at least until families are found for you.'

'Until families are found for us?' says Johann sharply. 'You mean until our families are found!'

'Yes, yes…Unfortunately, things never go as fast as we want them to,' the lady replies evasively. 'Now go unpack your suitcases, then come down to join the rest of us for supper, the dining room is over there.'

She beats a hasty retreat, so hasty that I wonder if she isn't on the verge of tears again.

I have no idea what's going on.

I recognise my bed in the girls' dormitory because my suitcase is lying on it.

I run over to the bed, fumble with the latches, throw the suitcase open.

Annabella is nowhere to be seen. I rummage through all my

clothes, she isn't there. I scrunch my whole body up into a ball and crush my fists into my eyes thinking *Now* what is left? The only person left in the world is Janek and they're going to take him away from me, too.

Janek says we're in a convent which is why the buildings look like churches and there are German nuns helping the Americans. I'm introduced to the other children at the centre but I don't care about them. Seventeen girls and twenty-nine boys, aged four to fourteen, all of us miserable because none of us want to be here, we know it isn't a real place, just a temporary stopping place between past and future. We're all thinking about the past—I want my life back with the clocktower the carousel the tiny coloured windmill wands the church the merry-go-round the jewellery box the piano and the Dresden picture postcards—and the future is nothing but an enormous question mark.

'How did Miss Mulyk recognise me from my birthmark?'

'You must have a file somewhere. She must have gotten her hands on your file.'

'But what does it *mean*?'

'I don't know.'

A new routine begins and the days slide by with it.

In the morning we make our beds and do exercises and go for hikes in the countryside. In the afternoon they divide us up into small groups and teach us this or that, I'm bored to tears during these classes because the other girls my age don't even know how to read yet and I have to start all over again with the alphabet and when I try to daydream instead of paying attention I don't know what to dream about, every train of thought I embark on runs into a dead end because I'm not the person I thought I was and I don't know who I am. After the reading class I get sent to an English class with only two other girls in it, the teacher is a man named Mr White which is funny because he's black, he's an American Negro and his skin is chocolate brown all over except for the insides of his hands and his lips which are pinkish brown or brownish pink. He teaches us to say 'Mummy' and 'Daddy,' 'please' and 'thank you,' 'what a nice day' and 'I am your daughter,' and he tells me I have a remarkable ear, my pronunciation is perfect.

'Are they teaching you English, too?'
    'No.'
    'Why are they teaching me English?'
    'I don't know, little sister.'
    Janek calls me little sister now, since I'm not Polish anymore and who knows if Miss Mulyk was right about my name being Klarysa?
    My seventh birthday comes and goes, I don't even mention it.

In bed at night my body keeps me company. I count my fingers and toes over and over again, trying to do the trick Grandpa taught me where it really seems like you've got eleven fingers but it's hard to fool yourself. I pick my nose which is one of the things you're allowed to do when no one is looking. I rub flecks of lint out of my navel and explore the warm cranny between my legs and smell my fingers afterwards and lick them. Sometimes I try to lick myself all over as if I were a mother cat licking her kitten but there are too many body parts I can't get at. I turn my lower lip inside out, remembering how when I used to pout Grandpa would say 'Be careful, Kristina, you'll trip over that lip!' That reminds me of the joke when he would ask people 'Can you stick out your tongue and touch your nose?' and they would try. Grandpa and I would go into gales of laughter watching them crossing their eyes and trying to get their tongues all the way up to their noses but then he'd say 'Look, it's easy!' and, quick as a wink, he'd stick out his tongue just a little way and touch his nose with his finger.

I stroke my birthmark and hum to myself under the covers and once a week I sing all the songs I can remember in my head with all the verses in the right order because I don't want to forget them, I lie there and sing to myself for hours without making a sound, the other girls whimper and snuffle in the dark and it disturbs me so when I run out of songs I start doing my multiplication tables and then I recite the alphabet backwards, a little faster every time, in a matter of days I can recite it backwards as fast as forwards, though I have doubts as to whether this talent will ever come in handy.

The leaves on the trees turn to russet and brown, they wrinkle and crinkle and allow the wind to carry them to the ground. I've never felt so sad in my life as now, standing at the dormitory window watching the leaves lose their colour and drift slowly to the ground one by one, my life has lost its colour too and sometimes I wish I could just wither up and drop to the cold ground with my head on my arms and die forever.

Then a day comes which is the Momentous Day, it is the eighteenth of October and we've been here for over two months, in the meantime quite a few children have disappeared and new ones have appeared and now our turn has come to disappear.

'So…' says Janek when we meet up for our after-dinner conversation.

We're sitting very close to each other on the front steps of the centre, it's almost completely dark out and also chilly and we haven't got our coats on which is a good thing because that way I have an excuse for shivering which is exactly what I feel like doing.

'So…' he repeats, looking intently at a spot between his feet where there is nothing at all. 'Did they tell you what's in store for you?'

'Yes. And you?'

'Yes.'

'Tell me, then.'

'You go first.'

'No, you.'

His jaw works and then he clenches it very hard as if he simply did not want to let any words squeeze through it.

'Tell me, Janek…'

He releases a lot of pent-up air in something halfway between a sigh and a sob, then draws a fresh breath of air into his lungs and holds it there, interminably, and at last he says, 'My parents are dead, my brother is dead, my whole family, they are certain of it now. I have no one left to go back to…so they've decided to send me to a boarding school.'

'*What?* Where?'

His hands are squeezing his knees but it's too dark for me to see if his knuckles are turning white, they turn white because when you squeeze hard like that the knucklebones come right up against the skin and all the blood vessels get shunted aside, I think that's the explanation.

'Where, Janek?'

'In Poznan. They want to take me there next week because I have an uncle there.'

'But how did your parents die?'

'They wouldn't tell me. They said they had proof but they wouldn't show me the proof. They said that for now I'll have to take their word for it and go to this boarding school and trust that they're acting in my best interest.'

I allow a long silence to surround Janek's words and hold them in its arms.

'What about you?' he asks, when the silence has done what it can which is not much, and I prepare to utter my own words which will require a lot of silence too.

'They're sending me to Canada,' I say.

'*Canada?* Why? I thought they knew who your parents were!'

'It's a mystery, Janek. When I was waiting in the hallway outside the office I heard them talking together in the director's office, they were speaking English in loud voices and they kept repeating themselves so I understood everything they said. The director said "But what about her mother's letter?" and Miss Mulyk: "The Ukraine is being taken over by the Reds!" And the director: "But the letter…" And Miss Mulyk: "That letter never existed, okay? I refuse to send Klarysa to the Reds!"… What does that mean?'

'I think… I think it means the Russians,' says Janek. 'So…?'

'Then they told me to come into the office, and the director left the room. Miss Mulyk told me she has a special feeling for me because she's Ukrainian, too… So… She has these Ukrainian friends in Toronto—the Kryswatys, a doctor and his wife—they've got no children of their own, and they'll be happy to adopt me. That way, she says, I'll be with my own people in a nice rich country and my name will be Kriswaty.'

Janek generously provides the silence I need.

Then he says, 'Poznan, Toronto.'

As he says the names of our future cities, a heaviness descends on me and presses and compresses me until I think I've become part of the cold cement we're sitting on and will never be able to budge from this spot.

'It's impossible,' I whisper.

He turns to me then on the steps and brushes my hair away from my face and gently touches my features with his two hands as if he were trying to memorise them.

'Well, you listen to me, Miss Kriswaty,' he says. 'They can send me to Poznan and you to Toronto, they can change our names, give us phoney papers and phoney parents and phoney nationalities, but there's one thing they can't do: *they can't separate us*, all right? We'll still be together and there's nothing they can do about it. We know who we really are and *right this minute we're going to invent real names for ourselves* and *that's* who we'll be from now on. Are you ready, little sister?'

I nod feebly.

'Good,' he says.

Taking my left arm, he pushes up the sleeve of my sweater and puts his lips to my birthmark, his lips are cold, his whole body is shaking.

'I'll be with you—*here*,' he says. 'My real name will be Lute because my father had a shop for stringed instruments in Szczecin. It doesn't matter what language, my name will be this instrument

303

in every language. All you need to do is touch this spot or even think of it and I'll be there, vibrating inside you like the strings of a lute to accompany your singing. Lute, Lute, Lute. Say it.'

'Lute,' I whisper. 'Lute, Lute.'

'Now choose your name.'

It drops into my mind out of nowhere and I say it: 'Erra.'

'Erra,' he repeats. 'Erra. Yes, perfect. I take Erra with me to Poznan and you take Lute with you to Toronto. All right? Erra and Lute.'

'Lute and Erra.'

'And later on…I'll come to you. When we're grown up. As soon as possible. I'll find you by your singing.'

'And we'll be together forever.'

'Yes. Let's swear.'

Putting two fingers on my birthmark, he says, 'I, Lute, swear that I will love Erra and find her again and be with her forever. Now you.'

'I, Erra, swear that I will love Lute and find him again and be with him forever.'

It's all very solemn and grave and the next day Janek vanishes, throwing the Centre into an uproar, and a week later I'm on an ocean liner staring out at the endless grey billowing pillows of the Atlantic Ocean.

Between 1940 and 1945, over two hundred thousand children were stolen from the territories occupied by the Wehrmacht: Poland, the Ukraine and the Baltic countries. This 'Germanisation' program was set up by Himmler in person to compensate for German losses due to war casualties. The older children were sent to specialised centres and given an 'Aryan' education; the younger ones, including thousands of babies, passed through the infamous Nazi 'stud farms' known as Lebensborn (fountains of life) and were then placed in German families.

In the years immediately following the war, several Displaced Persons organisations including the United Nations Relief and Rehabilitation Administration (UNRRA) returned some forty thousand of these stolen children to their birth families.

Sources:

Gitta Sereny, *The German Trauma: Experiences and Reflections 1938-2001,* London: Penguin, 2001.

Fernande Vincent, *Hitler, tu connais?* Besançon: L'Amitié par le Livre (no publication date).

Eva Warchawiak, *Comment je suis devenue démocrate,* Aigues-Vives (Gard): HB Editions, 1999.

Clarissa Henry and Marc Hillel, *Of Pure Blood*, trans. Eric Mossbacher, New York: McGraw Hill, 1975.

Also Chantal Lasbats's documentary film *Lebensborn* (1994) and numerous Internet sites...

REFERENCES TO LYRICS
(pages 112–13 and pages 172–73)

Fiddler on the Roof, by Joseph Stein, music by Jerry Bock, lyrics by Sheldon Harnick, based on short stories by Sholom Aleichem (permission granted by Arnold Perl), produced by Harold Prince, 1964. Excerpts from 'If I Were a Rich Man'.

The Wizard of Oz, a musical produced by L. Frank Baum and William W. Denslow, 1902. Adapted for film by Victor Fleming, screenplay L. Frank Baum, Noel Langley, Florence Ryerson & Edgar Allan Woolf, music by Harold Arlen, Goerge Bassman, George Stoll & Herbert Stothart, produced by Mervyn LeRoy, Metro-Goldwyn-Mayer, 1939, Warner Bros since 1998. Excerpts from 'Follow the Yellow Brick Road' and 'We're Off to See the Wizard'.

Porgy and Bess, composed by George Gershwin, libretto by Ira Gershwin and DuBose Heyward, 1935. Excerpts from 'It Ain't Necessarily So'.

On the Town, directed by Gene Kelly and Stanley Donen, screenplay and lyrics by Adolph Green & Betty Comden, music by Leonard Bernstein, produced by Arthur Freed, Metro-Goldwyn-Mayer, 1949. Excerpts from 'New York, New York'

Excerpts from 'Alabama Song', lyrics by Bertolt Brecht, music by Kurt Weill, composed in 1927 and used in the musical *Aufstieg und Fall der Stadt Mahagonny*.

Singin' in the Rain, directed by Stanley Donen and Gene Kelly, screenplay by Adolph Green and Betty Comden, produced by Arthur Freed, Metro–Goldwyn-Mayer, 1952. Excerpt from 'Moses Supposes'.

The Sound of Music, musical by Richard Rodgers and Oscar Hammerstein II, based on *The Story of the Trapp Family Singers* (1949) by Maria Von Trapp, libretto by Howard Lindsay, Russel Crouse, 1959. Film directed and produced by Robert Wise, 20th Century Fox, 1965. Excerpt from 'Edelweiss'.